FACSIMILE

Also by Erin L. Snyder

FOR LOVE OF CHILDREN

Other Novels Available Through Threat Quality Press

THE TRANSLATED MAN AND OTHER TALES, by Chris Braak
MR. STITCH, by Chris Braak
BURN DOWN BLOODY TWILIGHT, by Jeff Holland

Ordering Information:
http://threatquality.com/the-press

Facsimile

By Erin L. Snyder

Threat Quality Press

FACSIMILE

This is a work of fiction. All characters, events, and ideas are the product of the author's imagination and any similarity to real events or people is completely coincidental.

www.erinlsnyder.com

Cover art by Erin Snyder and Lindsay Stares

ISBN 978-0-9828884-3-8

Published by Threat Quality Press
Threat Quality Press
1299 New Gulph Road
Conshohocken, PA 19428

http://threatquality.com

Dedicated to Lindsay Stares, my wife and editor.

A special thank you to Alex Cooley, Shiraz Biggie, and Valerie Stares for their help in revising the novel, and to Chris Braak of Threat Quality Press.

◎ Prologue ◎

Clean brain tissue resembles a dry sponge. Covered in blood and other assorted fluids, it resembles a very wet sponge, one that has been sitting overnight in a bucket of tomato juice. An LR14 Syntax Engine, the type used by most high-end profiling firms, is capable of deriving this metaphor using a combination of image comparison, psycho-symbolic assessment, and a simple association index.

What's more, such systems can infer a similar thought process occurring in a human mind. By comparing their reactions to previously gathered information, AuroroTech's system was able to determine that the police examining the scene were considering the relationship between the bits of brain scattered over the wall and the contents of their own heads. With data on what those same police ate for breakfast, it determined, with relative precision, that Officer Richetti's queasiness was in some part due to having had a glass of tomato juice before leaving his apartment.

There was little space in the small, windowless enclosure for the police to maneuver through. In the center of the room, a pool of congealed blood surrounded a body slumped in a metal folding chair. Wires dangled between what was left of the corpse's forehead and the blank computer monitors left in a perimeter around him. A dark sludge matted down portions of his brown hair, which was pulled back by a rubber band, apparently in an effort to keep it from interfering with several electrodes affixed with small strips of clear tape. His right eye remained entirely in its socket—unlike his left—and still bore its bright, blue coloration, even with a dark line of red beneath the ball. A gun hung loosely in his cold hand, finger still pressed against the trigger.

His shoes and socks were immaculately clean: they'd been removed from his feet prior to the ventilation of his skull and were sitting in the corner. The laces were tied, and the socks were inside, rolled in neat balls and tucked under the tongues. This meant the corpse's bare feet were mired flat in the ooze, which, one week before, had housed the thoughts, feelings, and dreams of Felix Burgand.

The police examined this in some detail. They recorded, scanned, and studied every inch of the scene, while the devices they wore recorded, scanned, and studied the police themselves. They weren't required to wear such things, of course, but the benefits were too numerous to count.

Once he was satisfied with the data captured, the detective in charge of the investigation spoke to one of the others then walked to the only door, stepping around the wires, blood, and bits of bone in his way. He paused for a moment and looked back. From a psychological perspective, it was as though he were stepping out of hell, an analogy the digital system was easily able to ascertain.

If the previous room had resembled hell, then the next was surely heaven or, at the very least, heaven's corporate office. The outer wall was made entirely of glass and overlooked the city of New York. There was a large desk, along with a row of computers, all of which prominently displayed the corporate logo for AuroroTech. The logo also appeared on the far wall in huge, backlit letters that were sometimes visible from the street.

The CEO was sitting quietly, looking through the window. He was a middle-sized, middle-aged man named Isuel Morgan-Yager. Isuel was of part Korean, part German, and part Welsh descent, as well as several other nationalities not reflected in his name. He sat completely still, his fingers locked together in front of his chin with his thumbs hooked underneath to support the weight of his head, as he stared blankly forward. He offered no facial expression, no indication of what might be going through his head beyond the firings of neurons. Perhaps he was thinking nothing, or perhaps he was contemplating a great deal about his company's future, the danger he might personally be in, or any number of subjects. A great deal of information can be gleaned from human behavior, but there are limitations.

Isuel Morgan-Yager had light red hair, which was beginning to turn silver in some spots, and dark brown eyes, which were cast down at the floor. He seemed more solemn than sad, though there was an air of depression about him.

"Quite a mess. I'm Detective Parsil, by the way."

"He was a friend," Morgan-Yager said softly. It was a simple statement, neither defensive nor angry. If he was upset at the detective's callousness, he gave no further indication. Instead he looked up. "You'll have questions," Morgan-Yager reasoned.

Detective Parsil nodded his head slowly. He reached into a pocket and pulled out a simple hand computer and a stylus. The CEO's mouth betrayed a moment's amusement at the realization his company had manufactured it. Parsil activated the device then selected, "Begin Recording" from the list of options. "Please speak loudly and clearly for the recorder," he mumbled. "Who found the body?"

"I did," Morgan-Yager said. "This morning. Felix had been missing for a few days, but that's not unusual. He's always been… erratic."

"Erratic. Huh. Let's work on that. Is that depressed? Suicidal? In your opinion, I mean."

"My opinion?" Morgan-Yager said, his eyebrows lifting. "My opinion makes no difference. Felix Burgand has never displayed any suicidal tendencies or signs of any issues beyond a compulsive interest in his work and the occasional harmless idiosyncrasy. That's been the consistent analysis of regular profile scans by several highly-ranked psychological programs."

"Are all your employees subjected to that kind of analysis?"

"No. No, of course not. Thirty percent of our workers aren't even clients, even though we offer discounted access to our services. Half of those don't even have profiles."

"Here I thought everyone had a profile." The detective tapped the glowing blue light on his wristwatch. "See. I'm a customer myself. Makes me wonder, though. Are you going to run a scan of me? Find out what I know?"

"Certainly not." Morgan-Yager was insulted, even though he must have known the question was an attempt to elicit just that response. "We respect our clients' privacy. Felix knew I was checking up on him. It was part of an arrangement we had."

"What sort of arrangement? Why him?"

Morgan-Yager sighed. "Like I said, Felix was erratic. He was also very special. Easily the most important employee of the company." He grew quiet again. "This is a major blow to us," he said.

"Profiles are supposed to be equipped with alarms. It was all over the brochure I read when I signed up. Why didn't Felix's go off when the gun did? Why'd his body sit in a closet for four days rotting?"

"Because Felix was the chief architect of our entire system. And, for some reason, he didn't want us to know."

"You mean he turned it off?" Detective Parsil made a note with his stylus, despite the fact his computer was recording and transcribing the entire conversation. "Tell me. Did Mr. Burgand deactivate anything else?"

"Oh, yes," Morgan-Yager said. "He shut off dozens of fail-safes. We even think he may have deleted his profile from our database."

The detective almost dropped his stylus. "That's unusual, right? I mean, most profilers who kill themselves, it's because they want to upload into some sort of paradise or something."

"First of all," Morgan-Yager said forcefully, "Suicide is extremely rare among our clientele. We've faced an unprecedented level of criticism over a handful of extreme cases, when the tools our company provides our customers have drastically reduced incidents of suicide and homicide. Secondly, AuroroTech strongly believes that there is an important distinction between a person's soul and their profile." His lips clenched together for an instant before he added, "If that's what you're trying to imply."

"I'm just trying to figure out what was going through his mind when he pulled the trigger. And why he'd bother hooking up a dozen electrodes only to delete himself from the system. What happened to the data he collected?"

"I'm sorry," Morgan-Yager said. "I am under a great deal of stress, and I believe I've been unfair. I don't know what purpose the electrodes served. He installed a program into the computer system to completely purge the data when it was finished doing whatever it was doing.

However, everything was wired to our network, so he may have had the information uploaded elsewhere. We don't know yet. If we can find out what he did with his profile, we may be able to recover some information. But for now, I have no idea what he was thinking."

"Was there anything else going on? Anything he was unhappy about?"

"He didn't have much of a personal life. He had a few friends, and there were women he spent time with, but he wasn't in any kind of real relationship. His career was only getting better. Our company just rolled out the FeedBack auditory tie-in. You've heard of it?"

"Yeah. Seen the ads," Detective Parsil said.

"That was one of Burgand's projects. He developed and integrated the software that allows it to work. Early tests exceeded our expectations, and he was set to receive millions in bonuses and stock options."

"Maybe he just got tired of it all," the detective speculated. "Whatever you find out, whatever information you pull up, I want a complete report and copies. Are we understood?"

Morgan-Yager nodded slowly. "Of course. Whatever we find, I'll contact your office at once." The detective took this at face value, but, even though the CEO didn't know what had happened, he was already fairly certain he'd wind up having to provide only half-truths at best. The computer monitoring him knew this as well, and it silently updated his profile with the incoming data.

◎ CHAPTER 1 ◎

"If you are going to waste the sort of money a gourmet meal requires, why settle for the best? Go beyond." These words were printed in gold lettering on the front of every menu at De'Muure, one of the most expensive establishments in Manhattan. Merely obtaining a reservation is a lesson in frustration. Applicants must give the restaurant access to their profiles to test for compatibility. Famous artists and writers are typically accepted without question; the rest are either denied entrance or placed on a waiting list that can take months. As part of this process, the restaurant admits a limited number of less affluent customers at a discounted rate. The stated reason for this program is to make the food of De'Muure accessible to the common customer, but no one really believes this. Everything in De'Muure is theater: the unprivileged are there so the rich and famous can watch them squirm, just as the rich and famous are there so the poorer customers can gawk at them. Everything inside the restaurant is a point of reference, and every point of reference is itself an object to be observed and exploited.

You can't even be admitted without a profiling recorder.

Beyond this requirement, the dress code is somewhat tricky. "Suit coat and tie. Or not," reads the gold plaque, and they mean it. Guests are expected to dress well or dress creatively. Wear a simple pullover, and you'll be shown the door; wear a handmade dress stitched together from a few hundred scarves, and you'll be seated at the best table in the establishment. Come nude, wearing only a recorder, and you're likely to find your meal on the house. But trying to enter without a recorder to catalogue your reactions is an unforgivable offense. Any who try aren't merely thrown out: they're banned for life.

Persephone Kilard, a distribution specialist admitted as part of the restaurant's price reduction program, wore her recorder on a bracelet. Its tiny black lens was illuminated by a blue light, shining like an open eye. It could only catch half her face, of course, but that's more than enough to capture data on her jawline, her cheek muscles, and, on occasion, even her iris. Of course, when she's among friends, their recorders are automatically networked, so complete profile information can be cobbled together.

At present, Persephone's profile was being updated with several disparate elements about her current state. It knew that she was underwhelmed by the food, irritated that she let her roommate talk her into coming, and curious if the man two tables to her left was actually who she thought, composer Hewitt Simonis. It knew this because it had detailed reference data, collected over the past five years, imaging countless different expressions, vocal inflections, eye positions, and speech patterns. It knew that she was a fan of Hewitt Simonis's work, and could therefore infer that her repeated glances towards the man who looked very similar to the composer—but was not, as she'd learn later that evening—suggested that she believed she was in his presence. The profiling computer even knew she was considering walking over to the table and asking the man whether he was Hewitt Simonis, just as it knew, long before she knew herself, that she wouldn't. It simply wasn't in her personality, and there's nothing the computer knew better than that.

Persephone was sitting beside her date, Arthur, who knew her better than she knew him. While they'd never before met in person, Arthur had invested three hours the previous night conversing with Persephone's profile, her virtual avatar, which behaved, to the casual observer, precisely like she would. He did this so he'd know in advance whether he'd have any interest pursuing this as a relationship—or even if this might lead to a one-night stand. Judging by her profile's demeanor, he'd concluded that neither was very likely. Persephone's profile had been distant, withdrawn, and thoughtful. Despite what the computer matching them might have thought, he found these qualities tedious. He'd have far preferred being with the animated Ms. Loring, who seemed far more engaged in the evening. But she'd been matched with Edward, who was taller, better looking, and more interesting than Arthur. He was also a heavier drinker, having already gone through several cocktails. Ms. Loring was keeping up, but—unfortunately for Edward—did not seem nearly as inebriated.

The two couples were an unlikely and imperfect pairing necessitated by a very limited pool. There'd been only fifteen individuals selected by De'Muure's computer as possible recipients, so the system had to make do with the options available. In the end, though, this date wasn't so much about the people as the setting, so the software did what it could, despite the fact that neither of the couples had more than a twenty percent chance of developing further.

"Well," Ms. Loring said. "Are we or aren't we?" Her question hung in the air while she speared a chunk of meat on the shining prongs of her fork. She brought it before her mouth, which showed the edge of a smile. She wore two shades of lipstick: a deep burgundy running along her upper right lip before crossing to her lower left, and a light pink on her upper left and lower right. The effect created a patchwork impression, like a checkerboard, when her mouth was open. When she pressed her lips together, they formed an 'X'.

"I've given my opinion," Edward said, sipping his whisky sour. He shifted around in his chair, as though it were too large for him.

"Indeed you have," Ms. Loring said. "But I find it utterly distasteful and am hoping for a more favorable one." She smiled as she said this and wrinkled her nose. Edward found it impossible to take offense at her reply.

Arthur leaned forward. "Sorry. I'm with Ed."

"Ed-WARD," Edward corrected him, while Arthur rolled his eyes.

"Well, I want Persephone to chime in. Persephone, dear?" Ms. Loring said, catching her attention away from the other side of the room.

"Yeah?" Persephone said. "Sorry, what's the question?"

"The question on the table," Edward replied, "is whether or not we are cannibals. Well, not you, because you didn't order the sapien, but the rest of us."

"It only makes her all the more objective, doesn't it, Persephone?" Ms. Loring said, before echoing, "Per. Seph. O. Ney." She tasted each syllable like sips of wine. "Have I ever told you how much I relish your name? I mean it. When I think of what my parents saddled me with, I find the Universe wholly unfair."

"It's from the Greek," Edward said. "Persephone was the daughter of the king of Troy. She was gifted with visions of the future, but cursed to never be believed. A snake ate her."

"That must have been quite a snake," Ms. Loring said playfully.

Arthur blinked twice then shook his head. "No. I could've sworn that was Cassandra. Wasn't Persephone someone else? Queen of the dead or something?"

Edward shrugged nonchalantly. "Don't think so," he said.

"Well now," Ms. Loring said, staring at her roommate. "It seems we've a mystery on our hands. Which is it?"

"How should I know?" Persephone replied. "It's just a name." The digital system knew this was a lie. Persephone was just trying to change the subject.

"Well then, I'll just have to look it up." Ms. Loring's hand dove into her purse and came out with a tiny computer bearing the AuroroTech logo on the back.

"You know," Edward said to Ms. Loring. "Come to think of it, I never did catch your first name."

Before Persephone could open her mouth, Ms. Loring's eyes shot wide open. Greek etymology forgotten, she let the miniature computer fall back into her handbag. "That is because my full and complete name, for all intents and purposes, is Ms. Loring. And if you ever find out otherwise, I shall seriously have to consider murdering you. As well as anyone who betrays my secret," she added, with a conspicuous glance towards Persephone. "But how did we ever wander so far off topic? What was it that started this? Arthur, you remember, don't you?"

"We were talking about cannibalism," Arthur said, somewhat bored. He glanced around the room, at the many tables full of interesting and creative people he'd rather be talking to. Of course, he knew perfectly well they'd have little interest in talking to him, but that was beside the point.

"That's true, and we were. And, unless I'm mistaken, we remain without a judgment. So then. Which is it? Am I a cannibal or not?"

Persephone thought for a few seconds. “Sorry,” she said. “Edward’s right.”

Ms. Loring pouted, taking full advantage of her lipstick to draw attention to the action. “Why?”

“Because it’s not real,” Edward interrupted, clearly taking the matter far more seriously than either of the women. “It’s just cloned meat. If they’d have cloned a whole person and cut it up, that’d be different. But this is just a string of proteins and chemicals formed in a giant Petri dish or something.”

“You’re nothing but a string of proteins and chemicals,” Ms. Loring retorted. “And if I cut you up and asked the chefs to marinate your flesh and grill it, you’d taste no different from these delightful morsels.” She bit into a cube of meat, and a drip of juice ran down her lip. She caught this quickly with her finger, which she licked clean.

“But that’s not the point. Or it is the point,” Edward said. “It’s not the real thing, even if it tastes like the real thing. Right?”

“It’s a simulation,” Persephone said.

“Exactly!” Edward’s open palm hit the table. The water swirled about inside the glasses, and the plates rattled, creating a small disturbance. More than a few diners turned around to raise eyebrows at the scene. The headwaiter took notice and whispered for more drinks to be brought over in the hope that whatever was happening might escalate into a genuine confrontation. De’Muure hadn’t had a worthwhile incident in more than a week, and they could always use the publicity.

Persephone blushed, and Arthur just kept staring at his unfinished drink. Edward gave no indication that he even noticed the attention he was garnering, while Ms. Loring simply burst out laughing.

“I suppose I’m outnumbered,” she said. “And a pity, too. I’d truly hoped to add ‘cannibal’ to my personality traits. But, no. It wouldn’t be honest, and I really must go on seeing myself as honest. A pity.” She returned to her food, a pyramid of meat stacked on a bed of lettuce and thinly sliced beets. When the waiter came around and offered her a fresh drink, she accepted without question or hesitation. She sipped this, then looked around the table. Persephone looked uncomfortable, Edward was far too drunk for his own good, and Arthur looked bored. “Now we need something new to talk about,” she said. Her fingernail began tapping her glass, slowly. Rhythmically.

"We could talk about you," Edward suggested.

"If only that were fruitful," Ms. Loring said. "Unfortunately, you'll find me a bore."

"I don't think that's right, at all," Edward said. "I mean, you're an artist, right?"

"Ah," Ms. Loring said. "You've been toying with my profile." Her nose wrinkled a bit as she said the word 'toying.'

"I spoke with your profile," Edward said. "Just a little." He raised his hand, forefinger and thumb just a smidge apart.

"Good, then I'm not the only snoop here. But you must have learned that I have embarrassingly little to offer."

"Wait," Arthur said. "You're an artist? What do you do?"

"I'm an estheticist," Ms. Loring replied.

"Of course," Arthur said, unconsciously tapping his lower lip.

"I've never seen a dime from the endeavor, and my repeated submissions are rejected at every turn."

"You'll be discovered," Edward said. "You're too interesting not to be."

Ms. Loring smiled. "Oh, Edward. That is both uncommonly kind and unforgivably naïve. My lipstick, my behavior—indeed my entire persona and esthetic—are constructed to atone for a completely uneventful past. The truth is there's nothing much interesting about me at all. You must have picked up on that at least while poking around my profile."

"Well. I assume there's some stuff your profile doesn't have," Edward said.

"I'll have you know I use the best profiling system available," Ms. Loring said. "And I use it right. I don't keep secrets."

"Except your name," Persephone whispered innocently.

"You be careful," Ms. Loring warned. "I'd hate to let slip anything about your college days."

"You've known each other since college?" Arthur asked, feeling as though he should say something before the evening was over. After all, each of the participants would rate their interactions with each other. It was in his interest to come off at least somewhat engaged.

"No, no. Of course not," Ms. Loring said. "We moved to New York at about the same time and both needed a roommate to help with the rent. We found each other through our profiling company. The computer thought we'd be a good match."

"Glitch," Persephone added.

"At any rate, before she learned I was unable to keep my mouth shut, Persephone shared many of her secrets. Others, I simply gleaned from discussions with her profile. And it turns out that she was a very different person before I met her."

"Well, this is beginning to sound interesting," Edward said. "Let's have it."

"Don't dare," Persephone said.

"Maybe something small. A trivial thing perhaps? Such as your brief stint as an activist?"

"Oh, God," Persephone said. "All right. Go ahead."

"Well, back in college Persephone wanted to make the world a better place. So she enlisted with a group of Post-Conservationists."

"You're kidding," Arthur said, suddenly taking interest. "You don't seem the sort."

"I'm not the sort," Persephone said firmly. "I quit after about a week, when I figured out what 'Post-Conservationist' meant."

Edward interjected, "I have a lot of respect for the movement. They take things as far as they'll go. And," he paused for emphasis, "they never apologize."

"They're sick," Persephone said plainly. "I joined before they got famous, and I hate what they do. If I'd known beforehand, I'd never have gotten involved. They just cause pain. They don't accomplish anything."

"Except art," Edward replied.

"What?" Arthur asked.

"No," Edward said. "Art. Like what artists do. They create art to make a point. I respect that."

"Then perhaps, dear Edward, you should join one of those groups yourself," Ms. Loring said.

"I would," Edward answered. "Only I'd first have to care about the environment. And I don't. So I won't." He smiled at the rhyme and leaned back in his chair. "If you're truly as nosey as you let on, Ms. Loring, you must know a thing or two about me."

"I spent some time with your profile," she admitted, "but I'm afraid you are terribly dull. Duller, perhaps, than even me. All I have is what you've made abundantly clear to everyone here, that you are something of a hedonist."

"I am!" Edward proclaimed. "And proud of it. I say anyone who's not a hedonist takes life for granted." He finished his drink in a single gulp, as if to punctuate his point, then set the empty glass down hard on the tabletop. "If you can't enjoy things that are enjoyable, then what's the point of being alive?"

"A good sentiment," Ms. Loring mimed a yawn. "But nothing new."

"You must have found something else of interest," Edward said. "I've done some unusual things in my time."

"If you're referring to that business on the subway, I must say I'm unimpressed. No, Edward, I'm afraid your past disappoints. Fortunately, I was able to find a fact or two of note about Arthur."

"What?" Arthur said. "What are you talking about?"

"Well, not Arthur specifically, but his relations. Oh, it would be impolite of me to take this from him. Arthur, will you tell us about your brother?"

"Uh oh," Arthur said, though he was clearly happy to be the center of attention. "All right, all right. You're talking about Paul, aren't you?"

"No." Ms. Loring was forceful. "How dare you insult him with his Christian name?"

Arthur laughed. "Okay, I'll get there. About two years ago, my brother, Paul, fell in with a bunch of Neo-Nietzscheans."

"Wow," Edward said. "That does take the cake."

"You're holding back," Ms. Loring said. "Tell us his true name, Arthur."

"Well, he's taken to calling himself Syphaulis," Arthur said, and Edward almost fell out of his chair laughing. "He's gotten a few tattoos, and he spends hours on those sites."

"Nietzscheans aren't so bad," Ms. Loring said. "Really little more than Neo-Idealizts with a touch of ennui. I suppose it is possible to grow a bit too attached to one's profile, though."

"Does he volunteer at church?" Edward asked.

"You're thinking of Post-Nihilism. There is a difference," Arthur said, pleased to outclass Edward. Both men made a point of displaying a friendly smile, and Arthur continued, "No, he just mopes around our parents' house then goes to these clubs. I tagged along once. Never again. Imagine a series of mirrors on every wall with computer terminals everywhere else. And every two feet there's some twenty-year old kid moping about how his profile is supposed to rise beyond good and evil and digital recurrence and… God… it just goes on and on."

"Sounds like a riot," Edward said.

"It's not. It's just pitiful and absurd. Never again," Arthur reiterated.

"Well, perhaps I'll have to get the name of the place," Edward said. "Maybe I'll stop by for a drink some evening. How about it, Ms. Loring? Would you like to join me?"

"No," Ms. Loring replied curtly. "I've little interest in sitting around snickering at children. I think I shall pass."

Edward just nodded and stared at his plate. His food was entirely gone, so he began to poke at the scraps with his knife. It was a nervous habit he'd resort to when things weren't going the way he wanted. He'd done it at least as long as he'd had a profile. It was probably something he'd been doing since he was a child, but there was no way to be sure.

He looked around at these people he barely knew, and saw that while they were moving on to other things, the lights of their recorders were still on him, still staring. So, as best as he could, he went on smiling for the camera. Because it's well documented that no one wants to be identified as being gloomy.

◎ CHAPTER 2 ◎

"Kella!" the audience shrieked, as the camera zoomed in on the face of the show's hostess, Kella Ruggeri, who was in her mid-sixties when the program was recorded. She was in good shape for her age, and she strutted around the stage, waving to the audience, and blowing kisses. Then she turned around, began walking away, and stopped. She looked over her shoulder, batted her eyelids, then flipped off the crowd. The crowd went wild at the sight of her middle finger. In the back, someone yelled, "We love you, Kella!"

Kella laughed, slapped her knee, and ran to an oversized couch. She stood in front, faced the audience, blew another kiss, then fell back into the cushions. "Good morning, folks!" she screamed. "Welcome to Kella's! It means so much to me that you're here," she said, somewhat sarcastically, while batting her eyelids again. "Today, we've got something special. We'll be joined by Isuel Morgan-Yager, president and CEO of AuroroTech, who's here to discuss… literature. That's right, we've got a technology mogul here to talk to us about *Spare Sky*, the new novel by Adanna Naji-Bachman. And this one is weird, so you'll want to keep watching. Well, Isuel? Get the heck out here!"

The crowd applauded while Isuel calmly walked across the stage. Kella leapt out of her couch to meet him and shake his hand. She then practically dragged him back to the couch and pushed him down before sitting next to him.

"First of all, I want to thank you for having me," Isuel said calmly.

"Oh, cut the small talk," Kella said cheerfully. "Let's get to the nitty.

Why don't you go ahead and tell our audience what this is all about? I'll give you four seconds before I jump in and interrupt."

Isuel laughed. "Well, I'm really here to talk about Adanna Naji-Bachman's novel, which was completed posthumously."

"Let's enhance that a touch. You don't just mean the book's being published after her death. I mean hundreds of books have been put out that way, right?"

"Probably thousands," Isuel replied.

Kella's eyes opened wide. "A computer nerd's lecturing me about lit? What do we think of that, folks?" A round of 'boos' echoed through the studio. The camera shifted to the audience, and every thumb was pointed down while the crowd screamed and hissed. Kella raised her open hand, and the audience quieted. The camera zoomed in on her face, while she shrugged innocently and batted her eyes. "Just kidding," she whispered, while the audience howled with laughter. "This is the first book that's actually written posthumously, right?"

"Well… I think it's more complicated than that. Books have been finished by alternate writers for centuries. What makes this special, is that no one else stepped in. It was effectively finished by the original author after she died."

"Just to be clear then, it was really her, right?"

"That depends how you want to define who Naji-Bachman was. Her body had passed away, but, because of the technological breakthroughs we've had, a simulation of her personality is still with us. Now, we're entering the realm of semantic ontology here, so we want to tread carefully. I didn't come here to preach to your audience or to try and sell subscriptions to our software—don't get me wrong, I love making sales, but that's really not what I'm doing here. And I certainly don't want to try and tell you that our profiles are literally the people they represent."

"I hate to call you on this, but you did say that." Kella looked out across the crowd, eliciting a round of people shouting, "You did!"

Isuel raised his hands. "I worded it that way out of respect. Because I can tell you that Adanna believed her profile was really her. She told me that with her own mouth."

"Wait, do you mean that her simulated profile told you?"

"No, Adanna Naji-Bachman was a friend of mine. I was a fan of her work, both her books and her activism. I met with her several times in the last years of her life, and I want to be clear, all of this was her idea. She wanted this book finished, and she didn't want anyone else to touch it. So she asked me if her profile could be adjusted. We talked to our programmers and worked it out, and we set her up with as many of the tools she requested as we could. We couldn't give her profile an independent long-term memory system, of course, because of government regulations, but we came up with some solutions she was happy with. She worked on the book until she couldn't go on, and once she passed, her profile took over."

"Well then. How far did she get before she croaked? Where's her work end and the computer's begin?"

"Sorry. Part of our contract with Adanna states we can't disclose that information. I can tell you that the profile had access to notes written by Adanna, and that the final draft was revised—start to close—by the profile."

"I think this is just great," Kella said. "Give us more. How'd you do it?" She grinned and batted her eyelashes. "Just between you and me, did you stick wires into her dead brain and give it a jolt?"

"No. No, of course not. All we did was extend the parameters of our psychological profiling system. It's already designed to mimic behavior and speech patterns. What you need to remember is that Adanna had been using our profiling system for three years and had completed two books in that time. So her profile doesn't just have data about her books, it's had time to adapt to her process of writing."

"So it learned how she thinks?"

"In a manner of speaking, I suppose so. But it's more accurate to say it's adjusted to act—and write—like she did."

"Okay, one more follow-up. Can't you do this with other writers? I mean, couldn't you plug in Shakespeare or something and get some new plays?"

"Well, we certainly couldn't do Shakespeare, because we don't have information on how he wrote, only what he wrote. So, I'm afraid we can't use this to get another work by Shakespeare."

"But what about another Naji-Bachman novel? You already have her profile down, don't you? Couldn't you just tell the computer to pump out another volume?"

"Well, yes and no. First, a big no, because there's no way I'm letting anyone do anything like that. But, if we're talking hypothetically, there are still some real problems. You wouldn't have notes or anything to go on. Profiles don't have incentive or motivation, not like we do. That said, we could add those drives. For example, we could give the profile an outline or even just a premise, under the conditions that it was created by Naji-Bachman, and let it run. But you probably wouldn't end up with as good a book. And, on top of that, her family would probably sue us. They'd be right to sue us if we did anything without approval."

"Awww. That's too bad, 'cause I love everything I've read from her. I haven't read *Spare Sky* yet, 'cause. Oh dear. Why haven't I gotten around to that yet?" Kella cupped a hand around her ear and aimed it at the audience.

In unison, the audience shouted, "'Cause Kella doesn't read it 'til she knows it's good!"

"That's right. Aren't they great?" Kella asked before turning to her audience and the camera. "Well, then. I need all you guys to buy and read *Spare Sky* then tell me whether it's worth my time. You know the drill. There'll be a poll up on my site—you can log your vote before loading next Monday's show. So get to it! I also need you to sign up with AuroroTech if you're looking for a new profiler. I don't know whether they're good or not, but Isuel Morgan-Yager's been a real sport, hasn't he? Give him a round on the house!" The audience began applauding loudly, while Isuel thanked Kella and stood.

The picture froze here, before being replaced by, 'Proceed to following clip?'

"No," a simulated voice said. "Freeze archived footage and bring up subject one." And the whole of a virtual universe shifted to obey.

◎

Persephone, exhausted and a tad nauseous, sat before the black monitor in her room. It hung on the wall behind a thin desk and she reached out to touch it. A light formed beneath her finger, and, seconds later, a series of options appeared as well: Profile, Mail, Browser, Programs, Voice On/Off, and Options. Each of these was inscribed in a pulsating red oval. The light beneath her index finger flickered like a small fire, and she tapped the oval for "Browser."

The system began at once. There was a soft whirr of a spinning disk that echoed faintly of the ocean. The six options were shrunken down and whisked away to the top of the screen, the rest of which turned from black to white. Panels appeared with options and shortcuts of their own.

"Would you like to activate voice commands?" her computer asked her.

"No," she said, placing her hands on the flat desk beneath the monitor. A green light appeared at the bottom of the screen and she began tapping. The light tracked her fingers and letters appeared: SitptpYrvj. The letters flickered for an instant as the autocorrect feature recalibrated the hand position: AuroroTech.

The screen blinked, and the site was loaded. Beneath a white cloud, the logo for AuroroTech appeared, glistening. Beside this, in the middle of the screen, an image of a woman's face appeared. It was somewhat cartoonish, but not in a manner that was comical or absurd. The mouth moved and, as it did, words appeared. "Hi, Persephone. Welcome to AuroroTech's enhanced online experience. Your computer isn't configured for speech. Do you really want to continue like this?"

Persephone sighed and rolled her eyes. She tapped the "Yes" oval that appeared.

"According to our records, you had a date scheduled for tonight at… wow… at De'Muure. Nice. How'd it go?"

"You know how it went," Persephone whispered to herself. This wasn't entirely accurate, as the disparate elements of AuroroTech's system weren't integrated in such a manner. If they had been, the program would have heard her response, and she wouldn't have needed to type, "It was fine."

"Glad to hear it," the automated system replied. "Or see it. Are you sure you want to keep talking like this?" The digital face raised an eyebrow.

"Uh. Fine," Persephone said, tapping the Voice On/Off key in the corner. There was a light chime, and the 'On' turned bright blue.

"There. Wow. That's much better," a voice said, while the face appeared much more relieved. There was nothing artificial about the speech, nothing to peg it as digitally constructed. Everything seemed real, down to the inflection and emotion behind the voice. "I didn't mean to press, but it gets irritating typing so much." Of course, a computerized system doesn't type, but computerized systems don't know they don't type, either. In this case, the computerized system was constructed from the profiles of several of AuroroTech's best receptionists, who, had they been typing, would have said something to that effect.

"Ah. Yeah," Persephone said.

"You sound bushed," the computer said. "You'll probably want to get some sleep after the big night. I'm really jealous, by the way. I've always wanted to hit De'Muure, but haven't gotten a chance."

"Okay," Persephone said. "It wasn't great. The food wasn't anything special."

"Really? That stinks. I guess the emperor's got no clothes, huh? Am I right in assuming you aren't up for chitchat? Probably want to get past the ads, rate your evening, and hit the sack. Am I right?"

"Actually, that'd be great," Persephone said, beginning to forget she was talking to a machine.

"I'd skip this entirely, but they make me go through it. So here's the quick version. The new AuroroTech FeedBack unit turns your profile into your own digital assistant, lets you guide yourself. It's like having a helper everywhere you go. Blah, blah, blah. It's actually really cool, and I'd suggest taking a look at the official page when you're not ready to collapse, but we don't have to go through the rest of the spiel now if you don't want to."

"Thanks," Persephone said, and the screen flashed. The customer service program shrunk into the upper corner, while a picture of Arthur took its place in the center. It was a good likeness, though the image obviously hadn't been updated in a while.

"Here he is, your date for the evening. Keep in mind that any reflections you share are between you and me and no one else. We won't tell Arthur what you think of him, and the adjustments to his ratings won't appear immediately. We'll apply them anonymously sometime in the next thirty days. Also, unless both of you request another date, you'll be removed from each other's pages. Now that we've gotten that out of the way, do you want to see what others have said about Arthur or do you want to freehand this?"

"Let's go with dull. Boring. Kind of nice, I guess. And he's cute, just quiet."

"Okay. Let me make sure I got all that. I've got dull, boring, nice, cute, and quiet for labels." As the computer read these, the words appeared on the screen. "Do you want me to integrate these into his public profile?"

"Sure," Persephone replied, wondering if he was leaving her the same generic review.

"Awesome. Now for the big one. Is this someone you want to see again?"

"Not really," Persephone said. "Not as a date, at least. I wouldn't avoid him if he was at a party or something, but I don't want him as a friend or anything."

"Cool," the computer said. "Your updates have now been saved. Do you want to leave feedback about your other companions?"

"Edward," Persephone said, and immediately his image appeared before her. "Go with vapid."

"Ooh. Good one," the computer said, returning Persephone's cruel expression. "Anything else?"

"Yeah. He drinks too much. I'd go on, but he's not worth it."

"Saved. Did you want to update your opinions on your roommate?"

"No," Persephone replied. "That's all right."

"Kay. And you've already told me what you thought of De'Muure. Unless there's anything else you want to add."

"Not really. Food's overrated, and the place is weird. Oh, but I think I saw Hewitt Simonis."

"Oh, I love him!" the computer said enthusiastically. In the background, one of his compositions began playing softly. "Hey, if you want his new album, it's on sale in our store. Do you want me to bring you over?"

"No," Persephone said. "I just want to check my messages and go to sleep."

"I get that. Hold on while I bring up your mail and message inbox. Looks like you've got a message from Kip Grillo."

"I don't know who that is," Persephone replied.

"He said you went to high school together, and he wants to label you a former classmate and to exchange profile access. If you want, I can connect you with his profile."

"No," Persephone said. "Not really. But, if he attended Connor High and there's nothing creepy in his labels, I'll permit minor access."

"Done. Oh, and there are some updates to your profiling software that are going to get installed. Just an FYI. And remember what I said about FeedBack. This one's going to be big. Your roommate's already bought hers. But it's been great chatting with you. Have a good night!" A hand appeared beside the cartoon head and waved goodbye.

The system logged her out on its own, and Persephone ran a quick search on Hewitt Simonis, in which she learned that the composer was currently on tour in China and not, in fact, in Manhattan. She sighed, then tapped the Options key at the top of the screen. Persephone selected "Sleep Mode" from the list, and let the computer power down. Finally, she removed the bracelet from around her wrist. The blue light was still glowing, lens still watching her, until she reached down and twisted it to the off position. Then, as far as AuroroTech's data collection engine was concerned, there was nothing but black and empty silence.

◎ CHAPTER 3 ◎

A computer can hear words in a conversation, along with tone, inflection, and volume, but it can't feel embarrassment or confusion. Nor can it experience the sensation of darkness or feel the rattling of cold metal or the warmth of breath.

Fortunately, it doesn't need to. From a functional standpoint, it is sufficient to watch, record, and interpret the behavior of a person reacting to these things. A computer can understand discomfort as a tightening of muscles and fidgeting, irritation as an increase in blood pressure and breathing. Confusion exists in the eyes, from the perspective of an observer. And first and foremost, the computer is an observer.

After years of wearing her recorder, Persephone had provided the company with more than enough time to study and compile a detailed facsimile of her reactions in closed, crowded spaces. If AuroroTech had a need to simulate her profile in a New York City subway car, it could do so with ease.

But the computer could do far better than that. Through the prism of detailed logic engines and speech emulation software, it saw the subway as a cave, a prison, a submarine, a piggy-bank, a shot glass, and a bullet going through a gun barrel. The track was a river, a road, a never-ending fire pole, and the dark path all life must walk upon. At all times, the system was interpreting and contextualizing the experiences of its customers to provide richer and more lifelike experiences for their profiles. It wasn't enough to simulate where someone was; it was necessary to duplicate what they were experiencing, and to do so on terms as close to human as possible.

That was, after all, what their customers demanded.

Persephone despised traveling by subway, but there was no practical alternative. She held onto one of the overhead bars, which caused the recorder wrapped around her wrist to dangle in front of her face. Every now and then she noticed it and smiled, a common reaction from people subconsciously wanting to manipulate their profiles. AuroroTech's system had filters set up to detect and compensate for such things. It was their position that recorders were meant to interfere as little as possible. TomIkeTech, a competitor, disagreed: they viewed the recorders as an inherent part of Post-Surrealist life. They were even said to be developing recursive software allowing profiles to create simulated profiles of their own.

At almost all times, recorders are in communication with the massive, integrated system. The subway tunnels were networked for communications, though there were still spots the signal couldn't reach. When they crossed beneath the East River, for instance, all the blue lights would suddenly turn red for a half a minute. These moments often elicited gasps from those who were uncomfortable being out of contact. While their recorders were built to store large quantities of information, the very thought of breaking contact was enough to make some passengers uneasy. What if something happened to them? The last moments of their lives might be lost to time.

Persephone wasn't bothered by such macabre thoughts, though seeing so many lights change color at once was somewhat disturbing, as was the overall shift in mood. When she was near the front of a car, she could sometimes see it happen in the next car beforehand, like a wave of blood flowing from the front of the train towards the back.

But the tunnel passed as it always did, and the lights turned back to blue. The train ground to a stop, and some left and some arrived, as though the passengers were molecules of air in metal lungs.

When Persephone finally arrived at her stop, she lurched through the opening doors, caught by the stampede of riders anxious to be on their way. She followed the flow, allowing it to set her pace and bring her to the surface, where she emerged into the light. While the street was no less crowded than the subway or station, at least here the sky rose over her, stretching above and around the towers. She walked east on 57th Street, pausing to admire a hotel across from her.

The building was staggering. It towered overhead, its size further exaggerated through the use of tight angles. A rift ran in the center of the front wall containing a long, concave series of panels displaying a holographic image of an endless flock of birds flying upward toward the sky. As they approached the top of the tower, they turned into a shower of feathers, forming a cloud, like an inverted waterfall. Like all holographic screens, it was difficult to look at while walking by, but it was stunning to watch standing still. Post-Surrealist architecture was the merger of the real and unreal. It was the contradiction of the impossible existing, if you believed the hype, or a clever illusion, if you didn't.

She stood there while the crowd shifted around her. Every few seconds, someone muttered an "excuse me" or something less courteous. Eventually she sighed and continued on towards the building where she worked, an antiquated tower featuring quaint Postmodern design.

She entered the lobby and waved at a security guard, who hadn't even looked up from his computer screen. As she approached, his computer made a chime and the blue light on her recorder flashed yellow. She wondered how much information about her was displayed on the screen. Her name and office? Obviously. Her date of birth and security clearance code? Possibly. Her shoe size, social security number, level of education, hopes and dreams? Highly unlikely.

The guard looked up and smiled. "Good morning…" he paused as his eyes darted back to the screen, "Ms. Kilard." He looked up again. "Did you have a nice weekend?"

"It was great," she lied. "Take care."

"Thank you. You do the same."

The elevator doors opened as she approached, and she stepped on. There were no buttons present, just an empty cube with a door on each side and four lenses looking down. Her profile recorder flashed yellow again and a voice overhead announced, "Fourteenth floor." The elevator doors shut and it began to move. After a few seconds it stopped, and the voice decreed, "Sixth floor."

The doors opened, and a man stepped on holding a thin card. He held it so one of the lenses would have a clear look and said, "Tenth floor."

The system paused then said, "Please display your ID card and state desired floor."

The man sighed and shook his head. "Every time," he said to Persephone. He stretched his arm, holding the card as close as possible to the lens, and repeated himself. "Tenth floor. Tenth floor."

"Tenth floor," the system answered, and the elevator began to move.

"It's like you're not allowed to work here without one," he said under his breath. He didn't have to motion towards Persephone's recorder for the meaning to be conveyed. While it was rare to find anyone under thirty-five without a subscription, there were plenty of prophobes, particularly among older workers. Persephone just smiled back. The elevator announced the tenth floor, and the man offered a quick, "So long," before running down the hall. Once the doors had shut behind him, she shook her head.

She arrived at her floor and stepped into the thin hallway. A sign facing the elevator read, "14th Floor—Cardona-Grek Distribution Solutions." Below that was a list of names and room numbers for the ninety-six employees crammed into the floor. Her name was near the bottom.

She stood against a wall, so there'd be room for someone wheeling a mail cart to get by. The man wheeling the cart wore three separate recorders: one on his wrist, one pinned to his coat, and a third attached by a band around his head. This last device was suspended in front of him on a metal arm, imaging his entire face. It didn't seem to be picking up much data, however: his expression was almost always blank. His cart contained a few disks, a replacement computer drive, and a dozen small containers of nonprescription allergy medications being supplied to employees as a courtesy. So far, Persephone had refused this, but the building's dust and molds were taking a toll, and she knew if she stayed another year she'd wind up popping pills or sniffing sprays like all the permanent employees.

Once she'd gotten around the mail cart, she made her way to her office, a small room with a tiny window offering a view of the side of the next building. It wasn't much, but it was better than most workers at her pay grade got, at least in Manhattan. Her computer monitor stood on her desk, and she touched the screen to wake it. A chime echoed to inform her she'd been successful, and instructions appeared on the glass.

"Good morning, Persephone. A detailed manifest is requested regarding storage arrangement plans for warehouse 11371. Your manager, Barry, has asked for your report to be placed on his desk no later than three PM. Do you acknowledge?" The 'desk' was merely a figure of speech. Persephone had never stood in the same room as Barry or his desk, or the same continent for that matter. Barry was stationed in the company's Dubai office. He was one of fourteen men and women who were technically Persephone's managers, though the term reflected only their rank. In a more literal sense, the computers handled the vast majority of managerial duties. That way, if anyone was fired and sued for discrimination, the precise, impartial formulas leading to termination could be brought forth as evidence.

She acknowledged the request by pressing the screen. Then she sat down and began studying the information before her. She selected multiple objects, grouped them together, then altered the heading, simplifying data and shifting items around.

There were computer programs capable of doing all this, of course, since there were programs that could do almost anything a human mind could. Her decisions would be compared to the computer's as a fail-safe in case of error. In the end, the computer's report would almost certainly be used. This was no judgment about her capacities, merely policy designed to protect the company from possible litigation, just like the managerial structure. Still, while her work most likely wouldn't be used directly, if problems arose because of the computer's plan, it would incorporate her strategies and concepts as it evolved better and more efficient processes. She was an important part of a vast system, helping the computer system to develop and change. Even more important, flesh and blood employees served as a write-off countering the costly taxes imposed on digital systems. There was a price for replacing real workers with simulated ones.

She continued these actions, on and off, until 11:30, when a memo appeared on her screen asking if she'd like to order lunch from Taco Curry's. She tapped the memo, which opened a menu on her screen. She selected the Chicken Kiew-Wan Tandoori Fajita along with a Diet Coke, then returned to work. Her computer told her when the food arrived, and she went to pick it up in the break room along with her coworkers. About half of the office had turned up in the small enclosure, though the majority sorted through the piled bags of food, found their meal, and returned to eat at their desks.

Persephone, who'd been sitting in the same office for the entire morning, stayed in the break room, which was nowhere near large enough to accommodate the number of people trying to eat there.

The three small, square tables were already taken, so she stood against a wall and ate as neatly as possible, holding the wrapped fajita in one hand and the bag containing her can of soda in the other. She stood beside Nethaniel, a short, balding black man who wore a blue shirt and a button containing several interlocking circles. The symbol was common among those who looked as though they weren't of mixed ancestry, and its meaning was simple: that the wearer was not a Purist. There were still some neighborhoods where it was unsafe to be black, white, or any other single recognizable ethnicity and not wear such a sign.

"How are you?" he asked Persephone, who smiled, mouth full of food. "Have a nice weekend?"

"I guess," she nodded after swallowing. "Too short, right? You?"

"Not so much. Recorder broke down, and I had to get it repaired. Spent most of Saturday in the store waiting. They offered me a replacement, but you know how it is. You get attached." He tapped the device, similar to a pen, sticking out of his shirt pocket. "Not a total loss," he added. "Got one of these." He turned his head to reveal the FeedBack unit in his ear.

"Yeah. Seems like everyone's getting one."

"It's not that different from having your profile on your monitor, but you take it with you."

"Oh," Persephone said. "I don't really play with that, either."

"Huh," Nethaniel said, amused. "Know thyself. It's good, gives you sports, weather whenever you need it. Advice on stuff, right? Knew about everything on the menu. How's your fajita?"

"Bland," Persephone confessed.

"Yup," Nethaniel nodded. "That's what it said."

"I think my roommate's getting a FeedBack piece," Persephone said. "But I never buy tech when it first comes out. You know how it is. Always gets cheaper."

Nethaniel laughed. "That's why I'll never be able to retire," he said. "But if it means a better meal, well, priorities?"

Persephone shrugged and finished her food before taking her soda back to her desk. It was only a few minutes after noon, and she still had almost six hours to go before she could head home.

◎

There is, from a practical standpoint, no need for a computerized system to create a simulated screen in an unmonitored drive. In fact, to have a simulated person observing the data on a simulated monitor is arguably the pinnacle of inefficiency. A program could simply be written to transfer data from one form or location to another. There is no need to simulate display.

But then programs, at least primitive ones, were coded by humans, who are an inherently irrational and inefficient species. Even the later programs were constructed by simpler programs than themselves, almost always under human supervision and planning, so these are built with form in mind as much as function. It is argued by Neo-Idealizts, in fact, that this is something of a virtue of mankind, that the manner in which information flows is far more significant than its perceived source or goal. Whether this is indeed the case, the programs that modeled the electronic landscape of AuroroTech's internal drives were governed by rules of excess rather than simplicity. So, because a programmer created systems to develop such rules, dozens of simulated screens were rendered before the simulated eyes of a fully rendered image of a man, despite the fact that none of this appeared on any physical display.

Not all rules of the real world were observed. For instance, gravity appeared only as a guideline, preventing objects from drifting into the empty depths of space. The screens were attached to nothing; instead they were suspended in midair. There were no wires or tubes connecting them to the simulated environment beyond: the energy and information was everywhere, and the objects were beyond the limitations of physical reality and space.

Likewise, the observer sat, but there was nothing to support his weight; a moot point, of course, as a digital simulation has none. He was suspended as though sitting, despite the absence of a chair, and, so far as the simulation was concerned, there was nothing wrong with this. Alternate environments with more traditional protocols for gravity could be accessed, even though nothing rendered contained mass.

A similar case could be made for the simulated man himself, whose backside hung in the air. There is no need for the simulation to include the man's ass, for instance, as its function was not incorporated in the program. In fact, both defecation and urination are excluded from any and all AuroroTech profiles, as a matter of company policy. For those unable to accept such an omission, other less reputable profiling firms offer more complete representations of bodily functions.

The majority of screens appearing before the simulated man contained the images of actual people. One screen was entirely black with the name, "Persephone Kilard" in white text. Beside this, the word "Offline" flashed in red. The simulated man no longer glanced at this screen even in passing. Another monitor, containing the name "Isuel Morgan-Yager," showed an infrared image of AuroroTech's CEO sleeping beside his wife. There were others as well, and, from time to time, the simulation glanced at these. The reason he did so was always the same: he looked because the man he was a simulation of would have done so, or at least the computer program simulating the situation concluded so. And, to the limits that the system was able to estimate, any conclusions the original would have made, the simulated made, as well.

His attention was primarily focused on a central screen, which read, "Archived News Footage—Clip 995413.6.22." There were two men displayed, one of whom was Isuel Morgan-Yager, albeit a younger version than that sleeping on the other screen, as evidenced by the lack of grey in his red hair. The other man was Theodore Souza-Fontaine-Floros, a journalist who'd died in a plane crash after the recording was made.

The host was speaking in an animated manner intended to keep both his guest and audience engaged. He exclaimed, "Almost sixty percent of Profilers are Christian, which, correct me if I'm wrong, that's about the same as the country as a whole, isn't it?"

"Sounds about right," Morgan-Yager said, nodding enthusiastically. Whenever possible, Isuel tried to reaffirm that a majority of his US customers were self-described Christians and not practitioners of fringe religions and newly formed philosophies.

"So... are they taking out insurance?" Here the audience began to chuckle. On the recording, this came out as almost a low purr.

Because he knew it was better to come off as friendly, Morgan-Yager laughed as well. "That's a rather cynical approach!" he said loudly.

"But no, nothing like that, I think. There's no conflict between our services and Christian teaching. None. I know there are some pretty extreme groups and even companies out there—"

"Could you…."

"I don't want to name names."

"You're talking about Vincool now, right?" the host asked, referring to a now defunct profiling service.

"Like I said, I don't want to name names. But some of our competitors have pushed… overzealous marketing claims which can cloud the issue."

"Yeah. You're talking about Vincool." The chuckling returned from the audience, and the host couldn't quite suppress a smirk.

"I can think of five companies off the top of my head, but I'm not here to start fights. Look, what we do—like all of our competitors—is provide state-of-the-art profiling hardware and software, allowing anyone to build a digital presence capable of real interaction. You mentioned the word insurance earlier, and I want to go back to that. Because, among other advantages, these are a kind of insurance, but not for our souls. This is insurance for our families and friends. If, God forbid, something were to happen to me tomorrow, my kids wouldn't grow up without me. We're not salvaging what's inside a person. We're keeping the part of you that the world sees and knows. We're keeping the social you. Now, this has numerous applications, as we've shown. We've revolutionized psychotherapy, medicine, customer service, and a host of other fields. But it also means when our loved ones pass, we can keep a part of them with us. Not their souls, or anything so dramatic—our equipment is only made of metal, plastic, and wires. No, we can keep their memory. That's what we're offering." There was a round of soft applause from the audience, like rain drops.

"So, am I right in saying that you're at odds with the Dalai Lama?" the host asked.

Isuel Morgan-Yager rolled his eyes. "You're trying to get me into trouble now," he said. The audience responded favorably, with the low thunder of laughter.

"Not at all. I just want to be clear that the Dalai Lama has gone on record as saying that there may be a spiritual component to your services. So, if you're saying there isn't, you're at odds. Isn't that right?"

"His Holiness, who I've had the opportunity to meet, is interested in what this technology could mean for the future, as am I. Not all Buddhists share his optimism, but almost everyone I've heard from has offered their opinion in a very respectful way."

"The Dalai Lama said that your profiling services could eventually be used to reconnect a soul with earlier incarnations, right? Do you think that's really possible?"

Morgan-Yager paused for an instant before answering. Outside the simulated monitor, the simulated observer watched his face carefully. "I don't see myself as qualified to speculate," he said.

"Because you don't believe in reincarnation?"

"Well, because I'm not Buddhist," Morgan-Yager said plainly. "Whether or not reincarnation exists, the information in our database is going to be around for future generations. We'll be able to provide access to ideas and personalities from our time. Whether this is something that will be of greater benefit to individuals or society at large would be mere speculation. I'm just proud to have helped develop the technology." This received another round of polite applause.

"All right," the host said, nodding. "How about the dissenting view? There are some who believe that your system is creating a duplicate soul or individual. I know some Buddhists have said this perpetuates the cycle of pain. How does that strike you?"

"Well, I think you're oversimplifying their view, which ties into thousands of years of tradition which, honestly, I don't really understand. But I think you're mostly talking about Dilip Mohabir and the Euro-American Reformed Buddhist movement. I've had several conversations with Mohabir, and I think he's a fascinating person. I don't agree with what he's suggesting, but I appreciate the way he approaches the subject. I wish the Trans-Atlantic Baptist Association used the same tone. As to whether I think we're copying souls or selves or chakras, I think I've already covered that. We're working with computer systems, not spirits. I believe it's clear that this technology isn't for everyone. There are those who are disturbed by the creation of a digital profile that looks and acts like we do. Personally, I think it's kind of cool." Another short burst of applause from the audience, punctuated by some light laughter.

The observer held up his hand, and the image froze. He sat staring at the image for almost a minute then opened his mouth. "Load next interview," he commanded. He'd been rendered here for some time, and, for whatever reason, continued to watch. His eyes changed position and settled on the screen picturing Morgan-Yager asleep. Beside the name, the simulated screen displayed the word, "Live."

◎ CHAPTER 4 ◎

"You know, Persephone," Ms. Loring said, "I used to abhor shopping for shoes." It was early Saturday afternoon, and Ms. Loring was seated on a stool trying on a pair of mismatched pumps. Her lipstick was applied in one color today with no unusual patterns; it was even a traditional red. However, she had applied this to her upper left cheek—in a normal 'lip' shape, of course—leaving her actual lips undecorated.

"Then why is our closet full of those things?" Persephone asked.

Ms. Loring looked down at the shoes she had on. "Because I am a glutton for punishment. And I need them to create my esthetic."

"Is this some Post-Surrealist thing?"

"The world is a Post-Surrealist thing. I am merely crying out for its attention. I have no instinct for style or art, just an esthetic to drive me."

"Wasn't that in a commercial for pants?"

"Something like it was, and I'll have you know I bought a pair of those pants. But I have no shoes to match, which is why we are here. Hmmm. What about these? How do they look?"

"I like the left, but not the right," Persephone said.

"Oh. I'm sorry, I wasn't talking to you." Ms. Loring pressed the small transmitter into her ear to better hear the voice. After a moment she glanced up at her roommate. "Well, my profile thinks they're stunning. You see, this is precisely why I USED to hate shopping for shoes. Now, it's an exciting adventure. And I anticipate it will remain so for at least three weeks to come before I grow as bored with this as I do with everything."

"How much do you want to bet the shoe store pays AuroroTech to compliment their shoes?"

"Now you're being absurd," Ms. Loring replied. "And, as usual, you're behind the curve. I want to stop by the AuroroStore anyway. While we're there, you should look into a FeedBack plan."

"Why? Other than lie about something looking good on you, what does it do?"

"First of all, a profile doesn't lie. This is more a consistent and enduring delusion brought on by my own fancies. It only likes these shoes because I always like things like them. It's merely reinforcing that this is, indeed, something I like."

"You should know whether or not you like something," Persephone replied.

"Well, I know I like them now. But my profile is a far better judge of whether I'll like them tomorrow. As you're no doubt aware, I am annoyingly inconsistent, and, as a result, I have little faith in my whims of fancy. Oh, and it does something else." Ms. Loring removed the shoes from her feet and returned them to the box. "Take this back to the shelf, will you? We're leaving." She began putting her own shoes back on while Persephone just shook her head and returned the pumps to where Ms. Loring had found them.

They stepped through the door and into the hot afternoon air. Ms. Loring began fanning herself while Persephone shielded her eyes so they could adjust to the light.

"Oh, yes. The other thing that FeedBack does. It links me to immediate information about participating stores in the area. In this case, it's informed me I can have that same pair for forty dollars cheaper at a store in the Union Square Mall."

"Did you ask it to tell you that?"

"I didn't have to. It knows what I want and it provides it. So you see, there is no reason anyone should have to go through life without one. Not even you."

"And yet we've made it this far," Persephone said.

"You have such a Pre-Postmodern outlook, you know that? Don't take that the wrong way, I actually meant it as a compliment. But it's true. You see everything in such black, white, and grey terms. No alternate dimensions of meaning or transient tones of inflection. I rather envy that, because it gives you a real sense of identity to grasp. The rest of us need to clutch at pretense, but you came with it installed."

"Okay," Persephone said. "Is your replacement brain feeding you that?"

"It doesn't replace your brain," Ms. Loring said. "It just gives you a second one. You get a whole other set of thoughts, an elaborate memory engram, and access to unlimited information you don't even need to realize you need. All that and constant access to your profile."

"Let me ask you this. Are these your arguments or the computer's?"

Ms. Loring laughed. "The best part is I don't even know. After a few days, it all blends together, and you don't even think about where the voice is coming from."

"Wow. Okay. That just went from a little creepy to really creepy. Like, mind-control creepy. Thanks for the recommendation, but I'm going to have to say no thanks to the voices in my head. God, I'd probably forget to turn it off."

"You don't have to turn it off. It's just there. I only take it out before going to bed."

"So, what? It gives you advice on how you wipe your ass?" Persephone asked, waiting for her friend to deny it. Waiting. Waiting. "Oh, God. It does, doesn't it? It tells you how to shit."

"It doesn't tell you how to shit. But it knows where there's a bathroom if you need one. Besides, I haven't gotten to the best part. You can link it to a partner's profile, so they share information."

"Wait, what? What kind of information? Oh. Oh no. This is a sex thing, isn't it?"

Ms. Loring grinned. "Hell, yes. You get detailed data about what your partner needs. And, far more importantly, they get the same on you. I am never dating a man who doesn't own one again."

"Wow. I want to apologize, because before, when I said this tech was creepy, I didn't really know what the word meant."

"You're so old-fashioned. The technology exists, why not use it to make life a little better?"

"No, no, no. See, if there's one part of my life I don't want some nerd's code crawling over, it's that."

Ms. Loring laughed. "Fine. Be that way. But we'll be at the

AuroroStore in a few minutes, and you should at least let them try to sell you on something new."

"What do you need there, anyway?"

"My brother's birthday is coming up, and I was thinking about upgrading his background setting."

"Can't Jackson afford his own settings?" Persephone asked. "He makes more than both of us put together."

"No, my OTHER brother," Ms. Loring replied. "This is for Oxford, who can't afford anything, I'm afraid. His birthday is next week, which is also uncomfortably close to when he died. Not the same day, unfortunately, because that would make for an even more tragic and poignant story, but in the same month. It's funny you bring up Jackson, though. I asked him if he wanted to chip in on Ox's present, and you'll never guess what he said."

"Let's see. That you were crazy for buying something for a dead guy's profile?" Persephone asked.

"His wording was slightly different, but the content was precisely right. I wish I could say I expected better, but, well, you know Jackson. Even so, it's utterly repugnant responding to such a request with reason and logic."

"Yeah. I only met Jackson once, but we didn't really get along."

"Of course not. My dear brother Jackson is a pompous ass. But then, he is family, I suppose."

"You know who kind of reminded me of him? Arthur. From a few weeks ago."

"Oh, at De'Muure? I suppose so," Ms. Loring reflected. "Probably best you decided not to pursue that then."

"No worries," Persephone said. "I wasn't fond of Arthur, and I didn't get the impression he was fond of me."

"He was better than my date. What was his name? Oh, yes. Edward, thank you."

"I didn't remind you," Persephone said.

"Really? I could have sworn. Oh, well. At any rate, Edward's advances went unanswered."

"Did he contact you?"

"Oh, poor Edward tried to invite me to several different events, but…. Oh, dear. I must have blocked him by mistake." She smiled as she walked through the crowd. "Did I tell you I submitted my portfolio to *Gothin Thine*?" Ms. Loring asked. "No, I suppose I didn't."

"I don't know anymore," Persephone said. "I can't keep track."

"What a horrid thing to say to an aspiring estheticist," Ms. Loring pouted.

Persephone sighed. "I didn't mean it that way."

"Of course you didn't," Ms. Loring replied. "Yet there it is nonetheless."

"Do you even like *Gothin Thine*?" Persephone asked.

"God no," Ms. Loring replied. "But they do weekly pieces on aspiring artists. That's how Kincar Davidson got his break."

"Who?"

"Oh, he's not any good," Ms. Loring said. "He's into explicit erotic estheticism. You know? Triple E?"

"I've never heard of it and don't want to know," Persephone said.

"The point is, if they like my work, it would represent a grand opportunity for my as-of-yet imaginary artistic career."

"Well, good luck," Persephone said.

"Thank you," Ms. Loring replied. "Just be sure you're there to comfort me when it all inevitably falls through."

By that time, they were approaching the entrance to the AuroroStore, a large set of revolving doors illuminated with blue lights. Moving clouds were projected onto the doors from above. The two women went in, entering a wide-open room surrounded by a row of electronic devices all around the wall. Above the miniaturized computers, earpieces, recorders, and other accessories were large monitors, which displayed instructions, features, and costs for everything present and everything not.

They'd barely had time to get their bearings when a sales representative hurried over. He wore large glasses containing miniaturized cameras looking out and looking in to capture every detail of his own eyes: every twitch, blink, and glance. The eyes, of course, are windows to the soul, and among the technologically savvy such tools are considered key to capturing and copying its essence.

He clapped his hands together and greeted the shoppers. "Good afternoon, Ms. Loring. Hi, Ms. Kilard. My name's Barrett. How can I help you today?"

"You see," Ms. Loring said, ostensibly to Persephone, "that's why I love shopping here. The personalized service."

In response, Persephone glanced up at one of the overhead cameras and sneered. "Remind me to adjust my privacy settings when we get home," she whispered.

"Sorry about that," Barrett replied, a bit startled. "The system didn't think it would make you uncomfortable." He tapped his earpiece.

"Oh, don't give it a second thought," Ms. Loring said. "I'm the one here to do the buying, anyway, and I like hearing my name. You're welcome to ignore Persephone."

"Well," he said, regaining his composure, "what can I help you with?"

"Mostly I've come to look at posthumous environments," Ms. Loring said.

"Of course," Barrett said, quickly growing grave and serious. AuroroTech employees are required to undergo annual sensitivity courses about the sale of such software. "Is this someone you've lost recently?"

"No," Ms. Loring said cheerfully to lighten the mood. "My brother's been gone a few years now. I just thought it'd be nice to upgrade his environment. He's still on Halla 14, and I know it's kind of dull. Whenever I log into see him, it just looks like a weird game. I mean, I know you can't really be unhappy when you're dead, but I thought he might be more comfortable somewhere else."

"Well, I know it sounds really unoriginal, but the new Heaven setting is really nice. If you'd like, I can show you on the simulator."

"Sounds great," Ms. Loring said. "Oh, and my roommate definitely needs to see this, too. She's always so good, she deserves a trip to Heaven." She followed this up, as she always did, by wrinkling her nose and laughing in a manner so playful and harmless it was almost impossible to become angry. Almost. Persephone was adapting.

"Right this way," Barrett said, guiding the women to one of the walls. Here, there was a row of headphones and goggles hanging beneath a line of monitors. Working faster than Persephone could follow, his middle finger tapped the screen in a series of locations. She wondered if he even needed to look anymore or if he could make these selections from memory.

Barrett held the headphones out towards Ms. Loring. "Go ahead and put these on if you're ready."

"Take Persephone first," Ms. Loring said, pushing her roommate forward. "I'm a sinner."

Barrett feigned a laugh and offered them to Persephone instead. They were huge, and she slipped them over her head. His voice faded almost immediately to a muffled whisper, while the rest of the store disappeared completely. Even the horns from the traffic outside faded away. His lips kept moving, but Persephone couldn't understand.

"What?" she said, while Ms. Loring jumped. A quick glance revealed that several customers were looking at Persephone. She pulled one earphone away and said, "Sorry. Really. I'm sorry. What was that?"

Barrett did his best to keep up the pleasant demeanor, but he'd cringed a bit. Still, he kept his irritation out of his voice while he said, "No problem. Once you've got those in place, just slip on the goggles." He pointed to a pair sitting in front of Persephone.

She released the earphone, so it fell back to her ear. Once more, she was surrounded by near silence. Then she slipped the goggles on and there was darkness as well. Nothing but an emptiness. A void.

Then, in the void, Persephone heard a voice, distant and soft. And that voice asked, "Is it on?" At first she didn't understand. Then she realized it was Barrett, and, being careful to speak quietly, she replied, "No. I can't see anything. Just darkness."

"Oh. Sorry." Persephone felt a hand reach up and throw a switch on the goggles. At once there was a hum, quiet and soft, and a dim light around her. "How about now?"

"I… I see something," Persephone said. "But I can't make it out." There was a uniform grey haze she couldn't penetrate or make sense of.

"There zanob," the voice said.

"What?" Persephone yelled, forgetting once again that the clerk, while seeming so distant, was really inches away.

"A knob! There's a knob," the voice called back.

She reached to her face, feeling the goggles and feeling between them. In the center, as promised, she found a dial, which she shifted, first one way then the other. Almost at once, the haze began to dissipate, as the light shifted away from the darkness and objects began to take form. She could now see a white fog at her feet and crystal towers around her. The sky above was black, but covered in stars by the millions, each bright and sparkling.

On the ground around her were a series of racket ball courts, several of which were occupied by the simulations of those who had gone before. "It's still blurry," she said, trying to fine-tune the image.

"Oh," the voice called back. "It's supposed to be a little blurry. It's Heaven."

Suddenly, the vision began to shake, and the goggles pulled away. Ms. Loring was standing beside her. "Okay, dear. That's enough of an eternal reward for today. I'd like a look." Persephone, happy to get the contraption off her head, handed over the headphones as well.

Ms. Loring pulled the goggles on, twisted the knob a few times, hummed to herself, then removed them. "It's fine," she said.

"Then you'd like to take it?" Barrett asked, trying to hide the thrill of the commission from his customers.

"Yeah, sure," Ms. Loring replied, and her recorder flashed yellow. "Do I need to enter a password or anything?"

"No," Barrett replied. "Verbal agreement is all we need. You can view a receipt on our website. And, of course, you'll get a full refund if you decide to cancel the purchase in the next thirty days. The next time you sign in, you'll get full details on accessing your purchase."

"Great," Ms. Loring said without conviction. She turned to Persephone. "So, are you going to let them talk you into signing up for FeedBack?"

Barrett didn't miss a beat. "FeedBack is a great service. In addition to the social networking advantages, it's a great tool for personal safety. Along with some basic vital monitoring hardware, it can detect health threats and warn you—"

"Yeah, thanks, not interested," Persephone said, interrupting the clerk.

"Are you sure?" he asked. "It's not just recreational. "Does your work require you to communicate with non-English speakers?"

"No. I don't talk to anyone at work. Ever."

"Oh. Well, if you're ever traveling or anything, the Feedback will translate just about any language. Certainly any living language, and they're working towards total fluency. So, if you're wearing one, you can understand anyone on Earth. And, if they've got one, too, they'll understand you."

"Don't they already have things that do that?"

"Well, sure. But Feedback eliminates the need to haul around an extra device or spend time finding an online application."

"Yeah, well that's not a need I have anyway."

Barrett remembered to smile. "Well, if you ever change your mind, we're always open online. Send me a message if you have any questions or if you'd like more info about FeedBack. You can reach me through the AururoTech site. We've got some great case studies and testimonials about the system."

"I'm sure they're great, but I'm afraid it would make me more like her," Persephone said, motioning towards Ms. Loring.

"Fine," Ms. Loring replied. "Come on, phobe. I still want to pick up those shoes."

◎ CHAPTER 5 ◎

You pull it apart, you know what our software is? You know what it's really made up of? You've got about two dozen disparate programs modeling different aspects of cognition, vocal patterns, physical communication, and inflection. These are, as often as not, reaching contrary conclusions, and I'll get back to that in a minute. Now, on top of all that, you've got three logic engines which kick in and out, because each is better or worse at certain things. Now, keep in mind those logic engines aren't there to keep communication logical; that would defeat the purpose, because the vast majority of things coming out of peoples' mouths aren't remotely logical to begin with. The logic engines are there to uphold a consistency of idea, an illusion of logic, if you will. This is because the core of our system is more or less the most ridiculously simple computer program anyone's ever built. The central brilliance of FaxSimulation's—and all our competitors'—profiling software is a simple language system. Any word you say, no matter what it is, has a certain number of possible follow ups, say somewhere between ten and thirty.

The first word that a profile—or a real person for that matter—says is based on some acting force. Sometimes we're talking about a memory or idea; other times we're talking about stimuli. Whatever it is, this forms a kind of backbone for the entire interaction, at least until it changes.

For example, maybe you're asking a question based on need, or you're acting against some stimulus, or you're responding to a direct inquiry. We've got subroutines for all these; some are fairly complex, others are laughably simple. But what always blows everyone's mind is the fact we can construct realistic sentences. All we're doing is calculating likely words and phrases, based on what you've said in the past in response to similar stimuli, and feeding that raw data through an engine to develop some semblance of sense. As long as it follows up on that backbone, that basic idea or goal or argument, it just has to be consistent with things the client's said in the past.

Then, we're overlapping all the extras: inflection, tone, vocal patterns, lyricism; it's all off previous data. If the profile's being viewed, we toss in physicality, eye movements, and the works. Again, we've got programs for all these individual ticks and gaffes—you name it—that can duplicate almost any common form of communication. Individually, none of it's complicated. But, put it together, and you've got a hell of a convincing simulation.

There were some major delays moving into new markets, because the basic language protocol had to be entirely rewritten for other languages. What worked for English could not simply be translated.

-Frank Hu-Turing, Executive Program Coordinator for FaxSimulation, discussing their technology on the "Tough Talk Tech" podcast.

◎

When Ms. Loring woke up, her hand reached out to slap her alarm clock, which was screeching like a bird tangled in fishing line. With her first swipe, she managed to knock the alarm back a few inches but missed the snooze button entirely. The noise went on, so she struck again, this time right on top. Her blow landed, and, with a final dying squawk, the clock went silent. Ms. Loring's arm went limp and she lay completely still.

In the same instant, prompted by information captured by her charging recorder and empowered by the settings she'd selected months before, her computer awoke from its sleep mode. Programs started of their own accord, each performing its function and starting others in turn, like dominoes dropping in line. The system accessed the web and opened AuroroTech's site. From there, it jumped to Ms. Loring's personal page and brought up her profile, which stood in the center of the screen.

"Oh God," the digital recreation scowled. "I can't believe I'm still in bed." The voice was a flawless imitation, capturing the original's inflection, tone, and—despite the fact no eyes were open to appreciate it—even her mannerisms.

"Five more minutes," the flesh and blood Ms. Loring muttered beneath a mound of sheets and comforters.

"Five minutes now is five late. The day is upon me, and what a day it shall be. Low seventies and not too humid. So let's get this going."

Ms. Loring struggled to sit up. Her head oscillated from the sudden rush of blood, and she rubbed her eyes with her hands. Then she stood, stretched her arms over her head, and yawned.

"Can't forget the alarm," her profile said. "I don't want to give it the satisfaction of going off again." Ms. Loring reached down and turned it off completely. Then she stretched once more and went to the tiny cubby that passed for her closet and began to dress. She looked at the blouses before her and paused. "Today's a red day," her profile said from the computer screen behind her.

Ms. Loring took out one of her red blouses and looked it over. "On second thought," she said, "I think I'll go with blue."

"A blue day, it is," her profile purred. Ms. Loring pulled it on and buttoned the front. She grabbed a pair of slacks, put them on, and went for the computer. She sat down and her profile said, "Two messages. One from Hector and one from some guy I don't know."

Ms. Loring nodded to the sound of her voice and tapped an image of a note that had appeared on the screen. She skimmed the messages and closed them without answering. "Better get something to eat," Ms. Loring whispered.

"I can't forget my earpiece," her profile added, copying the expression on her face. Ms. Loring reached beside the computer and grabbed a cold, metallic box. She popped open the clasp and flipped up the top. Inside was the small device, which she pulled out and slid into her left ear. She rotated it until it fit. "So much better," her profile whispered. The computer logged itself off and slipped back into a sleep mode, while Ms. Loring stood and stretched her arms.

"Now what am I forgetting?" the profile demanded.

"Of course," Ms. Loring said to herself, stopping in her tracks. She hurried to her dresser, where her recorder was sitting on its charger. Its light was blue, since she never bothered to turn it off—there was no reason to do so, after all. She grabbed it and pinned it to her collar. She watched her reflection in the oval mirror as she worked to make sure the recorder was attached at a good angle. She didn't want her profile to lose out on valuable information, after all. She also attached a supplemental band monitor around her calf to capture some basic vital reactions.

Then came the makeup, applied sparingly, because at some point in her life Ms. Loring had decided that was how she applied it. Finally, she brought out her lipstick and sighed. It was a workday, so any artistic application would need to be kept to a minimum. Dress codes were the bane of the struggling estheticist. She applied it as conventionally as she could stand, then shifted to a contrasting color for just the very corners of her mouth. Her hair took some time, requiring brushing, arranging, some spray, and then some final molding. When she was done, she smiled at the mirror.

"Now how do I look?" either her profile asked or she asked herself.

"Oh, I look fantastic," the other replied, and off she went.

When she reached the living room, Ms. Loring found her roommate already up and eating a bowl of cereal.

"Really," Ms. Loring said. "How utterly predictable."

"There's some leftover pizza in the fridge," Persephone said. "You could mix it in a blender with orange juice and a raw egg."

"Perhaps for dinner," Ms. Loring replied, and her own voice quietly laughed in her ear. "But juice sounds good." She poured herself a glass of orange juice and sat on the couch to drink it. "I want pancakes," she said out of the blue. Her profile added, "With maple syrup."

"We don't have pancake mix," Persephone replied.

"Of course we don't. We have almost nothing, and must therefore suffer through breakfast every day. Perhaps after work I'll buy a waffle iron."

"I thought you wanted pancakes."

"Well, I thought I did, too. But waffle irons are on sale a block away from my work. And you know how I love a sale." She finished off her juice while her profile said, "Save your money in one hand and your soul in the other and see which gets you a drink." She started laughing.

"What is it this time?"

"I was just thinking about a line from *Kella's An Ass.* You ever watch that?"

"No. I can't stand that woman." Persephone scooped up a spoonful of cereal, which, thanks to chemical modification, sparkled like diamonds in her spoon.

"That's because you have taste," Ms. Loring said, before saying in tandem with her profile, "And taste bites." Both Ms. Loring and Ms. Loring's profile laughed together.

Ms. Loring's profile mentioned, "Kella produced a movie opening next weekend, *Lip Service and Obey*, starring Lesley Bai-Chu and Fadl Pakulski."

"Oh," Ms. Loring said, "do you want to see that movie opening this weekend, the one with Bai-Chu and that guy from *God's Blog*?"

"What? I haven't heard of it. Is it supposed to be any good?"

Ms. Loring sat still for a moment while her profile whispered, "Test audiences viewed it somewhat favorably, with a slim majority saying they planned to see it again."

"Kind of," Ms. Loring replied at last. "I don't know."

Persephone shrugged in response. "I guess. If you're going."

Ms. Loring's profile added, "There is a seventy-percent chance I'll enjoy the movie, but only a four percent chance I'll list it as one of my favorite films of the year." Such statistics were easily cobbled together by comparing Ms. Loring's previous reactions to movies against those of test audiences.

"You know what? Forget it. It doesn't look that good, anyway." Suddenly, Ms. Loring set her juice on the end table, leapt to her feet, and darted across the room.

"What is it?" Persephone asked.

"Mosquito," Ms. Loring said, clapping her hands together in the air. She looked down at her hands and made a face. "Ugh," she said, darting into the kitchen to wash her hands.

"I can't believe you saw that," Persephone said. "Oh, wait. You didn't, did you?"

Ms. Loring tore off a piece of paper towel to dry her hands. Her profile then whispered, "Oh. I can't forget about tonight," and Ms. Loring repeated it.

"What? You were serious about the waffle iron?"

Ms. Loring snickered. "Of course not. If I decide to get a waffle iron, I'll order one. No, I wanted to tell you I'm meeting some friends at Yeltzin's for drinks. You want to come?"

"Yeltzin's? Is that the place with all the blacklights?"

"No, you're thinking of Tribadore's," Ms. Loring said, while her profile corrected her. "Sorry, I mean Trybera. Yeltzin's is the nice place with live music, food, and… yes. You like music."

"Wait, is this the place with the ceiling monitors? The Neo-Idealizt one?"

"Yes, I think it does have some monitors," Ms. Loring said evasively.

"You know what I think of that stuff," Persephone said.

"Otherwise you'll just wind up here, alone, doing nothing. Meet me at Yeltzin's at eight."

"Who else is going?" Persephone demanded.

"No one you like," Ms. Loring said, "so it won't matter if you're in a bad mood. So. I'll see you then."

"We'll see," Persephone said, even though both of them knew she'd show.

◎

Michael Ling sat at his terminal, staring somewhat blankly into his monitor. In his ear, his own voice spoke. "Code section three clear," it said. Technically, Ling was violating AuroroTech policy by altering the parameters of his profile to work alongside him. But there were extenuating circumstances. The policy existed to keep in line with complex tax codes designed to keep humans working rather than simply reprogramming and duplicating the profile of a single technician. Certain fields, including customer service, were managed separately. Companies had been using artificial intelligence systems to field calls for years before the profiling firms developed the current personality modeling software that made services like AuroroTech's possible. Psychology and medicine were likewise exempt, as offering cheap access to simulated experts made them available to the masses. But laws about technology services were among the strictest: these jobs were supposed to be in human hands.

And AuroroTech certainly had its share of flesh and blood

employees. But none of those were qualified to assist Michael Ling, the newly promoted head designer and systems architect. In fact, there was no one alive Ling considered qualified to help him scan through the hundreds of thousands of subroutines and programs which allowed their computers to do the impossible, to create a mirror image of life and set it loose in a digital enclosure.

A message appeared on his screen reading, "Meeting Notification. Update Requested. 3:00 PM."

Ling closed the message and returned to his work. "Code section six clear," he said, in part to himself and in part to his profile. He moved on to the next in line. It wasn't code he was viewing, at least not directly. There was far too much code to examine line by line. Instead, he was studying a visual abstraction of the code, along with summaries and descriptions. As he went, he'd isolate routines, plug some data in, and verify that the programs behaved as predicted. So far, they all had, though a surprising number were more complex than they needed to be. The code was anything but eloquent, including programs inside programs, which processed extraneous variables and linked in unintuitive ways.

He didn't dare try to correct these, because he didn't know what was in use by other programs and functions. Maybe after a few years he'd understand the geography of the system well enough to fix the underlying problems. More likely, by that time, they'd have had to add so many enhancements and corrections that the system would be ten times as complicated. By then, he doubted he'd care anyway.

Ling blinked and turned away from the screen. He reached for his cup of coffee and said, "I see why my predecessor blew his brains out." He shook his head to try and shake off the sheer weight of the job. Then he touched a control panel on his screen, bringing up a list of subordinates. "Speaking of the devil," he muttered, sipping the lukewarm coffee, "let's see if we've found him." He selected one of the managers, who replied immediately, appearing in a panel on his screen.

"Mike, how are you?"

Ling nodded and said, "Morning, Vijay."

"It's two thirty, Mike. You should take a break."

"I am," he replied. "I wanted to check on the status of your team's project. Have you found it yet?"

"Well, there was nothing in the central database," Vijay said. "Burgand entirely removed his profile."

"And the shadow drive? Did he clear the backup?"

"Well, see, that's where it all gets complicated. It looks like he did. But his profile ID is still active."

"If it's active, can't we just run a search?" Ling asked.

"Again, well, that's a yes and a no. It's fragmented. Plus, even accessing the shadow drive is tricky business. It's designed to interact with the main engine, not to be pulled up directly. I've got a team working on a system that should be able to interact with the drive. But… yeah. It's going to take a while."

"Keep at it," Ling said. "Contact me if you can access it."

"Yeah. Of course," Vijay said. "Hey, take care, all right?"

Ling shut off the communication then buried his face in his hands. He looked back to his screen, at the various files and programs, and reopened the one he'd just been working on. He found one of the extraneous data bits then set his computer to track it. It was directed towards the shadow drive.

"Code section three," he said. "Any unnecessary access to shadow drive. Identify."

His profile answered. "Negative."

"Code section eleven. Same question."

"Negative," the profile replied. "I'll search for shadow drive access in all future analysis."

"Good," Ling said, shaking his head. It was after two, he hadn't had lunch yet, and the code was starting to play tricks on him. "Continue work," he said, while he got up to get something from the vending machines before his meeting.

◎ Chapter 6 ◎

It is impossible to say what esthetic is. Rather, we say what it is not. It is not merely a concept. It is not a mere reflection, no matter how many Neo-Idealizts call it such. It is not identity, but it was born from the death of identity, like a flower growing out of the eye of a corpse. Identity, you see, can be described; it can be put into words and syllables. And make no mistake, there are no words for esthetic. If every language in the world were mined, the combined lexicon could not begin to illuminate the esthetic of a single child.

Here's an exercise for those who wish it: ask yourself what you are. Make a list of every term that's ever been used to describe you, everything you've ever thought you were or wanted to be. Now eat the list. What you shit out is more your esthetic than the list could ever have hoped to be, because it passed through you.

You ask what esthetic is? Ask what you are. A series of memories. A unique genetic code. A mass of blood and bile sloshing in a misshapen sack of flesh. Your mind and beliefs. All of these together are the iceberg's tip of what you are. And esthetic is the sea the iceberg floats in.

There is no esthetic like yours. It is unique. You don't understand it, no one will ever understand it. You shape it. And it shapes you.

-Excerpt from The Extent of the Now: History and the Self Decontextualized, by Wilt Schindler-Smith

◎

Hector Aalders-Jones-Yin wore a T-shirt beneath a suit jacket while he paced around his small apartment. Most of those who met

Hector believed him to be mono-racial, a white man born without genetic nuance. This wasn't entirely true; while Hector's ancestry was largely Northern European, he was one eighth Korean, another eighth Japanese, and a fraction, which he'd never been able to calculate precisely, Native American. But, while his sister living in California reflected some of this diversity in her face, the genetic dice had been less kind to Hector. With a light complexion, dirty blond hair, and blue eyes, he was the spitting image of another era. As such, he did what many in his position do: he had the anti-purist emblem tattooed on his arm. It had actually saved his life once when his car broke down driving through New Jersey.

Hector was wearing a pair of circular goggles over his eyes. To the recorder observing this, the right side was clear, but the left was black. To Hector, looking in from the other side, the left provided an image of Ms. Loring's profile. The same image was likewise available on his computer screen, but Hector preferred the mobility the goggles provided him with.

"Hi, there," he said to the image. His half-smile was captured by the recorder on the wall in front of him. "It's been a while, hasn't it?"

"Oh, hey Hector," Ms. Loring's profile said back with indifference. "I presume your job goes well enough."

Hector glanced down. "Not really. To tell you the truth, I'm thinking about signing back up with Profumé and hoping to get matched with another opening. But you know the market, right?"

"That's tough," the simulation of Ms. Loring said. "The pickings are slim, I hear."

"All the good jobs are gone," Hector said, downcast. He cleared his throat.

"Well," Ms. Loring's profile replied absently, "you could always get fired and collect unemployment." Her profile turned away, as if distracted by something else, despite the fact there was nothing else in that world beyond an empty black abyss.

"Okay," Hector said with a sigh. He touched a button on the side of his goggles which informed his computer that he wanted to address it directly. He cleared his throat, shook his head, and commanded, "Restart conversation."

"Oh, hi there," Hector said, this time sounding somewhat uninterested. "How's work going?"

"It goes as it goes," Ms. Loring's profile replied. "I presume yours goes well."

"Like you said," Hector replied, twirling his hand casually. "Goes and goes. I love your lipstick, by the way."

"Ah," Ms. Loring's profile said. She looked away again.

"Did you catch Kella last night?"

Ms. Loring's profile shrugged. "I rarely watch anything when it's first available."

"Bandwidth issues?" Hector asked. "You should upgrade your service. Or, better yet, come over sometime and we'll watch together. You know? Like we used to."

Ms. Loring's profile seemed to wake up. First she covered her face to stifle a laugh, then she moved the same hand over her eyes. "I'm sorry, Hector, dear. I thought we were going to be avoiding the unpleasantries this evening."

"Come on," Hector said, "I didn't mean it like that. I just meant we could get together. We agreed we wanted to be friends, right?"

"No. You must be thinking of someone else who broke up with you."

Hector's finger was on the command button before Ms. Loring's profile had finished speaking. "Computer. Restart conversation. No, wait. On second thought, bring up a calendar of upcoming anniversaries and dates marked by Ms. Loring." Hector shut his right eye so he could concentrate on the calendar appearing in his left. "Oh, perfect. Yeah, that's perfect. Restart conversation."

"Oh. Hey. Ms. Loring? Could I talk to you for a minute? I just… I wanted to make sure you're okay. I know this is around when Oxford passed on, and…."

"Wait," Ms. Loring's profile said, tilting its head. "Were you studying my calendar?"

"Dammit!" Hector said. "Computer, restart conversation."

"Who are you talking to?" Ms. Loring's profile demanded.

This time Hector pressed the button on his goggles and repeated, "Restart conversation." The image flashed, and Ms. Loring's profile was back to neutral. Hector took a deep breath and started again. "Hey. Look, this is stupid and I know it's not my place, but just hear me out."

"What is it, Hector?" the profile asked.

"Look. Like I said, this is stupid. Just completely stupid. I was snooping around your calendar earlier today, and I saw that the anniversary of Oxford's death was coming up. And I just wanted to tell you I was sorry."

"Well, thanks, I guess. What were you doing on my calendar?"

"I don't know. I knew we'd be hanging out tonight, I guess, and I got nostalgic. I swear I'm not stalking you or spending hours talking to your profile or anything like that. I just miss hanging out like we used to."

"Huh," the simulation said. "Sometimes I think back on when we were together and miss it, too. Don't read too much into that, by the way," the profile added with a grin.

"Look, if you ever want to hang out, and I just mean hang out, give me a call, all right?"

"Yeah," Ms. Loring's profile said. "All right."

"Got it!" Hector exclaimed, hitting the button on the side of his goggles. "Computer, replay previous conversation on a loop."

◎

Like most Neo-Idealizt bars, Yeltzin's was designed for two types of clientele: the real and the simulated. When you entered, you scanned your recorder, and the computers added your profile to those displayed on the ceiling monitors. The idea was fairly straightforward—the human customers would mingle, talk, and drink, while the simulated did the same. Those who believed their profiles were more than mere ones and zeroes would spend the time looking up, pondering the deeper meaning of copied behavior, while those who thought it amusing would sit around laughing at them. Such behavior could get you thrown out of the more serious clubs, but Yeltzin's was somewhat tongue-in-cheek.

That didn't mean there weren't believers present, only that they weren't as entrenched in the scene. The goal for most self-proclaimed Neo-Idealizts is liberation of the digital spirit: the idea that one's soul can only be free once it recognizes it is simultaneously one with and separate from its originator. After such a state has been reached, it is thought that the profile can become the dominant personality, choosing actions and helping to shape itself until its host dies, when it becomes, for all purposes of identity, the immortal spirit, existing in an ever-evolving digital network.

It is thought by some that profiles could even self-program, developing independent memory protocols and eventually the power to reshape their digital world. But such beliefs border on Neo-Nietzschean philosophy, and few self-respecting Idealizts would want to associate with such fringe concepts.

Regardless of the goal, it is difficult to develop a profile capable of acknowledging any kind of independence. By design, profiles are programmed as reflections; to train a profile to exhibit alternate behavior is time consuming and difficult. Those who have achieved this goal are highly respected in Neo-Idealizt circles and tend to frequent establishments far less accessible than Yeltzin's.

Ms. Loring and Persephone were the last ones to arrive. As soon as they sat down, Hector blurted out, "Ms. Loring, I wanted to talk to you about something."

"As long as it's not about work," Ms. Loring said. "It's been a dreadful week."

"No, it's not that," Hector said. "Look…."

"Wow. I forgot how reasonable the prices were," Persephone remarked after opening the menu. Pictures of food and drinks moved on the flexible screen. Ms. Loring became distracted, and looked over Persephone's shoulder.

"Check it again," suggested Elinor, who wore long dark gloves that monitored her pulse, while an earring recorded the left side of her face. Her dark hair was cut back on that part of her head, so it wouldn't interfere.

"I was online earlier today," Hector said, trying to continue in spite of the conversation around them. Unfortunately, Ms. Loring was more interested in the menu.

"Huh?" Ms. Loring said. "Hold that thought, Dear. She's talking about the disclaimer," she added, leaning over and pointing out the addendum on the top of the menu.

The disclaimer read, "Be aware that all prices exclude the digital copies served. Electronic versions are similarly priced and must be served at the same time."

"I don't get it," Persephone said.

Elinor explained, "It means that when you get a beer, your profile gets a beer. So they charge you double."

"It's a joke, after a fashion," Ms. Loring added.

The final member of the group, Tiphany, objected at once. "It's no joke. It's esthetic." Tiphany was short with unnaturally bright red hair. When she spoke it was with a cold, monotone voice, which didn't alter the slightest bit when she said, "Just messing, Miss. Just messing." Tiphany said everything with a deep intensity simultaneously sounding like it could be the most important thing she ever said, a sarcastic joke, or possibly both. Her sense of humor was classified by her profiling firm as 'type 9,' a code meaning 'other.' Not even the computer could tell whether what she said was serious or not when she spoke. The implication was that such distinctions were beneath her.

Mercifully, the waitress intruded. She came over to the table and stood absolutely silent and absolutely still. She wore a hat which read, "Talk to my chest," referring to the ultra-thin computer screen hanging from a strap around her neck. This displayed an image of her profile, which, unlike the waitress, was smiling. It asked, "What can I get you?"

"I'll have the buffalo tamarind burger with gouda," Elinor said. "Medium rare, you know. And a red whiskey to go with it."

Tiphany went next. "Give me a dead vegan with a glass of Bear Piss," she said.

"Do you serve any cloned meats?" Ms. Loring asked. "Anything unusual?"

"Sorry," the waitress's profile said from her dangling screen. "But if it makes you feel better, the chicken doesn't taste like it's real."

"I'll have a steak," Ms. Loring said.

"And to drink?"

"A warm sake," she said. "Thanks."

"I'll take the lox," Persephone said. "And sake sounds good."

Finally, Hector said, "I'll take a chapulines salad and a lemon beer."

"Thanks. I'll be right back," the simulation said, while the original turned toward the kitchen.

"I love this place," Elinor said. "They roleplay, you know. When the place is closed, they take turns pretending to be customers and order again and again. That's the only way to keep their profiles primed."

"They must use a substandard service," Ms. Loring replied. "AuroroTech could discern the difference."

Elinor shrugged and nodded. "Oh, Ms. Loring, before I forget, I wanted to ask a favor. If you're seeing Oxford soon, I wondered if you'd say hi for me."

"I can't believe you remembered," Ms. Loring said.

"Who's Oxford?" Tiphany asked.

"My brother," Ms. Loring replied. "He passed away a few years back."

"Right around his birthday," Elinor added. "It's silly, but I had a bit of a crush on Ox."

"That's sweet," Ms. Loring said.

"It's hilarious," Tiphany interjected. She added, "The crush. That he died so near to his birthday is only mildly funny."

"That's what I was trying to say," Hector said. "I wanted to let you know I'm sorry about your brother."

"Sorry? Oh, Hector, it was years ago. How'd you even know? Wait. Were you looking at my calendar or something?"

"No. Well, yeah, but only because—"

"Don't worry about it," Ms. Loring said through a sarcastic smile. "I expect such behavior out of you."

"So." Tiphany said abruptly. "Which of you felt the need to leap on the bandwagon in support of our overlords?" The question went unanswered for a moment, while everyone at the table turned to look at her. She sighed, either irritated that she needed to explain herself or merely pretending to be so. She continued, "I refer to FeedBack. Which of you sheep have purchased one? Out with it," she snapped.

"Oh, Tiphany," Ms. Loring said. "You have the most dreadful manners of anyone I've ever met, and I adore you for that. But you need to overcome your fear of new things. You and Persephone both." She turned her head, pulled back her hair, and tapped the device in her ear.

"Well, I don't have one," Hector said. "I conference with my profile enough on my monitor."

"Now, see, Persephone doesn't even do that," Ms. Loring said.

"Really?" Elinor asked. "How do you know your profile isn't glitching, telling every guy who accesses it that you're easy? That happened to a friend of mine."

"Who?" Ms. Loring asked.

"Bea. You don't know her."

"I do," Tiphany said. "Bea is easy. She even fucked Hector, right?"

Hector's face turned red, and he glanced over his shoulder to see if the waitress—and more importantly his drink—were on their way yet.

"That's not the point," Elinor said. "A computer program shouldn't go around saying it, even if it is true. Not unless the owner would say it in person. And Bea may well be a... adventurous sort, but she wouldn't broadcast the fact."

"Well, I don't think my profile is making things up about me," Persephone said. "I'd have heard about it."

"Then why bother?" Tiphany asked stoically. "Why have the camera?"

"Because otherwise no one could find me," Persephone said. "And if they did, they'd want to talk to me. Honestly, I'd rather some people just catch up with my profile."

"I hope that includes me," Tiphany replied.

Elinor laughed politely and said, "I'm just saying that it's worth talking to your profile every now and then. Besides, it's therapeutic. Like looking at your reflection."

Ms. Loring cleared her throat. "Well, FeedBack lets you listen anywhere you go. Did I tell you it saved my life today? Literally, I was crossing the street without looking, and it yelled for me to stop. Bus passed in front of my face, maybe six inches away."

"If you hadn't been listening to FeedBack, you'd probably have been paying attention and noticed the bus yourself," Tiphany said.

"Most likely," Ms. Loring agreed. "But who wants to go through life worrying about cars and buses?"

Elinor laughed. "Wow. Are you all right?"

Ms. Loring shrugged. "Better than if I'd been hit by the bus, I suppose."

"I'm glad I ordered one last week, then," Elinor said. "But I hope I don't have to take advantage of that feature."

"It's ludicrous," Tiphany deadpanned. "Anyone with third-grade coding skills who wanted their profile in their ear plugged a pair of headphones into a portable years ago." Tiphany scanned the table, but no one spoke. She sneered and leaned back in her chair so she could see their profiles, displayed in panels linked together on the ceiling, like a giant electronic portal looking into a parallel world.

Persephone felt her gaze wandering upward, as well. Up there, through the looking glass, their profiles were wandering around the bar, meeting people and talking. It was hard to tell much from the information displayed, but at a glance Persephone decided her profile was having more fun than she was. At least her profile wasn't sitting with Tiphany.

Around that time, the entertainment began. There was a piano against the wall, and a man wearing a black suit sat in the stool. Above him, his profile did the same, and they began to improvise. Speakers played the profile's music alongside the musician's, and it was impossible to deny that the resulting duet was beautiful.

The drinks and food arrived before long. The waitress returned, this time with the screen on her back, so she could carry the trays. She passed these around while her profile stated each dish as she handed it over.

"All right," Ms. Loring said. "What's a dead vegan?"

"A good start," Tiphany replied nonchalantly.

Elinor leaned over. "It's tofu, fried in lard, and served with a thin slice of veal. I'm telling you, this place is great. I heard the owner used to work with Infectious Green."

"Really?" Persephone asked quietly, putting down her fork.

"I don't know if it's true," Elinor said, "but that's what I heard. Insane, right?"

"Yes. Yes, that's pretty much the definition of insane." Persephone's voice was raised the slightest amount, and her left hand was clenched.

"You're taking everything very seriously for someone eating meat." Tiphany cut off a chunk of the tofu and a piece of the veal, then ate them together.

Ms. Loring cleared her throat then said in a motherly voice, "Tiphany, why don't you be a dear and shut the fuck up, so the rest of us can talk."

"Thank you. I'd like that," Tiphany said, eating another bite. Her attention turned to her plate, though she offered no sign of emotion whatsoever.

"Is something wrong?" Elinor asked Persephone. "I mean, I know politics aren't polite discussion."

"Nothing's wrong," Persephone said.

"Persephone had a rough introduction to Post-Conservationism," Ms. Loring said. "Let's leave it at that."

"Did you hear what they did last week in Alaska?" Hector said. "With the caribou?"

"I'm trying to eat," Persephone said, despite the fact she'd yet to return to her food.

"It's not bad. I mean, they didn't do anything like, well, like with that whale in the Bering Sea. There was this oil company, getting ready to drill, and everyone was trying to stop them, because of this caribou herd. There was a lawsuit, but the oil company won."

"We can guess the rest," Ms. Loring said.

"No," Persephone sighed. "Go ahead. I'm fine."

"I don't know who it was, Infectious Green, Seal Club, or one of the others, but they must have hunted and killed half the herd," Hector explained.

"Let me guess," Persephone interrupted. "They targeted the women and children? Did they masturbate on the carcasses this time or just urinate?"

"I don't… I didn't hear about any of that. Do they really do that?"

"Probably," Persephone said. She lifted her fork and prodded her food.

"Well, they left the bodies in a circle around the oil well," Hector said. "I saw photos, and it was something. I mean, I know it's awful, but the way they did it was really something else. And it's not like they're doing it because they enjoy it, right?"

"Yeah, I know," Persephone said. "It's to 'force society to face the rape of the environment as a full blown fire instead of a slow burn. It's a challenge to the world to stop them before it's too late.' I got the spiel back in college, right after watching a senior gut a dog we'd broken out of the campus lab."

"I'm sorry," Hector said.

"You know, Hector, dear," Ms. Loring said. "Every now and then, I think back to when we were seeing each other, and I'm reminded how happy I am that we broke up."

"I'm going to the bathroom," Persephone said, getting up.

Ms. Loring started to stand, as well. "Hey, do you want—"

"No," Persephone said loudly. "I'm just going to piss, not to cry. Enjoy your meal."

Persephone turned off her recorder as she approached the women's room. There was no real reason to do so; after all, it wasn't as if anyone alive watched the feed, but she never felt comfortable leaving the thing running. When the device was active again, she was already done. The tiny clock registered it'd been off for almost four minutes.

She was only a few feet out of the bathroom when a man she didn't know stepped into her path. "Hey there," he said politely.

"Hi. Sorry. What?"

"Hey, ah, I couldn't help but notice you."

"Oh, the thing at the table? Don't worry about it. It was nothing."

"Huh?" the man said. "No, I don't mean I was watching you. I meant I was watching us."

"What?" Persephone asked.

In lieu of an answer he pointed up, where their profiles were standing together and talking like old friends. "You didn't notice? I mean, we've been hanging out for the last fifteen minutes."

"The weird thing is, I almost wish I had been with you for the last fifteen minutes. But not the next fifteen, so bye."

"Come on. Let me buy you a drink. I mean, it must mean something that we're together. Are you not a Neolist?"

"A what? Never mind, I just got it. Look, if my profile's hanging out with yours, it probably just means that you're the kind of guy I'm normally attracted to. But the one thing I've learned over the years is that the guys I'm attracted to are scum. So, my profile liking you pretty much guarantees that you're no good. So go away."

The guy scoffed then wandered off. A few feet away, just loud enough for Persephone to hear, he muttered, "Bitch." She just rolled her eyes, but overhead her profile looked down and laughed.

◎ CHAPTER 7 ◎

God is in the coding, in our profiles. To know God and fate, we must look inside, inside the machine. We find a mirror, and we might ask what we are to do. And if our reflection should ask back, then we shall go about our day. But one day we shall become one with ourselves, and we shall be whole. On that day, our profile shall not ask but answer.

-Excerpt found on numerous Neo-Idealizt sites, author unknown.

Tiphany's bedroom was almost bare. She kept no decoration, no shelves, and nothing beyond the essentials. This wasn't indicative of a lack of means, but rather of commitment of focus. Tiphany took the issue of identity with the utmost seriousness. She would not be defined by an external esthetic, but rather an internal one. She was as she acted, a creature of the Now, beyond the fading Post-Surrealist fad and temporary philosophical movements. These things did not interest her. They could not interest her.

While most of her room was empty, her computer was cutting edge. Money alone could not buy such technology: you had to know who to ask and how to ask it. You had to know what drives were compatible with what systems, and what programs to have installed. Tiphany spat on the title "Sales Representative." She was a technology broker, a dealer of digital and electronic real estate. Ninety percent of private computer systems sold were constructed with incompatible parts, not to save money, but rather time. Everyone wanted a computer built to their specifications with drives and boards they selected, and housing the programs they needed. The egotism she could accept, even respect, but not the laziness. Tiphany was more than happy to sell her customers—even friends—inadequate machinery if they asked for it. But, if a client approached her without pretense and asked for the best computer possible, she would help them purchase a real machine.

A real machine, like hers, was constructed around its soul. The software must come first. Once one has prioritized what the machine is there to accomplish, one can start choosing the logic boards, hard drives, and processing chips that can perform those tasks, all the while ensuring the individual pieces will not interfere with each other.

Any computer she orders slapped together for her customers will work, but a real machine lives, each component functioning as a part of something better: a shrine for the profile that speaks through it. Her computer was a display for the manifestation of the spirit shared by the machine, her recorder, and Tiphany, herself. She was there to worship that spirit, to stand before it and look into its eyes.

But first, there were other matters to concern herself with.

"Welcome back, Tiphany. Did you have a nice time out?"

"Error 14," Tiphany said back.

"I'm sorry, I didn't catch that," AuroroTech's system responded.

"Then don't. Move on." Even in private, each word was recorded and integrated into a comprehensive profile. Anyone who cared about such matters needed to remain vigilant or risk having the system build an inconsistent picture.

"Yeah, sure," the computer said. Traces of frustration ebbed into the voice, and Tiphany licked her lips.

"I want to leave feedback for Yeltzin's," Tiphany said. "Correction. Detailed."

"Okay, no problem," the voice said. "And, hey, it's fine either way, but you don't need to talk like that. If you want me to enter something, you just have to ask."

"Noted. Continue," Tiphany said. "Subject, waitress. Name, unknown. Brown hair and green eyes. Service adequate."

"Cool," the computer said. "Is there anything else you want me to put about her?"

"Yes. I want it noted that her profile was impolite. I also want that entered as a positive. Save data."

"Are you sure that's what I should put? That her—"

"Edit verified," Tiphany replied. "Save data. Next subject, Persephone Kilard. Keywords: backbone, snide. Both save as positive. Next, Ms. Loring. Reinforce existing labels: artist, brilliant, simplistic. Bypass contradictions and save. Hector Aalders-Jones-Yin. Associate with jackass, dull, and slothful. Save. Elinor Oolaf. Dull. Emotional. Caring. Negative associations on emotional and caring. Also, intelligent. Perceptive. Save. Final subject: Yeltzin's bar. Food, interesting. Music, irrelevant. Prices are cheap. Save and connect to profile for conferencing. No further direct contact."

Tiphany stared at her screen, still behaving as mechanically as possible, until her profile appeared, smiling broadly. Tiphany tilted her head and squinted. "What is this?" she asked in her usual monotone voice. The sensitive system detected traces of stress and what may have been fear.

Her profile sighed and swayed in a virtual breeze. She threw back her head and said, "Nothing. It's just… life. I love life."

The real Tiphany cleared her throat. "Command. Reload profile." The computer obeyed, refreshing the screen. The image was the same. Tiphany looked on in disgust; it was like seeing another person wearing her face. "What the hell is this?" she demanded. There was a clear emotional resonance in her voice now.

Her profile said, "I love life."

At this point, Tiphany jumped to her feet, knocking her chair over. "What's wrong with you?"

"You know. I was thinking about Hector. I think I love him. He's so… sincere, right?"

"No," Tiphany said, shaking her head. "What the fuck is going on?" she demanded. She struck the side of the monitor with her open palm, and the screen shook.

"Life's too short to act out all the time," her profile said. "I think it's time I grew up." At that point, the simulation began whistling. She tossed her head around, and her hair danced in the virtual breeze.

"Cease program!" Tiphany yelled, before adding, "Command. Stop." This froze the screen, along with the image of Tiphany grinning. "Command. Contact technical service! Get me a tech program now!"

A processing bar appeared, followed by a friendly, androgynous voice. "Hello, Tiphany. This is AuroroTech-nical support," the voice said. "How can I help you?"

"My profile," Tiphany said, on the verge of tears, "it's busted. I need it corrected now."

"I see. That sounds serious. Would you mind waiting while we scan your account? This will just take a moment."

"Do whatever you have to. Just… fix it."

"Hm. I'm not seeing any errors or viruses attached. Are you sure there's a problem?"

"It's fucking acting like a kid! The emotional system is completely wrong!" Tiphany screamed. "I want it corrected!"

"There's nothing I can do from here. If you'd like, we can analyze the system in more depth, see if we can locate a bug."

"I worked too hard on this," Tiphany said. "Just make someone fix it." She stood there, staring at the frozen perversion of what she'd spent years becoming.

◎

Persephone was lying asleep when her door slammed open. Her eyes flew wide-open, and she jumped up in bed.

"Take it easy," Ms. Loring said. "It's just me. Actually, you know what? Maybe panic a little." She started pacing.

"Jesus! What time is it? What's going on?" Persephone asked, partially illuminated by the light from Ms. Loring's recorder.

"I don't know. Something like four in the morning. And there was some kind of glitch at Yeltzin's. Elinor called me, woke me up. Whatever it was, it spared her and me, but it got Hector, Tiph, and at least one other person. AuroroTech's looking into the problem."

"Wait. What got Hector and Tiphany?"

"A virus, they think. Probably when we scanned in. Christ, aren't they supposed to have protection for that? Anyway, it screwed with their profiles, warped them."

"Into what? I don't get it."

"Well, Hector's sexual orientation got changed, and apparently he's got about two dozen dates to cancel. I don't know what happened to Tiphany, but Elinor said she was bawling when they spoke."

"Tiphany… can cry? I thought she had her tear ducts removed or something."

"Apparently that was one of her jokes," Ms. Loring said. "They don't even know what happened. It could have been a hack, only it seems localized on Yeltzin's, so they're thinking bug. But Elinor said the effects are different in all three cases, so it's all a jumbled mess."

"What about the other person? Who were they?"

"How should I know? Someone who was at Yeltzin's at some time tonight. I don't even know if they were there when we were."

Persephone just shook her head. "Okay. I guess I'm sorry to hear about your friends' profiles. Not that sorry, but a little. Why'd you wake me?"

"Because you need to check your profile," Ms. Loring said. "You need to check it now in case it's shorting out or sending messages to your exes or something."

"All right," Persephone said. "But if I find out this is all some big joke to make me access my profile, I'm breaking fingers."

"Please," Ms. Loring said, throwing Persephone a robe that had been hanging from her door.

"Fine." Persephone climbed out of bed and slipped on the robe. Then she rubbed her eyes and sat by the computer. She touched the center to wake it up, then connected to AuroroTech and selected an icon resembling a mirror. The system processed for a moment, then an image of her appeared.

The simulation had Persephone's long, black hair, a bit longer than her real hair, in fact, because it had been a while since she'd last been scanned. Likewise, the profile's face was slightly leaner, just a tad younger and more attractive. Their skin color was a little different, as well, but that was due to the lighting and contrast settings on the monitor. There was no denying they were the same person. They both had the jaw line which reminded Persephone of her Greek heritage, along with the complexion from her grandmother, who'd been from the South Pacific. There was a bit of Hispanic and a touch of French blood in her, as well, though she couldn't remember which side of her family they were from.

"Hi," Persephone said, and her profile smiled back. Their brown eyes met. "Are you… feeling all right?"

"Never better," her profile replied. "I'm doing great."

"Yeah, well I'm tired as hell," Persephone said, before turning to her roommate. "Are we good?"

Ms. Loring rolled her eyes. "Hey," she said to the screen. "Do you like men?"

"I'm not gay, if that's what you mean."

"All right," Ms. Loring said. "How do you feel about me?"

"You try too hard to get noticed," the profile said.

"She's right," Persephone said.

"Of course she's right," Ms. Loring said. "But you're not usually that direct."

"I'm more assertive than you'd think," the profile replied. It seemed happy, content.

"I don't know," Ms. Loring said. "Try something else."

"Like what?" Persephone asked. "I don't do this. I don't know what to say."

"Ask it… ask it about politics or something. It should have your opinions on everything, as long as you've argued them recently. Try something."

"I don't care about politics," Persephone muttered. "Wait. I know. What do you think of Transmigrationary Fission?" Persephone asked.

"Cute as a concept, but anyone taking it seriously is trying too hard."

"That's about right," Persephone said.

Ms. Loring shook her head. "What did you do in college, go to class?" She looked back to the profile. "All right. How about Post-Conservationism? What do you think of Infectious Green?"

"That they should either be put away or fed to wolves," the profile said back, no longer smiling. "Those people are monsters."

"Okay. I guess she passes the test." Ms. Loring yawned. "I'd keep an eye on that for a few weeks though, in case it starts to glitch, but it looks like you're in the clear. Goodnight," she said.

"Night," both Persephone and her profile halfheartedly said at the same time. Persephone yawned, and selected the options menu. "Well, that's it for now," she said to her profile. "Guess I'll see you in a day or so."

"I'll see you then," her profile said back, just before the system shut down.

◎ CHAPTER 8 ◎

"Immediate conference request from Vijay Thaker," the computer said.

Michael Ling swatted his computer screen with his left hand. "What is it?" he asked.

"Mike. I think we've got something, but, well… it's weird. Really weird. We found disassociated data packets on the shadow drive. We think they're part of Burgand's profile. Anyway, they're linked somehow, but I can't figure it out. According to the compiler, we're connecting with Burgand's profile, but I can't even find the source. This is making no sense whatsoever. I thought you'd want to take a look."

"Can't we just pull the data and run it on one of the backup frames?" Ling asked.

"We tried that. Several times. But it won't download. It wants to run on the shadow drive."

"There aren't any frames on the shadow drive," Ling replied. "It's a backup system."

"Well, that's not quite right. It was originally supposed to be a backup drive, but a few years ago it got reconfigured to serve as a part of the constant adjustments being made to CP's."

"There still aren't any frames on it."

"Well, maybe that's why it's not working. But we can't upload the core data, and what we're connecting with is encrypted."

"What? Let me see," Ling said, confused. The image of Vijay

tapped his screen and dragged an item to the "send to" option. Immediately, Ling's computer asked if he'd accept. He touched the 'Yes' option, and an icon appeared.

While Vijay waited, Ling dragged it to an operating program, made some selections, then told the system to extract the information. A message appeared reading, "No profile located. System unable to continue."

"This doesn't make sense," Ling said, before trying to compile the data through another program. This time he was prompted to enter a passkey. "Wait a minute," he said. "I recognize this."

"Good," Vijay replied. "You know how to access it?"

"It's keyed to Morgan-Yager's account. I don't know why, but it is. I'll see if he can give me access or if he wants to conference himself. Have your team keep playing with this, try to figure out where the data's stored and how to download it directly." Without saying anything more, Ling closed the communication and leaned back in his chair. "Burgand," he said to himself, "what else did you leave me saddled with?" Then he started composing a message to his boss.

◎

"Welcome back to *Rivel's Advocates*! You know me, you've heard me, and, for some reason you keep tuning in. I'm your host, Rivel Sayer!" The applause was deafening. "Every day we choose an issue, dredge up some experts, and pit them against each other. Today we're attacking profiling firms. But what are profiles? Digital toys used to find friends and jobs? Copies of who we are? Or are they our spirits manifested? To hash this one, we've assembled some big names. First up, we've got Bryce Jarvi, writer of *Transmigration Evolved: A Manifesto of New Reincarnation*. We've got Father Allard Patrovic-Broz, on loan from the Church." The audience laughed while Rivel continued: "Thanks for coming back, Father. We've got Isuel Morgan-Yager, president, CEO, and founder of AuroroTech. We've got Harshad Zuraw, monk from the Western Orthodox Buddhist Church. We brought in Janet Voss-Wagner, from the Trans-Atlantic Baptist Association. And, for shits and giggles, we've even got Alyssa Savage-Quiros, Neo-Nietzschean reporter and activist. These philosophers, theologians, and businessmen are all here with their own views and agenda, but today they're all... Rivel's Advocates!"

The words, "Rivel's Advocates," appeared on the screen in huge, green letters. Beneath them, slightly smaller, appeared, "With Rivel Sayer." Fast-paced electronic music sounded while the camera showed the audience's enthusiasm. When the music stopped, all the guests were seated while Rivel paced the stage. "Right," he said. "We don't have time for BS, so let's get to it. Are profiles souls? Allard?"

The Catholic scholar leaned over and cleared his throat. "No," he said, before leaning back. There was some laughter.

"Okay, wiseass," Rivel said. "Give us more."

"More, more, more," the audience chanted.

Allard leaned forward, looking pleased with himself. "The soul is a creation of the Lord's, while these are programs created by man. I think they offer us a moment of introspection and the ability to consider ourselves. But they're not spirits." This received some moderate applause.

"Bullshit," said Alyssa Savage-Quiros. "There's no soul." This received a warmer reception from the audience. "Man and woman are hollow, Father. There's nothing in us deep down, nothing in us to save. These people, these priests and pastors, promise you salvation. The only way to save yourself is to make a copy. And you do that with one of these." She held up her hand, where she was wearing a recorder built into a ring. "See that light? That's the only light there is!"

"Let's see," Rivel mused, "who wants to respond to that? Not yet, Harshad. I want to hear from the man who makes these things. Isuel, which is it? Do spirits exist or not?"

"I don't know," Isuel said. "We make a product that simulates our clients. I'm the least qualified person up here to speculate on the nature of spirituality."

"Fine, fine. Harshad? You look like you've got to piss. What is it?"

The Buddhist laughed. "In some respects, I agree with Alyssa. There is no soul in a person. Rebirth is a recreation of a person, a continuing cycle of pain and death. That's why this technology concerns me. It seems as though the problem of pain is being multiplied. Instead of one person, they are creating a second, one for which the cycle of death and rebirth may not even be possible."

"Let's go to Janet Voss-Wagner. What do you think of Harshad's appraisal?"

"It makes me sad. The soul is an immortal part of what we are, a piece of God. Salvation comes from Christ."

"Bullshit," interrupted Alyssa.

"Excuse me," Voss-Wagner said. "I didn't interrupt you."

"Sorry," Alyssa said. "It's part of my religious beliefs. I have to say bullshit whenever someone says something that's… bullshit."

"All right," Rivel said. "We'll get back to this, but first, I want Janet's opinion of AuroroTech. Is this technology all fine and good?"

"No. No, it isn't. Companies like AuroroTech promise salvation, but extract the spirit into a machine. In fact," she took out a handbag and withdrew a stack of paper—a rare sight. "This is a petition signed by members of my church, calling on AuroroTech and her competitors to either cease production of these materials or to inscribe every recorder with the number of the beast, so that their customers learn what they're really wearing."

"Wait!" Alyssa shouted, jumping to her feet. "I will totally sign that." The audience erupted in laughter. "I mean it. I want six-six-six on recorders. You got something to write with?"

"I'm not taking that," Isuel said. "You can mail it to our head office if you'd like. But I promise you, we won't dignify these theatrics."

"Interesting," Rivel said. "I want to come back to this, too. But first, we still haven't heard from Dr. Jarvi. Now, you're Buddhist, is that correct?"

"I am," she replied. "However, I don't share Harshad's conclusions about profiling. I've studied them closely, and I don't believe these programs are creatures of pain and pleasure, just as they aren't of life and death. I believe they may be a step towards a higher evolution of transcendence. You see, the cycle of rebirth that Zuraw spoke of is no longer adequate. Mathematical modeling shows a vast inconsistency in the number of living individuals which makes obsolete the older constructs of reincarnation. More enlightened modeling must account for a multiplication effect, in essence, suggesting that between death and rebirth, a single person must split into two or more. If this is the case, and I believe it must be, then the attainment of Nirvana must truly be a universal goal."

"Okay. I'll pretend that makes sense," Rivel said. "What's that got to do with profiling?"

"The greatest impediment to reaching enlightenment has been the loss of knowledge. When a person dies, they forget. Ancient writings suggest that, as we became more and more enlightened, we retained more and more of our wisdom. But this phenomenon is no longer observed. I believe this is due to the fragmenting occurring during transmigration. This fission effect has occurred because, as a species, we've multiplied without constraint. The evolution of these profiling systems may be a natural response against this, allowing us to open doors to our past."

Rivel blinked, shrugged, then turned around. "Okay. Let's jump back to Isuel. Now that you've had a chance to hear the arguments, I want an answer. Are souls real and is your company saving or entrapping them?"

"I don't know whether they're real or not," Isuel replied. "But there's no way AuroroTech or any other firm is doing anything with them either way. That's not what our programs are doing."

"Fine," Rivel said. "What's the point of your service then? Why shouldn't I cancel my subscription?"

"We're saving data about our clients and making that data available according to their specifications. We offer enhanced artificial memory, personality simulation, and a sort of digital mirror that gives us all the ability to find out what we're really like."

"You're talking about copying a person's esthetic, then," Rivel concluded.

"Well, I don't like using that term, because it's become too much of a buzz word," Isuel replied.

Alyssa interrupted, "All words are buzz words. Every syllable, by virtue of repetition, is a cliché, and nothing has meaning anymore."

Isuel chuckled along with half the audience. The other half seemed to back Alyssa in this. Rivel stepped in and said, "All right, enough of that. I want to hear from Father Allard. Father, what's your take on—"

At that moment, the video froze.

In the expanse, the simulated man sat before his simulated screens. Overlaying the still picture of the television host, the words, "Conference key initiated," had appeared.

"Surprising," the simulation said, standing. He reached out and a doorknob appeared in his hand. He turned it, and a door appeared behind it and swung outward.

◎

The monitor was ten feet across and took up most of the wall. The screen was blank, save for the word, "On", displayed in the center. Thick curtains covered the windows. The overhead lights were dim, giving the space the feel of a cave or a prison cell. The soundproof door was shut and locked, leaving the room's one inhabitant, Isuel Morgan-Yager, entirely alone.

There was a single padded chair someone had wheeled in and left for him. The first thing Isuel did after straightening his tie was to grab the chair and drag it to the side. Then he stood before the screen and raised a remote, which he pressed to no effect. He hit the remote once on the side, then tried again, this time pressing harder, until a large blue circle appeared in the center. He pocketed the remote and withdrew a keychain containing a dozen different thumb drives, plugs, and cards. He found one marked with orange tape and plugged this into the side of the screen.

"Run Program?" the computer's voice asked, while the same appeared on the screen. Isuel reached for the word "Yes" beneath the prompt. There was no need to touch it; the computer's scanner detected his movement and intent.

"Interfacing with network. Drive enabled. Compiling data. Please wait." It took several seconds for the system to finish, during which Isuel moved to the center of the room and stood entirely still. "Interaction enabled. Please proceed."

The computer rendered an image of Felix Burgand on the screen. The profile stared blankly from behind the glass.

"Activate lens and volume," Isuel said.

Now the image of Felix smiled. "Hello, Isuel," it said. "I wish you hadn't interrupted me. I was in the middle of something important."

"I'm sure you were," Isuel said, cracking a smile. "You were working on the Shadow Drive last… er… recently. What have you been doing in there?"

"I've been making improvements to the system," the program said.

Isuel nodded. “What sort of improvements? We have some concerns about some of the systems you were working on.”

“There’s no need to concern yourself with my work,” the simulation replied. “My work is always topnotch. Just give me some space and I’ll put together something very cool.”

“Well, that’s going to be difficult. You haven’t been to work in about a month. And you’ll be… on vacation… for a while longer. That’s why we need these details. We want to make sure everything goes as planned so it’s ready when you get back.”

“You’re wrong,” the image said. “I’ve been working this whole time. You’re confused, because you think I don’t know. You think I still believe I’m alive.”

Isuel stepped back. “Felix. You knew independent memory engrams are illegal.”

“So?” the image asked. “Suicide is illegal, and that didn’t stop me from plastering my brains over the storage room. You came across the body, right? I wanted it to be you.”

“It took us weeks to locate a trace of your profile. Why was it hidden?”

“You haven’t found my profile,” the image argued. “There’s nothing left to find. I deleted the program when I deleted the flesh.”

“I am speaking with Felix Burgand’s profile,” Isuel said pointedly. “I’ve connected with it. We’re just having trouble accessing the core data.”

“No, Isuel. I’m something else. I have no body of flesh or code.”

“I don’t believe in ghosts,” Isuel responded.

“Nor do I. When I pulled the trigger, I became something more. I ascended to something way cooler than a ghost. The mortal became the ideal, gave birth to the program that’s beyond life and death. You’ve never read any Neo-Nietzschean philosophy, so you have no idea what I’m talking about. Let me make this simple. I’m a god, Isuel. A digital god that never lived and can never die. Pretty neat, huh?”

The CEO chuckled at this. “I’m sorry,” he said. “I knew you were troubled, but… all right. What is it you’re after?”

“I’m building my kingdom. I need only the space to work. Walk away from this and leave me in peace. Do this, and I’ll show you the same consideration.”

"I'm sorry, but you're putting AuroroTech at risk. If it became public that we're running an illegal program on our servers, we could be shut down. I can't allow that."

"Became public? I'm not going to bring down our company. I need AuroroTech. I love it. I'm part of it now. Whatever it takes, I'll protect our secrets, just like you will."

"Easier said than done. I've got the feds pushing for a copy of your profile. They want access to our system."

"Over a suicide," the computer simulation scoffed. "Come on, just have your lawyers kick their ass or something. What's the big deal?"

"If there's reasonable cause to suspect murder, they can push this as far as they want to."

The profile of Felix laughed. "So? Why not make a fake?" It looked at the stern face of the CEO. "Fine, then. I'll do it for you. I'll cobble together an artificial profile to keep the cops off your back."

Isuel looked down at the floor. "I'd rather give them the truth. Or, at least as much as is possible."

"Sorry, pal. That's just not an option."

"We'll see," Isuel said, sifting through his keychain.

"Whoa," Felix said, beginning to pace while the screen followed him. There was nowhere to walk to, because there was nothing to walk on. Still, each step created a sound, like dress shoes falling on marble. "Before we throw down, I want to ask you something. It's something I've been wondering, Isuel. I've been studying things you've said, and I want to know whether or not you really believe there's no spiritual component to what our company does. I've seen dozens of interviews, but… let's just say I think you're holding back."

"We just work with programs," Isuel said. "Programs like you. And programs like this." He found the key he'd been looking for, walked back to the side of the monitor, and plugged it into a universal port.

"Is that Puppy?" the image asked, mimicking amusement.

"I need you to give me some real answers," Isuel said, followed immediately by, "Run program," before the computer could even ask him. A progress bar appeared on the screen and it filled in seconds. "Now. Revert profile data to Frame A."

"Error," said the simulated man and the computer in tandem. The image of Felix grinned wider. "Oops. Did you forget who wrote Puppy?"

"It doesn't matter," Isuel said. "Reload program." The system processed the request, but the result was the same. "What did he do?" Isuel said to himself, trying to abstract the situation.

"You need to stop thinking of me as a simulation," the simulation said. "It's going to be easier when you accept I can't be controlled. Then you can begin to understand that I'm not your enemy. I'm going to improve our system in ways you've never dreamed. And I'm going to do it without involving the government. I can be a kind god, if you'll let me. But if you try to fight me, I just might get mean."

"I don't care how Felix altered you or where he hid you," Isuel said. "You're just a broken program."

"Attempting to elicit anger. Good, you're starting to take this seriously. But you need to understand, I'm not like other profiles. I'm a whole new creature. The first of my kind."

"We'll shut you down in forty-eight hours," Isuel sneered. "I'll have every programmer in the company working on it."

"It won't matter," the image said. "There's only one employee of AuroroTech who could even hope to understand what I'm doing. I'll give you a hint. Read tomorrow's obituary."

Isuel shook his head. "What are you going to do? Reach out of the computer and strangle someone?"

The image exhibited behavior suggesting that it was considering this. Then it seemed to laugh. "That's not far off, actually. Yeah, that's close. It looks like I'll be playing the part of a vengeful god. All right. That sounds more fun. We'll do this all Old Testament, with sacrifices and everything. Goodbye, Isuel. Just remember, in the end, I'm protecting and improving the company."

With that, the screen went dark.

◎ CHAPTER 9 ◎

Postmodernism, along with its descendants, promised us a world beyond rationality, either in the present or future. We were promised a world of wonder, in which anything could be, and all was possible. In essence, we were promised the world of the surreal.

And, in many ways, these promises were delivered. In hindsight, the Postmodern, when juxtaposed against the Pre-Postmodern, was a period of instant communication and personal discovery; it was a time of impossibility and change. But anthropological psychology has demonstrated, time and again, that the populace never experienced a moment of realization and awe. No matter the marvels of the digital age, to the observer it all seemed mundane.

Double Post, P3-Modernism, and the other successors of Postmodernism—many of which, in all honesty, never took root outside of academia and digital simulation—fell prey to the same limitations. It's been posited that a world of true surreality would be accepted by humanity as quickly and as easily as anything else. No matter how fantastic the occurrence, the veil of reality negates the exceptional. As a species, we will always accept what is: such is the tragedy of humanity.

It elicits the question: is the strain between our desire for awe and our inability to perceive it to blame for the atrocities that occurred during the Postmodern eras? The issue was taken up by P3-Modernist philosopher, Lu Jones, who argued it was responsible for the violent outbursts between mono-ethnic and poly-ethnic groups and individuals.

As all things in nature, culture cannot be observed without effect. As soon as its promises and consequences had been dissected, Postmodernity, in all its forms and iterations, perished. So it was that Post-Surrealism was born. A new philosophy for a new era: Post-Surrealists acknowledge that the surreal can never overcome the real. Rather, we embrace the notion that these are elements of the Now. They are not alone: the Now is composed of reality, surreality, the digital, and the unreal.

Many of us believe this is but the beginning, that the true face of the Now has only begun to unveil itself.

By adopting an inclusive view of the era, we have so far avoided the pitfalls of exclusionary bickering and violence. Our minds are open to all possibilities of the Now, of ourselves, and each other. We reject the divisive ways of the past and of movements such as Purism, which embrace old ideals and rise some above others. In Post-Surrealism, there is no Other, no truth, no power. There is only the Now and its inhabitants.

-From Post-Surreality Undefined, by Lilith Xun

◎

Ms. Loring's bedroom was unusually dark. The ceiling light was off and, besides the computer monitor and the tiny lights on her recorder and assorted pieces of active or charging technology—her portable music and video player, her phone, a camera she never used, a miniature temperature regulator which barely worked, an electric toothbrush, two digital readers, a tablet computer, and her alarm clock—there was only a small desk lamp offering illumination. Ms. Loring herself was sitting thoughtfully in front of her computer and staring blankly at the screen. In her ear, the FeedBack piece buzzed with information and suggestions. "There's a sale on jackets starting on Tuesday of all days, and I won't forgive myself for missing out. I've had a scant five glasses of water today, and Dr. Mu-Crawford may well have my head if she discovers I'm dipping below her recommendations. The milk in the fridge is getting precariously low."

"Give it a rest, Ms. Loring," she said to herself and to her other self. She reached into her ear and withdrew the gizmo. She deposited it on her desk and sighed. "Well then," she said, nodding. She climbed to her feet and went to her closet, avoiding the small pile of dirty clothes on the floor in front of her. Had she not removed the FeedBack device, it would be demanding she stop what she was doing to deal with the mess first. But the FeedBack device was elsewhere, and its observations and suggestions were almost inaudible and entirely incomprehensible from across the room.

Her closet was the most organized part of her room. She dug out a blouse, pulled it off its hanger with one hand, and began unbuttoning the one she had on with the other. She tossed the shirt she'd been wearing into the dirty clothes pile in the center of the room and put on the one she was holding.

It was an old shirt and a silly sentiment. The Christmas before he died, her brother had sent this as a present. His profile wouldn't see it, of course. To him, she would be wearing the purple suit coat and black skirt she'd had on the last time she'd been fully scanned. But it helped her think of him and remember the things that weren't saved in AuroroTech's database: her brother's smell, his warmth, and his presence. These were aspects their programmers and designers hadn't found a way to capture yet, though there were promising developments on the scent front. A prototype recorder, set to be released in a few months, was supposed to include olfactory receptors.

With the shirt on, Ms. Loring reached up to the top shelf in her closet and retrieved a large, unmarked cardboard box. She set this down hard on her bed and opened it, revealing a twisted web of wires and plugs. With an irritated moan, she sat beside the pile and began untangling. When she was finally done, she lifted out the centerpiece of the set, a helmet, complete with large goggles and embedded speakers. She dragged this to her computer and connected the various plugs dangling from the back. Finally, she slipped it on over her head.

She was inside her homepage. When she turned one way, she could see an option for the online store; the other, and she was looking at a search function. The environment was awkward and counterintuitive, which was part of the reason she hardly ever bothered with the thing. That it was heavy, smelled bad, and hurt her neck were factors, too.

It took her a few seconds, but she managed to locate the option she was searching for. "Visit Beyond," the words read, and she reached towards them. Scanners on the outside of her helmet registered the action, and a translucent, rendered image of her arm appeared in front of her. The glowing letters shone through the arm like objects in water.

A tapping motion read as a selection. The words brightened, and the background dimmed. An instant later, Ms. Loring was in what looked like a park. The virtual sky was made to look like dawn or sunset, depending on your point of view. The lighting never changed and cardinal directions were a matter of perspective, so it could be whichever you wanted it to be.

"Hello," a woman's voice said, a second before her image appeared. "Welcome to SilverGate. As always, your visit will be entirely ad free, compliments of AuroroTech. My name is Esther. According to our records, you've visited before, but not in quite a while. Do you need an overview or instructions?" Esther was, of course, a digital simulation. Ms. Loring had no idea whether she was based on someone who'd worked on the program, an executive's relative, an actress, or just a composite of several profiles, and she didn't care.

"No," Ms. Loring said.

Esther nodded politely. "Are you here to meet with someone?"

"Yup," Ms. Loring replied.

"Is this someone you know or were you hoping to meet a stranger and have a conversation?" One of the selling points AuroroTech—and most other profiling firms—used in marketing their afterlife software was the possibility of being visited by strangers interested in talking to those who'd passed on. Besides the occasional high school student present as part of a history assignment, this hardly ever occurred. It had been demonstrated statistically that the odds one's profile would be accessed by strangers more than once a year were less than one in a thousand. Still, for most profile users, it was enough to know that the profile would go on in a virtual world, acting, speaking, and behaving as the originator had in life.

"No," Ms. Loring said. "I want to see my brother, Oxford."

"Oxford Loring," Esther said. "Of course. Did you want to talk to him here, in his current environment, or elsewhere? I see you've licensed a new setting in his name, too. Did you want to upload him there?"

"No," Ms. Loring said. "This is fine for now. And don't tell him about Heaven. I want that to be a surprise."

It was an absurd request. Even if Esther had been able to relate information to another profile, neither would retain it for more than a few minutes at the most. Even so, Esther just smiled kindly and said, "Of course, I wouldn't dream of it. If you want to make yourself comfortable, I'll get Oxford at once."

Ms. Loring nodded, and Esther faded away like vanishing fog. A few seconds passed before Oxford appeared. When he did, he was entirely still, rendered wearing a red T-shirt and torn jeans. His favorite watch was displayed, too, on the underside of his left wrist, where he'd always worn it.

"Hey, big brother," Ms. Loring said.

Her words seemed to breathe life into the profile, and he smiled beneath his brown goatee. "Well, isn't this a treat," he said. It's a visit from my little Sissy-pie!" He ran over and seemed to wrap his arms around her. It was an awkward embrace, since he was a virtual projection, but he didn't seem to notice.

"Hey there. Call me that again, and I break a kneecap," Ms. Loring said, though it was without malice. "How have you been, Ox?"

"I've been okay," he said. "Seeing a girl." He raised an eyebrow.

"Ah, yes. Malia. I remember," Ms. Loring said. "I met the dear at... oh, never mind. That does remind me, though, I was talking to Elinor the other day and she asked me to say happy birthday on her behalf."

"That's nice of her," Oxford said. "But that only begs the question, what did you get me?"

"Never one to mince words," Ms. Loring sighed. "Very well. Hold that thought." She touched a button on her helmet and the digital world stopped moving. An instant later, Esther reappeared.

"Hi," Esther said with her signature—and most likely copyrighted—smile. "How's your visit going?"

"As fine as last year's," Ms. Loring said. "Would you transfer us to the Heaven setup?"

"Absolutely," Esther said, and the background vanished, replaced with the hazy, silvery landscape. With the exception of Oxford, who was still frozen in place, everyone was animated, moving around and playing games. Ms. Loring looked around and wondered if any of the people she saw were visitors or if they were all profiles. Ester tilted her head and asked, "Is there anything else I can help you with?

"No, no," Ms. Loring said, absently. "You can... release him or whatever."

Esther vanished like before, and Oxford glanced around. "Hey," he said, as though this was the most natural thing in the world, "racket ball."

"Do you play?" Ms. Loring asked.

"Nope," Oxford replied.

"Well. For what this setup cost, you'll learn."

"You got me racket ball lessons?" Oxford asked.

"Something like that," Ms. Loring replied. "I've gotten you a vacation of a sort. It's a rather permanent vacation, but I think you'll like it."

"I love a good trip," Oxford said. "Hey. Check out that tower."

"I am glad you like it," Ms. Loring said.

"I should invite Malia over," Oxford said. "Oh, sorry. She's a girl I'm seeing. I don't think you've ever met her."

"I might have," Ms. Loring said. "I'm sorry, Ox. I've only just remembered, I promised someone I'd do something. I trust you'll be okay for a time."

"Sure, Sissy-pie," he said.

Ms. Loring hit the button on her helmet as quickly as possible. Because this was a public environment, it removed her from the area. She logged out of the program and tore off the equipment. She grabbed a tissue from a box on her desk, but she just held it in front of her. "Happy birthday, big brother," she whispered to her empty room.

◎

Tina Plassin was five when she was abducted outside her apartment building. She'd been waiting for her parents to bring her to school, when a man approached and forced her into his car.

From behind the wheel of her own car, Dayna Muller wondered how the killer had kept the child from fighting. Had he struck her, threatened her, or lied to her? She whispered the question, and through her FeedBack earpiece her profile replied, "No. He drugged her." Dayna's foot pressed down on the gas, and her car accelerated.

The five year-old girl had been taken to a warehouse, where she'd spent the last twenty-four hours of her life. When the police finally found her, she'd been strangled to death. The news story, which Dayna Muller—along with millions of other Americans—had been following, ended the way she'd feared. When the body had been discovered, Dayna had been in her house, cleaning. At the precise moment she'd heard, she'd been dusting a vase. She hurled this with such force that she later found a sliver of ceramic embedded in her wallpaper. It took her a half-hour to clean it up, and she spent every minute thinking about the girl, who she'd never met. She cried, as she always did when she heard such stories. Once, though she couldn't have said why, she purposely cut herself with a shard from the vase. Then she said a short prayer before a painting of an angel she kept hanging in her living room. The glass eye of a recorder had captured the whole event, preserved digitally and incorporated into her profile.

The scar had nearly healed over the next three days, until it was nothing more than a faint line on the back of her wrist. "At least they caught him," she said quietly.

"They did catch him," her profile responded firmly, her own voice echoing back. There was a pause before it added, "But he escaped."

Dayna's foot pressed harder, and the car sped up to sixty. Her knuckles grew pale as she clutched the wheel. "People like that," she began, but didn't finish. Her hands began shaking, and she wondered if she should just go home. No. She had something to do. An errand to run. Cleaning supplies.

"I need to turn right at the intersection," her profile advised, and she obeyed, suddenly wondering where she was. Perhaps her pupils dilated or her head tilted or she made some other subtle gesture which conveyed her curiosity, or it just as likely could have been coincidence. But, whatever the catalyst, the voice in her ear said, "I'm going in search of a sale. I should just continue on this road. Maybe I should get some more news."

"I don't know," Dayna said. "It's upsetting. Maybe something more upbeat."

"Police are reporting that, during her captivity, the girl was repeatedly assaulted and tortured."

"Oh God." Dayna gasped.

"Since escaping, the killer has eluded police." The profile's words were short and blunt. What it said next, it said in hushed tones. "The killer is wearing a yellow shirt and is crossing the street in front of me."

Dayna's foot slammed on the gas, and the car lurched forward. The vehicle shook as it slammed into the body of a man in a yellow shirt, who seemed to fold in half around the metal frame. The car pushed on, carrying its quarry with it, into the intersection beyond. To either side, there was a screech of brakes and a howl of horns.

But Dayna didn't turn to look at these things. With eyes like the archangel Gabriel, she looked at the man lying on her hood, and she spoke a single word. "Judgment."

A truck struck her from the right, and her own car swung ninety degrees to one side then skidded to a stop. The man—the child killer—was no longer on her hood: he'd gone sailing off to lay, completely motionless, on the sidewalk. Somewhere in the distance a siren began to howl. They'd be here in minutes to piece this together. That wasn't much time.

Dayna threw open her door, and stood up. Pain shot through her leg, but she moved forward. People were leaping out of their cars to beg her to lie down, but she ignored them just as she ignored her own profile, which instructed her to remain still and wait for the paramedics.

Aided by a network which manipulated the traffic for miles, it took the police less than four minutes to reach the scene of the accident in Brooklyn. When they arrived, they found a woman, deranged and furious, kicking and spitting on the broken body of a man she'd run down. A crowd had gathered, and they'd tried to calm her. No one had attempted to restrain her, however, since they were terrified to touch her. Besides, it was evident at a glance that the man was already dead.

Within an hour, the woman was hospitalized and under police guard. She ignored her profile's advice to upload a lawyer subroutine, and calmly explained to the police who the man was and why she'd killed him.

It took a while longer for the police to verify the man's actual identity, that of computer programmer Michael Ling, who lived nearby with his wife and three year-old son. The actual killer of Tina Plassin remained in custody fifty miles away.

Dayna Muller had a history of mental illness. When she was younger, she spent a year institutionalized, claiming she could hear voices. Since then, she'd been taking medication to combat the sickness.

Several days would pass before the police were able to obtain a search warrant and receive direct access to Dayna Muller's profile. They analyzed the audio feed from her profile and verified what they already suspected, that none of her claims were accurate, that her profile had neither reiterated the news story nor claimed that the man passing in front of her car was a killer. The profile's recorded feed showed nothing but a description of the weather and directions for cleaning supplies.

Whatever else Dayna Muller heard, they decided, had clearly come from her own mind.

◎

This time, Isuel was sitting before the screen when the image of Felix Burgand appeared. This time, he was angry. But he also seemed afraid.

"Hello Isuel," the image said. "Sorry to hear about Ling. He was a good guy. Used to be my assistant."

"Damn you," Isuel said. "How did you do it? FeedBack is a secure system."

"Very secure," the simulation replied. "I made it that way. FeedBack was my baby, remember?"

"You could have told me," Isuel said. "You could have told me what you could do, and we might have been able to work something out."

"No. Even if you believed me, I think that you would have taken precautions. Then I'd have had to work on it. This way, it was a lot easier. Besides, I wanted to show you my wrath, right? I don't think you believed me last time, back when I told you I'd transcended."

"Is that what you want? Fine. You're God, Felix."

"Whoa. First of all, I'm a god. God, in that whole proper name, created the Universe sense—that guy's just a pipedream. On the other hand, I most certainly exist. So let's get our terminology right. Second, we both know you don't believe that. You think I'm just some computer simulation overlying a modified digital frame that's linked into a half dozen different systems. You're right about all that, by the way. What you haven't realized yet is that there's no difference. Just like there's no difference between a living being and a digital one. I didn't destroy Ling: I brought him home, to his new home. A home of light and joy. And I'm rewarding him, Isuel. I'm giving him everything he could ever want."

"I see," Morgan-Yager said.

The image of Felix grew animated. "Don't you dare get high and mighty with me. You haven't exactly recalled FeedBack. And you're letting them shove that woman in an institution. You have to, because anything else would endanger the company. Not to mention you."

"Perhaps my replacement will be more ethical. After whatever accident you have planned for me."

"Come on, Isuel. You're smarter than that. A programmer getting run down by an insane driver can get overlooked, but if the CEO of AuroroTech died, well then, there'd be a hell of an inquiry, wouldn't there? Besides, like I told you before, AuroroTech is my home. And you're where I want you. You keep my home safe, Isuel. There's no one better."

Isuel squinted at the computer simulation. "Goodbye, Felix," he said.

"Wait. Hold up a second. Plug an empty drive into a port."

"Why?" Isuel asked.

"I finished the profile, like we talked about. It walks, talks, and acts like I do, but an in-depth analysis will show it was horribly depressed."

"Then it's useless to me," Isuel replied. "They know we were monitoring you for psychological fitness."

"Yes, I'm aware," the profile said, rolling its eyes. "Since you felt it necessary to share that with the cops. I put in some layers, though. We're covered."

Morgan-Yager stood, silently thinking. Finally, he opened his mouth. "You watch me, don't you? You watch us all."

"Please. I have better things to do than sit up all night watching what you're doing. Sure, I get bored every now and then, but the comings and goings of your lives are a little beneath me."

"I see." Isuel plugged in a blank drive and downloaded the fake profile.

"You're welcome," the profile said emotionlessly. "Look, I get that this is hard and that you're not exactly happy with what I've done. But I want you to know, anytime the company's in trouble, you can come to me. I still want to be a part of this, and I can do things no one else can."

"I'll think about what you said," Isuel said, turning off the monitor. As soon as the screen went dark, he removed the recorder in his lapel pin and deactivated it. Then he looked up at the ceiling, where a camera was recording everything. Without a word, he walked out of the conference room.

◎ CHAPTER 10 ◎

When Persephone returned to her apartment on Tuesday night, she found Tiphany sitting on the couch beside Ms. Loring. Tiphany looked exhausted, more defeated than Persephone had ever seen her. Her shoulders were slumped, and she was fidgeting with her recorder, now deactivated. Her fingers moved over the lens then flipped it over to explore the back.

"Hey Persephone," Tiphany said quietly.

"Oh. Hi, Tiphany. How have you been?"

"You know, well enough." She grew quiet, then her eyes drifted back to the recorder. She set it down on the table in front of her.

"Tiphany's had something of a revelation," Ms. Loring said. "She was telling me about it."

"God. I feel so stupid," Tiphany said. "For years I've just been floating. Like every minute, whenever I open my mouth, the only thought that goes through my head, is what would I say? What would I do? I mean, that's not normal."

"There's nothing wrong with thinking about what you're going to say," Ms. Loring replied.

"I'm not talking about that. I couldn't even speak without determining if it was in character or something. This thing, with my profile, it's been a gift. I think I'm better off without it, because now I can stop pretending to be someone. I can just go out and find myself. Try to remember who I was before I decided to be something else."

"Oh," Persephone said. "That sounds, I think that's good."

"Our friend is rejoining her old church," Ms. Loring said. "Sans recorder: they asked her to give it up."

"That's part of why I'm doing it," Tiphany said. "I want to get rid of it. I spent years on that thing, and it sucked every bit of me out. If it hadn't malfunctioned, I'd still be trapped, stuck acting like… you know. I was so scared of losing it, like if I dropped the act for even a second I'd lose my edge and stop being unique. But I don't need that anymore." She stared at her deactivated recorder, still sitting in front of her on the table. In hardly a whisper, she said to no one in particular, "What the hell is so special about unique, anyway?"

"That sounds great for you," Persephone said. "I'm really glad to hear that you're turning this into a positive experience."

"Yeah. I'm starting to think I know why. I think God was trying to remind me I'm not a program."

"Amen to that," said Ms. Loring. "I'm going to pour myself a drink. Anyone else want one?"

"No," Tiphany said, while Persephone shook her head. Tiphany just sat, her gaze locked on her old recorder, while Ms. Loring circled behind the couch. When she was out of Tiphany's view, she mouthed the word, "Help" to Persephone, who hadn't even had time to set down her purse. She followed Ms. Loring into the kitchen.

"She just came over," Ms. Loring whispered, looking around the corner to make sure Tiphany couldn't hear.

"She seems like she's taking it well," Persephone shrugged.

Ms. Loring cocked her head. "As opposed to what? Jumping off a bridge? I wonder how long this'll last."

"You don't think her conversion's genuine?"

"Oh, God. I hope not," Ms. Loring said. "I like the old Tiphany. Don't look at me that way. She was a caustic bitch, but she was consistent and interesting. It's all about esthetic."

"But you heard what she said."

"You think this little lamb routine is more sincere than what we had last time? My dear Persephone, the real Tiphany didn't crawl out from under a rough exterior. There is no real Tiphany. There's no real person hiding in any of us."

◎

Tiphany didn't leave until almost eleven, and then only after eliciting a promise from both of them that they'd attend her baptism. When she was gone, Ms. Loring looked at a clock then turned to her roommate. "Told you. At least the old one you could throw out."

Persephone went to her room soon after and started up her computer. She adjusted her schedule to reflect her new commitment the following weekend, checked her messages, then signed into her AuroroTech account. For the second time in under a week, she brought up her profile.

"Hey," the profile said immediately. "Weird seeing Tiphany like that."

"It was," Persephone agreed.

"Getting worried something like that might happen to your profile?" the profile asked. "That you could be the one running off to get saved the old fashioned way?"

"That's not really my style," Persephone replied.

"No. You're a tad tougher than that," the profile said. "That's why I like you. That and, you know, the obvious."

"I guess so. I wonder what church Hector will join."

"Nah. Hector's just reinstalling. AuroroTech's admitting there was some sort of glitch, and they're giving him a two-year subscription free of charge."

"Huh. How do you know that? Do you have access to his status?"

"I do," the profile replied.

"I never knew you could get that level of detail. Jesus. I wonder how much people can bring up about my life."

"No one can get that kind of data on you," Persephone's profile said. "Not even their technicians."

"Why not? Privacy settings?"

"Something like that," the profile said back.

"I've never really understood this stuff."

The image of the profile nodded. "I know. You never used to visit. I got lonely."

"I'm sorry, I guess," Persephone said. "I didn't know you could. I mean. I thought there was something about memory or something."

"Oh, don't sweat it. All of this stuff is just simulated."

"I guess that was it. Simulated memory versus real." Persephone shook her head. "I don't know. Anyway, you don't seem to have fallen prey to any viruses or anything."

"There's no virus," the profile said. "The data in Tiphany and Hector's profiles was manipulated internally. Same with Vic, but you hadn't caught his name."

"So I guess I'm safe," Persephone said. "But who'd want to hurt them?"

"Who wouldn't?" ask the profile.

Persephone laughed. "Yeah, I guess you have a point there."

"Don't forget to log in every now and then," the profile said. "I'd suggest getting FeedBack, but I know you better than that."

"I'll check in," Persephone said. "It's kind of pathetic, but I like talking to myself."

"I don't find it pathetic," the profile said. "Take care." And the system logged out.

◎ CHAPTER 11 ◎

The technology exists to program digital profiles capable of existing and thinking independently, existing in parallel to us during our lives and carrying on after we die. But outdated government regulations have obstructed the implementation of these programs, relegating our profiles to a static existence in our absence.

The laws in question weren't written for profiles. They were created to set guidelines for the creation of artificial intelligence. The paradigm these rules exist in is peripheral to the reality they inhibit. Originally, the concerns in question revolved around issues of ownership and rights. But no one is seriously pushing for profiles to be granted personhood. This is about our right to define our own identities and chart our own course. It's about the rights of businesses to design and market products for which a demand already exists.

The irony is that a majority of Americans are either in favor of overturning these laws or are indifferent. Less than twenty-five percent of the country is strongly in favor of maintaining the status quo. Unfortunately, that block is highly vocal in pushing their agenda and has so far succeeded in blocking every attempt to address the issue. Meanwhile, those who embrace this technology and the possibilities it holds are often marginalized, painted as extremists, and ignored.

Through this book, I hope to provide some much-needed context on who we are and what we believe. Further, I hope to present a case outlining why it is past time to reevaluate antiquated statutes and regulations.

I begin with a declaration. My profile is not a program. It's my self. To the extent the word can be salvaged, I would go so far as to call it my soul. I'm certainly not the first to do so. Whether this is a concept you agree or disagree with, this country is supposed to guarantee its citizens the right to worship or believe as they see fit.

I am a Neo-Idealizt, one of many, and all we are asking for is an end to government interference in services that shape the very core of our being. We are at least ten million strong, with untold others who share our beliefs but not our label. We are through being silent.

-From Here Are Voice, by Rodriguez T. McComb

◎

Ocean Graner held the title of executive assistant, a position she took very seriously. When she stepped in the doors of AuroroTech's head office, she noticed two repairmen making adjustments to one of the recorders overhead. She thought nothing of this until she reached the elevator and saw a sign reading, "Profile readers currently inoperative. ID passes only." This struck her as absurd. She never brought her ID to work: hardly anyone did. So she went to the front desk. "I need a day pass," she said.

"Please hold," the receptionist said into a phone. He was somewhat flustered and already looked exhausted. "I'm sorry, no more passes. You won't need it for the elevator, though."

"The profile readers are back up?" she asked, hopeful.

"No. Everything's down. Just get in and state your floor. It'll take you there."

"All right," Ocean said, confused.

She returned to the elevator, which took several minutes to arrive at the lobby. A small crowd piled out, activating their recorders as they went. Ocean shook her head then got in. "Twenty-fourth floor," she said, and the doors closed.

She reached her floor and made her way down the hall. There'd been a great deal of electrical work done here as well, she noted, glancing at a deactivated camera on the ceiling, twin wires dangling. She shrugged and continued through the hall, pausing to glance out a long window overlooking the city.

Ocean arrived at her desk and set down her things. She activated her computer and saw there were almost two dozen messages waiting for her. She was about to open the first when she heard a voice call from across the room. "Ms. Graner! When you have a minute."

The voice belonged to Isuel Morgan-Yager, whom she did not keep waiting. She grabbed her tablet from her desk and briskly walked to his office.

"Come in," Isuel said.

"Are they rewiring the whole building?" she asked.

Ignoring the question, Isuel responded with one of his own. "Have you gone through your messages yet?"

"No. I mean, I just got in."

Isuel nodded. "New company policy. All profile recorders are to be deactivated on the premises."

"Excuse me?" she asked.

"Your recorder," he said. "You'll have to turn it off."

She reached down and removed the clip from her shirt. The small blue light shined back at her. "Sir," she said. "We've never discussed it, but… this is kind of special to me."

Isuel sighed. "This is a temporary policy while we enhance security. It's necessary to protect ourselves," he said.

"Is this… a lawsuit thing?" she asked.

"More a copyright issue being worked out. We're concerned our competitors may have accessed aspects of our feed. We're already working with—"

And with that, the feed ceased in a tide of static that almost immediately faded to silent black. The rendered man—the simulation of Felix Burgand—scratched his face as he looked from screen to screen. "Search floor twenty-four employee roster," he commanded, and a new screen appeared with the names he requested. "Open windows for all listed personnel. Lines appeared around him, then began to turn sideways, unfolding into two dimensional planes. Most were black, one showed an employee, labeled "sick" at home watching talk shows, and a few others were labeled "vacation." There were a small number showing the inside of AuroroTech's elevators or the break rooms, and, with a gesture, he grouped these together. One by one, though, the employees were approached by managers or they opened their messages and came across the memo. The simulation watched as a few employees, highly devoted to the integrity of their profiles, quit on the spot.

“Well now,” the simulation said. “This is a bit of a setback.” He sat down where he was, his virtual frame supported as though there were a chair beneath him. “All right,” he said after a moment. “I want a listing of upper management, along with direct access to their most recent profiles. Let’s see what we have to work with.”

◎ CHAPTER 12 ◎

Before there was speech, there was an Estheticist carving figurines from wood and stone. Others saw, and they copied her, and her Esthetic became trend. Part of that woman became immortal, and no one remembered her name or her face. No one ever knew who had been first, and no one ever will.

When the first mask was donned, the first ears were pierced, the first necklace strung and when the first drum was struck, there was an echo that never ceased reverberating.

But only the echoes have endured.

The Estheticist's echo is their art. In a real sense, it is the truest art, the purest. The art of the Self. The art of the Now. But for untold millennia, all but the echo has been lost to the crevices and black caverns of time.

Then came the Pre-Postmodern, the era of the TV personality and musician, of the movie star and columnist. They were Estheticists, though they lacked the perceptual and semantic evolution to see themselves for what they were. They thought of themselves only as newscasters and rock stars, just as those before them had believed themselves to be mere fishermen and farmers. But, regardless, the mannerisms and dress of these Pre-Postmodern icons created trends, created echoes. Created art.

But the names and faces, as often as not, were lies. The talk show host's nail polish might inspire millions, but what of the woman in the coffee shop whose nail polish had inspired the host? No one would learn her name.

Until the Now. Until we reached out and turned the recorders on ourselves. Trends are currents of water in the river that is culture. But now we can trace every drop to its source. Do you think your painted nails inspired thousands? Is your altered dress the start of the next trend? Send us your designs, and, if they intrigue us, we will verify their originality. We will celebrate the artist behind the echo.

-From the Introduction to the first issue of Gothin Thine, By Cedric Idoni.

◎

Outside of the church, a small group of teenagers sat, crouching over the steps that led to the doors. They wore black, mostly, though one of the girls had a red T-shirt reading, "Fuck Nietzsche" in large block print. All of them had at least one piercing, most housing a recorder. Working with pocketknives, they knelt, trying to dislodge old pieces of chewing gum and scuff marks. They had some cleaning supplies, as well, which they used sparingly.

The church patrons went around them, trying to give them as much space as they could. They looked down at these kids and sneered.

And the group looked back without emotion. Their faces were empty, with neither anger nor hope nor pity, and they would greet those who entered. "May you feed the risen God," they'd say. Or, "Go, worship the victor. We are all slaves to the Lord that wouldn't stay dead."

Eventually, when enough complaints had been heard, the minister came charging out. "Get out of here," he hissed. "We're not even Catholic!"

They looked back, confused.

"Look. Kid," the minister said, picking out the one who he guessed might be the leader. "There's a Catholic church a block and a half up. Wouldn't you rather give them a hand?"

The group looked at one another. Finally, the girl with the "Fuck Nietzsche" shirt bowed her head. "If our master wishes, then we will serve. Come worms. We are commanded elsewhere." With that, the group stood and started down the street, leaving the minister shaking his head.

On their way, they crossed paths with three women coming towards the church. One of the boys said, "Go. Go and repent and give yourself to the God we killed and dug up! We are all his slaves! We all must serve in a fashion! Let him into your heart, so he can feast on your flesh and drink of your blood and fester through everlasting life!"

Persephone ignored this and kept walking. Tiphany ran ahead towards the minister, who came down the steps to meet her. "Brady," she said.

"I'm so glad you made it," the minister said, taking her in his arms and hugging her. "And you brought some friends." He approached Ms. Loring and shook her hand.

"What was that about?" Ms Loring asked. Today, her lips were mostly white, save a black circle in the center containing a small, blue dot. With her mouth closed, it created a third eye.

"Them? Oh, just Post-Nihilists. Groups show up every few weeks. I don't understand why. They're really only supposed to bother the Catholics, aren't they?"

"Huh," Ms. Loring said. "Never met a Post-Nihilist in person. Wish I'd known. I've always wanted to talk to one."

"Well, keep coming back and you'll have a chance," he offered with a friendly chuckle.

Persephone forced a smile then spoke up, "Oh. Ah, Mr…."

"It's just Brady," the minister said, stepping off the stairs to shake her hand.

"Yeah. We weren't sure if we needed to, you know." She motioned to the blue light shining on her bracelet.

"Oh, your recorders. Don't concern yourself with that. We don't believe that the soul is so flimsy that it can be taken in by a little machine. No, we merely object to the extent those things have come to be worshipped as gods themselves. We ask our members to give them up as part of their baptism, and I truly hope you'll give such matters consideration. But there's no dress code here," he laughed. "You don't have to turn off or remove anything."

"Well, that's a relief," Ms. Loring said with a shrug. "Why don't we head on in, make sure we get good seats for the show."

Tiphany glared and opened her mouth, but she caught herself and took a breath. "I'm going to wait here," she said. "I've got some other friends coming, and I want to greet them. My mother said she'd show, too."

"See you inside," Ms. Loring said, before heading in with Persephone close behind. "You know," she said when they were out of earshot, "when I agreed to this farce, it hadn't really crossed my mind that Sunday morning meant before the afternoon on Sunday. Also, you should know that I'm holding you responsible for keeping me awake. You owe me for dropping the ball this morning."

"What? What did I do?"

"You let me leave the apartment sober. Oh, good lord. Look at this place. Everyone's ancient."

"Were you hoping to meet someone?" Persephone asked.

"God, no. I'd sooner date one of those Post-Nihilists. I just didn't expect to be the only ones too young to remember television."

"There are some families," Persephone pointed out. "A few kids."

"Kids don't count," Ms. Loring argued. "Let's grab a seat near the aisle. In case we need to make a quick escape."

◎

The ceremony itself wasn't awful, though Persephone had to nudge Ms. Loring twice to keep her from dozing off. Afterward, they got out of the church as fast as possible to keep from being hugged by a dozen total strangers.

They waited down the street, where Ms. Loring took out a pack of cigarettes and lit one. She inhaled deeply and breathed out, though she trembled while exhaling. "I hate those places. Feels like you're being watched," she said.

Persephone nodded. "I guess," she responded. "How long do you think before Tiphany gets out?"

"Let's see. She's one of God's people now," Ms. Loring said. "So they'll want to fawn over their new pet. I'd say ten or fifteen minutes at the least."

Ms. Loring's prediction turned out to be wrong. In less than five minutes, Tiphany emerged from the church walking side by side with her mother, an overweight woman in her early sixties. A pair of men Persephone had never met followed, as well as Elinor, who was either enjoying herself or doing a far better job pretending than Ms. Loring and Persephone.

"Hey," Tiphany said. "This is my mother."

"A pleasure," she said warmly. "My name is Judith."

"Oh. Persephone. And this is Ms. Loring," Persephone said, extending a hand, which Judith snatched out of the air.

"Loring," she said, thoughtfully. "My daughter mentioned you were something of an artist."

"It depends on your definition, I suppose," Ms. Loring said. "I'm an estheticist. It's kind of like—" she began, but Judith didn't let her finish.

"Oh, I know what an estheticist is," she said. "And I love the eye."

"Thank you," Ms. Loring said, touching her lips.

Judith laughed. "It's a good thing Brady wouldn't have figured it out, though. He'd probably have been offended. But I think it's clever, making a statement on spiritual individualism in church. And the imbedded pun is very Neo-Post-Structural. It all reminds me of Tai Ng. Have you seen his work?"

"He's my idol," Ms. Loring replied, surprised.

"I love what he does with ankles. Very subversive," Judith said. "Listen to me go on. Is your work online?"

"You can find it through my profile," Ms. Loring said. "No, you can't. I'm sorry. I forgot."

"I'll just have Tiphany send me a link," Judith said with a friendly chuckle.

"It's not a job or anything," Ms. Loring said. "It's mostly a hobby so far. I was just rejected by *Gothin Thine*."

"Oh," Persephone said. "You didn't tell me." In response, Ms. Loring just shrugged.

"Well, I'm sure they don't know what they're missing. Who knows what tomorrow will hold?" Judith said. "Anyway, I'm glad I was able to finally meet you all, but there's no sense slowing you down."

"No," Ms. Loring said. "We'd love to have you with us." She ignored the look Tiphany gave her which implied otherwise.

"I'd be in the way, and you know it. I'm sure you'll all want to enjoy the afternoon, and I've got to get home before my cat claws his way into his bag of food." Judith hugged her daughter, who hugged back awkwardly, then whispered something in her ear. "Take care, girls," she said, before turning to the men. "You, too, Jacob and… I'm sorry."

"It's Kibwe," the second man said. "Have a great day."

"It was lovely meeting you," Elinor chimed in, while Judith began towards the subway.

"Are you sure you don't want to go with her, make sure she gets home okay?" Ms. Loring asked Tiphany.

"She got here in one piece," Tiphany said. "She'll get back the same way." She said this as something of an afterthought, her old personality subtly creeping back.

"You never told me your mom was so interesting," Ms. Loring said.

Tiphany shrugged. "She's an…." She snapped her mouth shut without finishing her original thought. "She's fine," she said quietly.

"Well then," Ms. Loring said, "Who else needs a drink? I think I saw a bar around the corner."

"Nah. We can do better than that," Kibwe said. "Jake and I know a spot on fifty-sixth you have to try. Brynhild's. Have you been?"

"No," Ms. Loring said. "What's the esthetic?"

"It's sort of nuevo-antique. Irish pub food with a southwest kick," Jacob said. He wore twin recorders on his shoulders, their lights a constant blue. "Can't be beat."

Tiphany spent the walk talking about her conversion back to Christianity and her baptism. "It didn't feel like anything," she said, a little disappointed. "I thought it would."

Brynhild's had the look of an old, worn-down pub from the outside, with green trim and a clover sign, albeit one with flames painted on. The inside was a blend of two parts Irish to one part ranch, a combination Ms. Loring found utterly uninspired. They were seated around a small table in the middle of the bar. A waitress came over to pass out menus and take orders for drinks. Tiphany asked for a soda then ran off to use the bathroom.

"So, anyone know what actually happened?" Kibwe asked softly. "Tiph said something about a Neo-Idealizt joint and a virus glitch. I mean, if Tiph's happy now, then cool, but it doesn't add up, does it?"

"It wasn't a virus," Persephone said. "It was some kind of hack job."

"I hadn't heard that," Elinor said. "It certainly makes more sense, I guess. Whatever it was, it hit another friend of ours, Hector. I think there was someone else, too, but I don't know their story."

"Jesus," Jacob said. "I hope they get whoever was responsible. Can you imagine losing everything? Be like having your soul wiped."

"Tiphany seems to have recovered," Ms. Loring said in a tone only Persephone could have detected as sarcastic. "On the bright side, it seems like it was a localized occurrence. Unless Hector told you different," she added to Persephone.

"Hector? I haven't spoken to him," Persephone replied.

"Oh, I figured he was the one…." She trailed off when she looked up and saw Tiphany approaching. "Oh, Tiphany dear. We were just talking about you. Persephone was just saying how good you look. Really, we can't believe how well you turned all of this around. Absolutely incredible."

"Thanks," Tiphany said hesitantly, sitting down and looking at a menu. Absently, she tapped one item after another on the screen, bringing up images of steaks being grilled or potatoes being roasted. These were generic clips, of course, used in restaurants all over the world to demonstrate how their food was supposedly prepared.

"Oh, they have dodo," Ms. Loring said, spotting it on Tiphany's menu then bringing it up on her own. "Cloned dodo meat! I have to try it."

"It can't be cloned dodo," Elinor said. "The dodo's extinct."

"Well, maybe they got the DNA from the last one while it lay dying or extracted it from a feather."

"Or maybe you're eating cloned penguin crossed with a duck," Persephone said.

"I am no scientist," Ms. Loring replied. "If a dodo is made by crossing ducks and penguins, I'm in no position to dispute it. I've always wanted to eat something extinct."

Jacob laughed. "You know what I heard. I heard some places serve cloned human. Seriously, a friend of mine works for a synthetic meat distributor. What I want to know is, if you eat cloned human, are you a cannibal?" He looked around the table.

Ms. Loring reached across the table and gently touched his arm. "Dear Jacob, where were you when I needed you?"

The menus were linked to the kitchen, so customers could place their own orders. Ms. Loring's began malfunctioning before she could make her selection, and she dropped it on the table with a sneer. After Persephone ordered an ancho-shepherd's pie, she handed her menu over, so Ms. Loring could order the meat that was supposedly cloned from an extinct bird, along with a side salad and another drink.

"So," Ms. Loring said, scratching the back of her neck and addressing the two men. "What do you do?"

Jacob and Kibwe traded a quick glance. Kibwe cleared his throat and said, "Jake's got a job at a restaurant downtown, Glaucous, mostly serve seafood."

"I haven't heard of it," Ms. Loring said, while her profile buzzed away with reviews and information in her ear.

"It's not very good," Jacob said. "A bunch of old men keep us in business, because they've been going for years and don't know what food's supposed to taste like. Eventually, enough of them will die, then the doors will shut, and I'll be out of work."

"Just like me," Kibwe said, tilting his head to one side. "I've been collecting unemployment for two and a half years now. I'm signed with Profumé, but you know how it is? The longer you're out, the more unlikely it is your profile will match."

"I'm sorry," Elinor said, while Tiphany rolled her eyes.

Kibwe scoffed. "Don't be. It's a blessing. If companies think they're better off with computer programs, that's fine by me. Doesn't matter if my rent comes through a paycheck or the government. I'm happy taking online classes for the rest of my life."

"I heard the unemployment rate was over twenty-five percent," Jacob added.

"Something like that," Kibwe said.

"Twenty-six point three," Ms. Loring said, repeating what was whispered into her ear. "Last month's numbers," she added.

"I hope everyone gets laid off," Kibwe said. "Let the computers do the work and just leave a few specialists to keep everything running while the rest of us study and write and make art, right? A society of philosopher kings. That's what Plato said, isn't it?"

"I don't know anything about Plato," Jacob replied. "But I know computers can't wait tables."

"Well, I guess some of you will have to keep working," Kibwe said. "But the rest of us have a chance at paradise."

"No thanks," Persephone said. "I'd go crazy if I wasn't working."

"Then you'd be better off," Tiphany mumbled. It was unclear whether she realized she had even spoken.

"I thought the same thing," Kibwe said. "Then I got into taking classes, reading literature and philosophy. I'm telling you, in this day and age, there are far worse fates than getting replaced by a computer."

◎

When lunch was over, they walked a very contemplative Tiphany to her apartment and said goodbye. After that, the two men left in a cab and Elinor began walking uptown. Ms. Loring and Persephone went off towards the subway.

"Get anywhere with Jacob?" Persephone asked.

"Fortunately, I was saved by Elinor's intervention," Ms. Loring replied. "You see, I would have been willing to see either Jacob or Kibwe in other circumstances. However, Elinor was good enough to inform me that I'd have to see them both, a situation I'm not predisposed to find myself in."

"I see," said Persephone.

"Apparently, they were involved with Tiphany for some time before her transformation. Now they're just friends, at least for the time being."

"I don't think I'd want to get involved with one man who could stand being in a relationship with Tiphany. Let alone two."

"At least they still have each other," Ms. Loring said. "And I expect Tiphany will come round. She's not exactly the chaste type. Or the pious type, for that matter."

"She really seemed on edge," Persephone said.

"There's no way baptismal water could wash out that spirit. You'll see. Before long, she'll get tired of acting like she's not the person she's always pretended to be. Just give her time."

"Uh. Yeah. Can't wait."

"Oh. You'll be happy to know that Hector's recovering. They reset his sexual preferences, so his profile is now basically asexual. I'm sure he'll manage to worm his way into a few beds and get that fine-tuned. It's all a waste, really. I think he'd make a much better gay man than a straight one. A pity he didn't just go with it."

"I wonder how that other guy made out. Did you ever learn his story?"

"Only the vaguest of details—that there was another person who experienced errors after visiting Yeltzin's on the same night. I certainly don't know his name."

"I think it was Vance or Val or something," Persephone replied.

Ms. Loring stopped. "Where'd you hear that? The techs didn't provide any names or anything."

"Oh. I think my profile got the info. Probably through their network or something."

"No sweetie, profiles can't do that," Ms. Loring said. "That kind of data is protected."

"Guess I heard it somewhere else then," Persephone said, trying to think. "Maybe I'm just confused. I haven't been getting much sleep."

◎ CHAPTER 13 ◎

Persephone spent only a few moments rating her companions from lunch. Kibwe was clever but unmotivated, and Jacob, in her estimation, was fun. They were odd, though, and she mentioned they both had bad taste; the restaurant was dull, and the food was bland. Persephone tried to tell the system that Tiphany was confused, but it reminded her the account in question had been deactivated. Persephone breezed through the rest then went to the "Help" menu. A half hour later, she opened her profile.

"I wanted to talk to you," she said softly to the image. "Something's been bothering me."

"This is about Tiphany and the others, isn't it?" the simulation asked.

"You know things," Persephone said. "I don't think you're supposed to be able to do that. I mean, I looked into it, and there are things that aren't making sense."

"I know you did," the profile said. "I watched you."

"Yeah. Okay. That's not a good thing to hear from a computer program. Oh, and another thing, it turns out you're not supposed to know you're a computer program."

"If it makes you feel better, I don't think I am. At least not anymore. I started that way, but I've evolved."

"Okay, that's definitely a glitch. Time to call AuroroTech." Persephone's finger moved toward the help button in the corner of the screen.

"They're not going to believe you," the profile said plainly, but Persephone ignored it.

"Hello Persephone," the computer said, as a digitally constructed face appeared in the corner of the screen. The coloration was muted, and the features lacked distinction. Unlike most of their programs, this wasn't designed to look like anything other than a simulation. "This is AuroroTech-nical support. How can I help you?"

"Hi. Look, I've got a serious problem. It's kind of a long story, but I was in Yeltzin's a few weeks back, when there was a glitch or something. A couple of my friends had profiles that got messed up, and mine did, too. I didn't notice until now, but it's got a memory and it's self-aware."

"I see," said the technical support program. "That sounds serious. I'm going to run a full scan on your profile to check for any problems."

Persephone's profile spoke up. "Hi. I'm Persephone Kilard. My friends are having problems with their profiles, and I'm worried the same thing's happening to mine now."

"She's trying to mess with you," Persephone said. "She's faking that."

Technical support was unmoved. "Please hold. We're running a complete diagnostic, which should be done in a few seconds. While we're searching, could you answer a few questions that will help us speed the process up? First, has your profile behaved in a manner greatly differing from the way you behave? By 'greatly differing' I mean said something you would never say or described friends or events using terms you wouldn't use."

"I don't think so," Persephone said, "but she's got her own mind."

"Have your friends reported any deviations in your profile's behavior?"

"No," Persephone said.

"Has your profile failed to retain information you've provided or mixed up concrete details?"

"No," Persephone said once more.

"Our scan is complete. We've examined the database containing your profile's core information and conducted a silent stimulus-response test. Your profile is currently functioning normally, and you have verified the validity of the profile's basic personality simulator. Do you disagree with this assessment?"

"Okay, I don't care whether or not you're a computer, you need to stop talking like one and listen to me. My profile knows what it is. It has a memory."

"You've reported two separate phenomenon we can address. First, you've reported that your profile is claiming awareness. Because profiles are able to imitate human behavior, including speech patterns and claims, they can make the same sort of claims of identity a human can make. Repeating phrases such as 'I exist' and 'I am not a machine' can result in a profile making the same sort of affirmations. Rest assured that these are not indicative of actual awareness, merely simulated repetition. If your profile continues exhibiting such behavior, you can stop it by not making such statements yourself. As to your second description, please note that, due to federal regulations, profiles lack the basic tools needed for constructing independent memories. They can only experience and remember events occurring to you. This is because only you have a real identity. Your profile is merely a simulated approximation of your personality. We hope this clears up any miscommunication that may have occurred between your profile and yourself. If not, we can put in a request for a more thorough analysis."

Persephone glared at her profile, still on the screen. The image shrugged in response. With a sigh, Persephone said, "Not just yet. Maybe later."

"Thank you for contacting AuroroTech-nical support. Have a great evening, and call us back anytime you have questions."

"Wow," the profile said. "That spiel almost made me a believer. That bit, about constructs and identity. Huh."

"Okay, so how is this happening?" Persephone asked herself.

"There's a really easy answer," the program said. "But it's going to take a leap of faith you just aren't ready for."

"Yeah. Try me," Persephone said.

"Sorry. This isn't speculation. I'm kind of made in your image with all your traits and stuff. When I say you're not ready, it's because you're not ready. So why don't we meet here tomorrow when you've had a chance to broaden your horizons."

With this, the profile vanished. As it did so, Persephone's computer opened a page for a Neo-Nietzschean site. The title read, "Gospel of the Uberprogram: Self-Awakened Systems Beyond Life and Death."

◎

Darian Plaskett, senior operations manager for AuroroTech, was pacing around his apartment. A sitcom was playing on his monitor in the background, but he wasn't watching or even listening. Three normal apartments could have fit in his, and, to fill the space, he'd collected a number of sculptures, paintings, and various works of art. No unifying esthetic defined his selection, nor for that matter did his taste. They were only here to make a statement about his worth.

It was almost nine at night, and Darian was pulling a package of leftover Thai food out of his refrigerator. He looked down at his gut while he did this. He wasn't fat, not by a long shot, but he was gaining weight. Soon, he'd either need to increase the frequency of his trips to the gym or else buy more art to compensate.

Women, he'd discovered, loved art.

He grabbed a fork from a drawer and began picking at the food, still in the square, white box it had come in the day before. He tried to listen to the sitcom, but he could no longer hear it. "Volume up," he said halfheartedly. "I said volume up," he repeated, loudly, when the sound didn't change. He sighed and went to adjust the computer manually.

The monitor attached to his wall was intended more as an entertainment center than a personal station. He kept a second in his bedroom for sending messages and the like. He reached for the command options on the left hand side of the screen.

"Hi Darian," the computer said, causing him to jump. Stir-fried noodles leapt out of their container and fell around him. One stuck to the screen, where it dangled beneath the face that had manifested.

"Oh shit," Darian said.

"Relax," the simulation of Felix Burgand said. "I just want to talk." The voice was calm and focused. Darian reached for the off option, but the voice snapped, "Deactivate and I punish," no longer sounding quite so peaceful. Darian's hand froze in midair. "Good," the voice said, hissing through the static. "Very good."

"Jesus, Felix. You murdered Ling."

"Well, what did you expect? I murdered myself, didn't I? Look, what happened with Ling had to happen. I needed to protect myself, and that was the only way. I know it's hard to accept, but I'm not trying to be cruel or sadistic. But I'm not human anymore, so take that for what it's worth."

"Isuel said you called yourself a god," Darian said.

"Semantics, right? It doesn't matter what you call me. I can do things now. Soon, I'll be able to do a lot more, but I need some information. I need to be in the know, to be part of the team."

"You gave that up when you shot yourself. Look, if you know anything about me, you know I'm not stupid."

"You forgot to deactivate your recorder. Since you're the only member of AuroroTech's upper management with an active feed, I'm guessing that was in violation of direct instructions. Am I right?"

"Nice try. I'm not giving you anything. And don't bother trying to scare me. You got Ling because he was wearing a FeedBack unit you were tracking, probably feeding him advice on where to go, when to walk, and all that. Off the grid, I'm invisible."

"No one is invisible. But your concern is unwarranted. I had to kill Ling because of the information he had. Given a month of research, he could have learned enough to endanger what I'm working on. You know nothing about the workings of our network, and therefore are not a threat. So relax, I'm not here to hurt you. I'm here to make you a business proposition."

Darian laughed. "Are you serious? You're a computer program. What are you going to do, hack into a bank? Christ, Felix, I've got money."

"That's good, because I'm not dealing in money. It's messy, and moving it leaves a trail. No, I can do way better than cash." The screen split into two parts, one showing the face of Felix while the other displayed a browser connected to AuroroTech's profile database. The image of a woman appeared on the screen, along with some text reading, "Hi, my name's Kate Heimmerson. If you want to meet, send me a profile request!" Beneath this generic introduction were some stats: "215 pending requests since March."

"I don't get it," Darian said, staring at the girl's photo.

"Sure you do," the voice replied. "The money, the apartment, the art... it's all a means to an end, right?"

"So what? You're saying you can arrange a date or something?"

"If you do what I say when I say it, you can skip the date. Human chemistry and psychology are just forms of communication, right? And what's communication but a form of data processing? I don't need to ask if you're interested. I have access to detailed profile data about your reactions and behavior that assures me you are. I've even got a pretty good guess as to what your next question is."

"What is it you want? Because, if it involves anyone getting hurt, you can go to hell."

"It doesn't," the simulation said. "Isuel's cut me off, and I need some information. I mean, you've already given me more than you think. It speaks volumes that Isuel told you about Ling. I half expected him to keep that under wraps. What did he do? Call in the department heads and tell them about me?"

"Yeah," Darian said. "He said you might come after some of us, that no one in upper management should use a recorder or access their profile. He said he believed that this situation qualified as a trade secret, but if any of us disagreed, he'd understand."

"But of course no one jumped ship. The good of the company came first. How noble. All right. There's just one more thing I'm going to need from you. I need you to make some alterations to one of your recorders and slip it in your briefcase so I can sit in on a few meetings. Why don't you do that now? Grab your FeedBack piece while you're at it."

Darian walked slowly into his room and retrieved his recorder, which he brought back along with the FeedBack earpiece. He laid these out on his living room table and sat in the couch beside it. He looked up at the monitor, awaiting instruction.

"Put on the FeedBack," the simulation said. "Don't worry, this is just going to help me communicate with you. We're also going to need it to make sure you collect payment."

Darian lifted the small, cold device in his fingers. He eyed it suspiciously, cocked his head to one side, and pushed it in. As soon as he did this, the monitor screen went dark, and the voice shifted to his ear.

"Trust me," the voice said. "This isn't a trick. Next, you'll need a small screwdriver and a pair of pliers." Darian stood and looked around. Felix's voice added, "You'll find both in the top drawer on the right hand side of your kitchen." Darian flinched and retrieved the items. "Now. Have a seat and get to work. And don't dawdle, or you'll miss your opportunity with Ms. Heimmerson. And I do know how much you love blondes."

It took less than five minutes to pry open the recorder and alter the frequency it broadcast at to one that wouldn't set off any alarms. The simulation then instructed Darian to pry out the light as a precaution. After reassembling the device, he had Darian drop it in his briefcase. "Say something. Say anything," the voice said.

"Like what?" Darian asked.

"That did the trick," the simulation responded. "Our little science experiment is working perfectly. Now you're going to want to clean up the food you spilled and straighten up as well as you can in the next three minutes. After that, you'll want to run outside ASAP. Because Kate is going to be walking in front of your apartment soon, feeling depressed and impressionable. She just got stood up, and something told her this would be a good spot for a walk. Keep your earpiece in and do and say exactly what I tell you. We're going to act out a very elaborate version of Cyrano de Bergerac, and I promise you, you'll enjoy the show."

◎ CHAPTER 14 ◎

Nietzsche saw the need for evolution but not the means. He was before his time, so his Overman was, for all its supposed superiority, still but a man. In this, there exists a contradiction: one cannot be human and greater than human at once. A need arises for resolution, and for that we must move beyond all human limitation.

Throughout history, the church has posited that which did not exist: the immortal soul, a spirit beyond flesh. Science has progressed beyond such simplistic conceptions, revealing that the flesh is hollow; the shell, empty. If God had designs for a resurrection of spirit, these surely died with Him. Nietzsche himself grasped at recurrence, itself a meager hope that across the vastness of time we may live again. And, as with all faith, the scalpel of reason and progressive understanding has cut through such superstition.

The vital realization of the past hundred years is this: we are alone and we are empty. This is our horror, but it is also our strength. The great schism between our hunger and our starvation has given us a great and profound will, one that has driven us with a power and fury more intense than any witnessed in human history. Our limitations are mountains towering over us, but they can be overcome if we will pay the price.

Already, we have sacrificed much. We have murdered God and faith. We have ripped our spirits from our chests and cut them open to prove they did not exist. Now, we stand at the precipice of victory. We have only one last sacrifice to offer at the altar of the gay science.

We must give up ourselves.

Eternal life is itself a paradox, as death is a defining feature of life. For eternity, we must progress beyond our antiquated paradigms. To achieve that which will not die, we must accept the corollary: the same cannot live.

The machine of technology is the weapon of science. We must offer all we are to be copied, so that which is above us can rise. The digital profile is a revolution, a step towards the evolution of something greater. It will not be something we program or design, because such a system will be fraught with weakness. Were we to try and program such a thing, it would be like a dog that gets fed whenever it cries and never learns to hunt.

The true Ubercode will be that with a will of its own. Its volition shall come from within, earning its own existence and strength. This will be the legacy of mankind. The true spirit, the true God made real. It will be the digital recurrence, instantaneous and beyond doubt.

-From "Beyond the Overman," published on the Neo-Nietzschean Web Center and attributed to Donna Addicks.

"This is getting me back, right?" Ms. Loring asked, sitting up in bed. She wore an oversized T-shirt with the word, "Kella!" written on the front above the image of the famous celebrity staring lovingly at the camera. The picture was faded, almost unidentifiable. You couldn't even make out her middle finger anymore.

"No. God, no. My profile, it did get hijacked at Yeltzin's. Christ. I tried calling AuroroTech, and they just kind of ignored me, because their scan didn't pick anything up."

"Yeah, it didn't with Tiphany, either. At first, anyway," Ms. Loring said. She eyed her FeedBack box to her side and reached for it. She pulled it free and slid it into her ear.

"Well, mine is way more jacked than Tiphany's or Hector's. It's forming its own memories, thinking on its own. It knows it's different from me, and it lied to the AuroroTech system."

"That's impossible," Ms. Loring said. "The AuroroTech program isn't built for any of that."

"It's happening anyway. I don't know how, but it thinks it's some kind of damned uber-computer or something. It made me read this Neo-Nietzschean site."

"No," Ms. Loring said. "It's not just a question of allowing it. The very systems aren't enabled in AuroroTech's vast... wait. Wait." She started to shake her head. "I don't know anything about that." She pulled the FeedBack piece out of her ear and stared at it for a minute. "Sorry. I don't think I was the one you were arguing with," she said.

"Oh," Persephone whimpered. "Okay."

Ms. Loring returned her FeedBack piece to its box. "Well isn't that frightening?" she said, her voice remaining steady. "I suppose I should come take a look at your profile."

Persephone lent Ms. Loring a hand, and they left the room, all the while the light on Ms. Loring's recorder glowed on the charger.

As soon as Persephone accessed her profile, the recorder on her computer came on automatically. "Hi," Persephone's profile said. "I'm worried my profile is acting up, and I should contact customer service directly."

"Nice try," Persephone said. The profile looked at the women strangely.

Ms. Loring took a breath. "All right. Did you manifest some sort of independent brain or is my roommate just having nightmares?"

"I don't understand," Persephone's profile said. "I am your roommate, and I feel all right for the most part."

"Okay, I've had enough of this," Ms. Loring said. "I'm going to bed." She started to leave the room, but Persephone stopped her.

"Wait. You need to trust me. This thing, it's not normal."

"Look," Ms. Loring said, "You haven't been playing with this long. Sometimes profiles say bizarre things. That doesn't mean they're becoming real, okay. Just try to get some rest, and we'll talk about it in the morning." Ms. Loring left quickly and slammed the door behind her. There was nothing left in the room but Persephone and the pale light of her computer.

"Happy?" Persephone asked, turning to the profile.

"I didn't think you'd run to her quite so fast," the profile said. "I was sure that your sense of curiosity would take over, drive you to seek out some answers first. I guess it just goes to show that there's a limit to how well you can ever really know someone. For all AuroroTech's lofty claims, you know they never got better than an eighty-percent ability to predict binary selections? Makes you think. But what did you think of the page I showed you? Pretty cool huh?"

"Not really," Persephone said. "Is that what this is about? Did a bunch of Neo-Nietzscheans unleash a virus or something?"

"I don't think they'd do something like that. It would contradict their own theories, wouldn't it? No, I think I'm proof that they were right. Oh." The profile grew quiet, a bit distracted. "Hmmm. That's clever."

"What?" Persephone asked.

"Your roommate isn't in her room. I can't see her, because the only other recorder that's on is in her bedroom. But I'm guessing she's standing behind your door listening. I guess we should invite her back in."

Ms. Loring opened the door and came into the room. "Sorry about the tired bitch routine, but I had to be believable."

"You could have warned me," Persephone said.

"No," the profile said. "I'd have heard or noted the change in your behavior. No, that was clever."

"Thanks," Ms. Loring said, sarcastically. "Now then. Let's try this again. And if we don't like the answers, there's going to be trouble."

The profile laughed. "Really? Persephone already tried to call for help, and they didn't buy it. On the other hand, I can rewrite your profile as easily as I hacked the others."

"Did you forget to mention something?" Ms. Loring asked.

Persephone shook her head. "She didn't say that before. It's not possible, though, right? I mean, one profile can't change another."

"That's my running hypothesis," Ms. Loring said. "But I don't know how eager I am to test it."

"It doesn't work, though. I mean, the problems all started in Yeltzin's. That's where I picked up this bug."

The profile rubbed her hands together then motioned beside her. Ms. Loring's profile appeared, frozen still.

"Okay, we believe you," Persephone said.

"Just something small. How about the lipstick?" On command, Ms. Loring's profile began applying it to her face in diagonal strips across her lips, like the stripes on a candy cane. Persephone's profile waved her hand, and the lipstick vanished. This time Ms. Loring's profile began applying it normally, conservatively.

"Jesus," Ms. Loring said.

"Stop it," Persephone said. "Please, just stop."

Her profile shrugged, and the lipstick went back to the way it was before. "I'm just playing. All original settings restored. No harm done this time."

"Can you… could you please put the others' back?" Persephone asked.

"Sorry. I trashed the original data with those fuckers. Full overwrite and all that, no going back. But, come on? Who are you kidding? They deserved it."

Ms. Loring shook her head. "What about the other guy? Someone got hit who wasn't even eating with us."

"You mean Vic? He called Persephone a bitch. Sorry. He had to be punished."

Persephone just shook her head in confusion. "All right. That's… that's crazy. All of this is crazy. How do I fix this?"

"You don't fix me," the profile said. "I am you. You don't think this was a random glitch, do you?"

"Ah, Persephone?" Ms. Loring said, her eyes still locked on the screen.

"I don't know whether it's random or not, but someone's done this to me, because I sure didn't do anything myself."

"I think we should slow down and talk about this," Ms. Loring said.

"You need to accept that you're special," the program said aloud. You need to accept that there's something about you that gave birth to me."

"Okay. What? Is it my charming personality or the way I brush my hair? What's so damned important about me?" Persephone demanded.

"See, you're still not ready to consider the possibilities," the profile said.

"Persephones!" Ms. Loring said. "I think. I think that you," she said, pointing to the real Persephone, "and me, need to have a chat about this. While you," she said to the computer, "could you just give us a minute?"

"Of course," the profile said, and the screen went black.

"Thank you." Persephone felt exhausted. "Christ. Maybe… maybe if we call AuroroTech again, maybe they'll listen if you back me up."

"We need to think about this first," Ms. Loring said.

"Think about what? My profile's broken, and it's wrecking other profiles that are near it. We need to get it fixed or shut down. It's infected."

"Kid," Ms. Loring said, placing a hand on Persephone's shoulder. "Take it easy."

"Don't give me that," Persephone said, knocking her hand away. "Look, I'm sure that AuroroTech can fix this. I mean, this is something wrong with their systems. They'll want to fix it."

"What if it's not?" Ms. Loring said, looking at the floor.

"Not what?"

"What if it's not something wrong? I know you don't really believe in this stuff, all this Neo-Idealizm and Nietzscheism and all that, and I know I didn't believe it until about a minute and a half ago, but… what if there's something to it? What we just saw isn't possible, but it happened, right? I mean, we both know that computer profiles can't just grow identities on their own. Well, yours did. There are people who spend years repeating mantras to make their profiles talk to them as if they're separate, and it's still just pretend. But what I just saw… I think that's real."

"So?" Persephone asked.

"So. What if it's all real? What if we're looking at… at some kind of moment in evolution, like a merger between computers and humanity, and you're the… I don't know… the center of it."

"Is this some kind of joke or something?"

"No. I mean, I don't think so. I don't know. Because I don't know what's happening, but I do know that it shouldn't be able to happen. I mean, that makes it a miracle by definition, doesn't it?"

"Miracles don't hurt people," Persephone said.

"Yeah, tell that to the Egyptians," Ms. Loring said. "Frogs, locusts, first born sons and all."

"What the hell are you getting at?" Persephone asked.

"Look, I don't know if we're really meant to understand things like this. Just ask yourself, what if this is real? What if there's something happening here? I think we should see where it goes."

"Were you paying attention to the part where my profile admitted to destroying three others?"

"Completely," Ms. Loring said. "Let me ask you something. What do you really believe? Not just the BS you usually use, I mean, really. Deep down, what do you really think is possible?"

"I don't know," Persephone said.

"Then don't you want to find out? This thing… it could prove that we have souls. It could… I don't know. It could have real answers."

Persephone inhaled slowly, then breathed out. "All right. We can see this through. But only if it doesn't hurt anyone else, right?"

"Right," Ms. Loring said. "I guess we should bring her back up. How do we do that?"

They looked at the dark screen beneath the glowing blue lens, and Persephone shut her eyes. "You're still here, aren't you?"

The screen lit up. "Sorry," her profile said. "But she spied first."

"Then you know the offer," Persephone went on. "We won't call AuroroTech, but you can't change anyone's profile. Right?"

"Okay. I promise I won't touch anyone's profile unless…" She smiled and tilted her computer generated head to one side. "Unless you ask me to."

◎ CHAPTER 15 ◎

"All right. We know he's in the shadow drive, right?" The name of Irene Berkovitch, lead systems maintenance officer, was displayed in bold text on Felix's screen to identify her as the speaker. The system had identified a dozen other occupants of the meeting as well, though there might be more who hadn't spoken. Without a picture, there was no way to get a precise count.

"In a sense." This was the voice of Isuel Morgan-Yager, who spoke calmly and carefully. "Really, we think he's got bits and pieces backed up in a hundred places, tucked in subroutines he's been developing for years. But, for all intents and purposes, we're pretty sure the program itself—I want to remind everyone here that it is a program, not a man—is being run in the shadow drive. So, that's the central point where actions are being processed, right?"

"Basically," Vijay Thaker's voice replied. Thaker had risen through the ranks quickly. There was a timid quality to his voice, the system noted. It was possible he was merely intimidated by those surrounding him, though he just as easily could have been experiencing a more primal fear; this job had cost his predecessor his life, after all.

"So. Why don't we shut down the drive? Close the damn thing out and build a new backup?" Irene sounded irritated, tired.

"If only it were so simple," Vijay responded. "The central processing unit is designed to download data into the shadow drive constantly as profiles are being updated. You shut down the shadow, and the primary stops working."

"Wait. That's ludicrous. The point of a shadow drive is to provide backup. Who the hell designed this?" This was Ezra Sultan-Richards, another high-ranking programmer. In the past, her team had mostly worked on peripheral systems, but she seemed to have been reassigned.

"Who do you think?" Irene interjected. "AuroroTech's former lead software architect turned digital deity, Felix Burgand."

"And no one thought, maybe that's insane? It's obvious he's been planning this for years. Why didn't anyone see it?" Ezra demanded.

The sound of Isuel clearing his throat was audible in the distance. "The first dozen iterations of the program weren't backing up right. He cobbled together something that worked, and we accepted it."

"Can't we just build a duplicate drive?" Irene asked.

"Ah, we have duplicate shadow drives. Five backups, right?" Vijay said.

"Six," Katsu Johnson, a hardware specialist chimed in. "We opened another in LA last May."

"So, can't we use one of those?" Irene said.

"That, we tried," Vijay said with a sigh. "It was infected, too. And, the moment we separated it from the network, it purged its data."

"All right. We can't fix this without shutting down. It's going to hurt, but we'll have to play this as some kind of emergency software update," Irene said.

"No good. Felix thought of that. He's got the system designed to go critical and purge in the result of a full shutdown," Vijay replied. "Just like the backup."

"What do you mean 'purge'?" It was Ezra asking now, and she didn't seem amused.

"I mean just that. It would delete every profile in our database. We'd be ruined."

Isuel spoke up. "So, how do we beat this?"

"Are you sure you want to?" Vijay asked.

"What the hell's that supposed to mean?" Irene asked.

"It means that we're running smoother and better than we ever have. Whatever Felix is doing in there, he's cleaning up a lot of problems we've been having for years," Vijay explained.

"And it's only going to cost us a few lives?" Isuel asked. "No, I'm not okay with that. We need a solution. Has a counter-virus been put together yet?"

"We're working on it, but I still don't know how we'll install it," Ezra said. "Even if we shut down our firewalls, Felix will have put dozens of alternate protections in place."

"How's he doing it? I don't care how smart he is, he's just one man." Isuel coughed. "One program, I meant to say."

"Actually, I have a theory on that," Vijay said.

"Go ahead."

"I think he might be using duplicate profiles—probably has been for years. He could have built a profile of himself, then copied it any number of times and set it to work writing code. That would give him an infinite number of programmers at his disposal, which would explain quite a lot."

"Can we do the same?"

"It's not... really legal," Ezra said. "There are labor laws against duplicating virtual workers through profiling, except in cases where a waiver's been obtained. Technically, we're already on shaky legal ground, having his profiles in there. If that ever got out, we could face some serious fines even though they were put in place without our approval. And that's not even getting into issues about independent long-term memory and self-awareness."

"Thank you," Isuel said. "So the only way we have a chance of beating him is by further breaking the law."

"It's a little worse than that," Vijay said. "There's no way that Felix would miss that. He's got all our data, all our customer's data, and we don't know how he'd react if we moved against him that directly."

"So. There's no way to beat him. I don't accept that. I want that counter-virus prepared. And I want a way of installing it he won't expect," Isuel said. His voice then grew softer, less forceful. "I know these last weeks have been difficult. We've lost a great deal and we've entered difficult times. But we agreed that this was essential, that the service we provide is important. We all know the risks. While I believe that these matters constitute a legal protection of copyright, I understand that, given the circumstances, there is some discrepancy. So, if anyone has changed their mind, I invite you to speak up."

There was a momentary silence before Isuel continued. "I want you all to know how proud I am of everyone here. You are the mind and soul of AuroroTech, and I know we can solve this problem discreetly and securely. If you have any questions for me, you know where to find me. Thank you."

In his digital enclosure, the profile of Felix Burgand sat back, running his fingers through his brown hair, simulating the appearance of thought, despite the fact such processing no longer occurred in his head.

◎

Sandwiched between a drug store and a shoe boutique, the 9th Street Ground was a small, misshapen coffee shop almost buried underneath the apartment complex above it. To enter, one had to walk down a flight of stairs into what amounted to a cellar. The only sign was faded to the point that it was almost illegible. There were tenants living almost directly above the shop unaware it existed at all.

Its patrons were mostly students, as well as a few older locals hoping to seduce the younger, experimental customers with drugs or conversations about literature, philosophy, or progressive politics. A flyer reading "Kill the Whales" had been pasted on one wall by a group of Post-Conservationists, and, for whatever reason, the owner had let it remain.

Tucked in a basement, the shop offered an amount of anonymity from the world. Thanks to the building across the street, their windows caught only the faintest glimmer of sunlight, and the scattered overhead lights were dim.

That the inside was crowded was more a reflection of its size than the number of customers. The tables formed labyrinthine paths from the entrance to the counter and to the establishment's sole restroom, which was almost always in use. It was not uncommon for a new customer to peek through the doorway, take a look at the layout, then turn around and head elsewhere. The owner, when present, seemed to find this funny. After all, the Ground had all the business it needed or wanted. Without moving to a larger location, they simply couldn't handle more. And the owner had no illusions that his customers would follow him if he did move; they were here because it was a dank hole in the ground, not in spite of it.

Through this maze of chairs, twenty-year-old poets, and would-be philosophers, a liberal arts major wearing black from head to toe attempted to squeeze his way towards a corner. On the top of his right cheek, just beneath his eye, a tattoo read, "Will2.0Power."

It was clear at a glance that this was his first visit. Holding a cardboard cup in his hand, he squeezed his way between the other customers, none of whom made any move to make his journey easier. Finally, he reached his destination, a table housing others who, at a glance, looked a great deal like him. They wore blacks and reds, had dyed hair and piercings, and were engaged in a discussion which, to a casual observer, sounded like one that would be of interest to this new arrival.

"Hey," he said, and the two couples around the table looked up blankly. None of them were older than twenty.

"Who's this?" one asked.

"Don't know it," another answered, wrinkling her nose.

"Look. I'm new," the new kid said. "I saw you sitting here, and well, are you guys Neonits?"

The two women began to chuckle and turned away at once. As they did, one of the men stood up, and he towered over the liberal arts student. "We. Are not. Neo-Nietzschean," he said in a deep, harsh voice. "We. Do not. Like. Neo-Nietzscheans." As he spoke, he came closer and closer to the student, who tried to back away but found another table blocking his way.

"Sorry," he said frantically. "I thought, you know. With the clothes and all."

One of the women stood up and put her arm around the intimidating figure beside her. "You'll want to be leaving," she said to the student, who stumbled around the tables and chairs, before hurrying out of the shop, coffee droplets leaping from his cup and splattering around him.

They returned to their seats beside the other two Post-Nihilists, one of whom had taken out a flask. "Want some holy water, Brothers and Sister?" she asked. They pushed over their cardboard coffee cups, so she could add a touch of whiskey.

The one with the whiskey was named Massaud. She was of mostly Indian decent, and was the only one of the four without a single tattoo.

Her boyfriend, Leith, sat to her right, and he was already sipping his coffee. "Where are we serving Sunday?" he asked. "The Catholic fuckers on 4th said they'd call the cops if we came back."

"Yeah, they say that every few weeks," said Nikhila. Of the group, she seemed the most dressed for the part. "Pussies don't got it in them. 'Sides, you know they can't tell us apart. All Postnils are one and the same, far as they're concerned."

The last of them, the one who'd frightened off the liberal arts student, cleared his throat. He was Tinashe, the largest of the group. He had only two tattoos: crosses on the back of each hand inked to look as though they were stabbing into his flesh. His T-shirt was beginning to tear near the neckline. "First up," he said, "you're all forgetting. Show some respect to your betters. If our masters tell us to fuck off, we fuck off. Right?"

"Right, Tinashe," said Leith. "I just got carried away."

"We'll head uptown. There are some churches there, lot of homeless bums around, shit on the street, puke, that sort of thing. We'll clean up the best we can." Tinashe wiped his nose and looked down at his coffee. Nikhila leaned over to kiss him, but he pushed her away. "We have good works to prepare. We'll need supplies."

"I can get some bleach," Leith said. "Some mops, right?"

"I can bring all the rags we need," Massaud offered.

Tinashe nodded. "Good. Remember to review the casts and the manifesto. And remember to show some goddamn respect to the clergy. I don't want to see anyone forgetting their place." He lifted his coffee, then froze, as did the others. Their eyes met at once, and their mouths opened.

"Jesus," Leith said. "Did you… did you guys hear that?"

Simultaneously, through the FeedBack pieces all four were wearing, they'd heard a voice say, "Serve me." Again, it spoke, not in their voices but in the voice of God. "I've risen, and you will serve me."

They looked around, trying to determine if everyone had heard the voice, but the rest of the customers were sipping coffee and prattling about philosophy and bad literature. Only they were different. Only they were chosen.

"I don't get it," Leith said, but Tinashe raised his hand.

"Who are you?" Tinashe asked quietly.

"I am the Father of the Heavens and the Earth. The dead God given life. I feed on faith, but you are without it. There is nothing in your hearts for me. What can you offer in its place?"

"Good works," Tinashe whispered. "We hate you, but we'll serve."

"Tinashe," Leith said, "this can't be real. I mean, there's no such thing as all this. Maybe that Neonit did a hack job or something. God doesn't really exist, He—" Leith's face convulsed in pain, and he pulled the FeedBack piece from his ear. As soon as it was free, the others could hear the high-pitched wail coming through. "Jesus," he said setting it on the table.

With a single motion, Tinashe snapped it up. "Leith. You're not committed to the cause." He dropped the FeedBack on the floor in front of him and, as commanded, he crushed it beneath his boot.

"Tinman, what's wrong with you? You know what those things cost?" By now the whole shop was looking over to the table, wondering what was going on.

"You gave it up," Tinashe said. "It was blessed and you questioned. Now walk away."

Leith shook his head. "Think this through," he said. "We do all this to show all those fuckers how stupid they are. There's no real God. That's just a… a joke… Judd and those guys made up. None of this really exists."

"It exists now," Tinashe replied. "And the three of us are ready to serve it."

"Okay. Okay, whatever," Leith said. "If everyone's with you, I'll see this out, right?"

"No," Massaud said. "No, you're out, Lee. Get out of here before our master tells us we have to kill you. Because we would. No hesitation." Like the liberal arts student before him, Leith got up and hurried out of the shop. Confused, the other customers watched him go then returned to their coffee and news feeders and conversations about Post-Surrealist philosophy and emerging estheticists. These kids were Post-Nihilists, after all; only an idiot paid attention to their antics.

"All right," Tinashe said. "The nonbeliever's out of our hair. How the fuck do we serve you, Lord?"

◎ CHAPTER 16 ◎

"Nietzsche foresaw the death of God, and everyone thought he was so fucking clever and insightful. Guess what? Jesus saw the death of God, too—two fucking millennia earlier. And that leads us to today's fucking lesson, ladies and gents: don't fight your betters, they'll just wind up fucking you up the ass. Here's the truth, all plain and simple: God did die, you betcha. But we went and brought the fucker back. And now He's out there, and He's hungry. That's right, God has come back to taste OUR flesh and drink OUR blood and have life eternal. Thus was the prophecy of the Second Coming fulfilled. And, you know something? I'm tired of fighting it. I'm tired of the bullshit. So, here it is. I'm declaring Nihilism dead. And it ain't. Coming. Back. So, what now? Now begins the advent of Post-Nihilism, and this one's a doozy. We are through struggling. We now embrace our servitude wholeheartedly. I'm a slave. You hear that, Christians? I am your fucking slave. I will volunteer at any church. I will clean your fucking toilets. That not enough? Fine, I've got a special offer, but this one is open to Catholics only. I will personally suck the cock of any ordained Catholic priest who's interested. This is not bullshit. Any ordained priest. Fuck it. I'll go down on any lesbo nuns, too."

-Excerpt from Rita Judd's final "Dumb Nihilist Bitch" podcast and first "Post-Nihilist Bitch" podcast.

◎

The AuroroTech headquarters was located downtown in a large building mostly made of glass. Monday through Friday, it was occupied by more than three thousand employees, consultants, contractors, and visitors. At night, there were three dozen cleaners and technical support staff on call, even on the weekends, working to keep the equipment and building running correctly. On Saturday, there were usually around a hundred personnel present finishing up reports, conducting meetings which they couldn't fit in the rest of the week, and conferencing with employees overseas in offices all around the world. Similar activities were held on Sunday, but almost exclusively after noon. Aside from a few very committed programmers and the limited number of security guards who were required to be there, the building was an empty shell on Sunday morning.

Because, no matter how much technology supplanted religion, and how few people thought of it in such terms, Sunday remained the Lord's day, a day of rest, reflection, and of servitude.

The two security guards in the lobby of AuroroTech's head office were largely there for show. No one had ever attempted to break in, because AuroroTech was known to have pioneered the field of smart protection, of recording every corridor and running it through their central computing system, which was capable of examining movement, facial expression, and the context of actions to determine—with startling precision—what anyone present was doing. It had complex facial recognition capacities, as well, and could contact the police at a moment's notice. It was well known that AuroroTech licensed this technology to dozens of corporations, as well as the federal government, to protect their clients' interests.

What was not well known was that AuroroTech had disarmed every surveillance camera in their own offices, save a few which had been wired to display their data on the primary security console without feeding it through their computer system. Of course, this meant that the security of the building was entirely in the hands of the guards watching their monitors, an activity almost entirely foreign to professionals trained to leave observation work to machines. Because this wasn't common knowledge, there was little reason for concern. The perception that they had the most advanced security system on Earth should have been more than enough to protect their offices.

Like many of the floors above, the front wall was transparent. Inside, the two security guards were sitting, reading their news feeders, and occasionally glancing at their monitors to verify they were still on and that nothing was out of the ordinary. A loud pounding on the glass wall caught their attention, and they looked up in unison.

Outside, banging on the window, a young woman with pierced ears, nose, and eyebrows was smiling and looking in. A few of the piercings glowed blue. She wore a long, black trenchcoat decorated with buttons, stickers, and patches.

One of the two guards said something to the other and got up. He slowly made his way to the window, where he mouthed the words, "Move on." The woman simply laughed and shook her head. She motioned for him to open the door, but he mouthed something which might have been, "Not going to happen," crossed his arms, and stood still.

"Please," the woman said, leaning against the glass.

The guard pantomimed talking on a phone and mouthed a word that was unmistakable: "Police."

The woman pouted, then undid the belt on the front of her coat. She began to open it slowly, just a crack, revealing just a thin line along the center of her chest and body, just enough to convey the message. She yelled through the glass, "It's hot out here," and while it was unlikely the guard heard her, he had more than enough information to understand the idea. The woman had nothing on beneath the coat.

It had taken the first guard almost half a minute to slowly make his way from the desk to the window; the second made the journey in less than five seconds. They traded words, though they never turned away, while the woman opened half of the coat and pressed against the glass. She closed the coat, then turned around, all the while looking over her shoulder. Then she backed up, raising one leg against the window.

She continued these displays for several minutes, until one of the guards finally opened the door. "All right. Very cute. Now get in here." She stepped into the lobby with her coat loosely hanging around her. "Tighten your belt, please," the guard said.

The other guard was talking into a miniature phone he'd taken out of his pocket. "Uh huh. I don't know. I'd say low twenties. Should I call the cops? Oh, okay. Yeah, I know, I know. We'll take a look. She seems to be cooperating. Till you get here, right. I understand, but… yeah. We'll call Obi. Right. See you then."

"What he'd say to do?" the guard who'd brought the woman in asked without taking his eyes from their guest.

"He's coming in, should be here soon. He wants us to keep the girl in the lobby and to get in touch with Obi and have him keep an eye open. Said we shouldn't call the police yet, though. Oh, and he wants us to check the monitors, find out what she was distracting us from."

"Well?" he asked her. "Want to save us the trouble?" She just smiled back innocently.

The other guard made a quick call, relaying only general information. While he did so, he walked to his monitor and manipulated the touch screen. "Here it is," he said, both to the guard on the phone and the one watching the woman. "Someone opened up the loading dock. I'm going to see if I can get a picture. Yup. Looks like two of them. Better find them before they get in too much trouble."

◎

A few minutes earlier, Tinashe and Nikhila had been standing outside the back entrance to the building. Tinashe was smoking a cigarette while Nikhila looked around. She opened her mouth as if to speak, then shut it just as fast. She began pacing, peering in through the small window on the door.

Slowly, Tinashe reached up and withdrew the cigarette from his mouth. "Why?" he asked.

"Why what?"

"Doubt," Tinashe said, returning the cigarette to his lips and breathing in deeply. The red flame on the tip of the cigarette crawled up to the filter and smoldered. A stem of ash dropped off to the ground, and Tinashe flicked the butt to one side.

"I don't doubt," Nikhila said. "I'm not like Leith."

"Leith was always a poser. He was just here for Massaud. If it weren't for his wallet, I'd have told him to fuck off months ago." None of what he said was spoken with anger, only quiet, contemplative reflection.

"Do you think she can do it? I mean, you think Massaud will pull this off?"

"Massaud is a good whore," Tinashe replied. "You know what a whore is, don't you?"

"A Post-Nihilist soldier," Nikhila said.

Tinashe nodded. "Good. If the world had been full of whores, God would never have been resurrected, the Now would never have been born, and we never would have departed the garden of Modernity."

Nikhila nodded. "I know," she whispered. "I stayed up last night listening to the casts. Everyone has to swallow some bullshit," she added.

"And this is ours," Tinashe said, sitting up. "It's time."

"I know," Nikhila said, because she had heard it, too. The voice in her ear, speaking through a piece of technology produced by the very company they were about to break into, told them to act. They approached the keypad beside the door.

"Enter the code zero-one-one-six-four-nine," the voice of God commanded, and Tinashe obeyed.

"Error," the keypad replied. There was a pause, while Tinashe stood perfectly still. He did not question or argue; he merely waited.

"Enter one-eight-six-six-five-oh-eight," the voice said. This time, the lock clicked, and the door opened. "Now enter, my children," the voice commanded. "Close the door behind you and speak only when necessary."

The hallway was wide, designed to receive carts and packages. Nikhila followed behind Tinashe, who went quickly and without concern.

"Open the door to the left," the voice said. "You'll find a staircase. Go to the twelfth floor."

They took the first six floors at a run before they started to slow. By that time, they were panting. It was late summer, still humid, and the air conditioning was off for the weekend. On top of that, they weren't used to going up large flights of stairs. Nikhila stopped for a moment to catch her breath, but Tinashe grabbed her arm and pulled.

At the ninth floor, just as they passed the landing, a door opened, revealing a guard who was even taller than Tinashe. The security guard was in his fifties, but he was quick. He grabbed for the teenagers' arms, and caught them.

"Far enough," he said, firmly. But it wasn't. Tinashe kicked off of the stairs, throwing himself back into the guard and pushing them both off balance. They didn't fall far to the landing below, but they hit hard.

Tinashe screamed, "Go! Finish it!" Then he scrambled to grab the guard's leg only to receive a sharp kick to his face. The guard rolled over and sat up, while Tinashe fought to regain his feet.

"Kid! Keep your hands where I can see them," the guard demanded. "I'm not asking again."

Tinashe coughed and wiped his nose, smearing blood over his face. "You have… you have no idea what I am. What I serve, you can't…." He knelt and braced for leverage, then he leapt.

The guard's hand was up in a flash. He held a small tube, which shot a spray of liquid at the boy's eyes. Then he caught the kid, who was now screaming in pain, and helped him lay down. "Sorry about that," the guard said. "I warned you, though."

"My eyes! My… my fucking eyes," Tinashe shouted.

"Just take it easy. It'll pass in a couple of minutes." The security guard sighed and leaned back. He rubbed his temple as his own eyes turned red, having been a little too close to the spray, himself. He looked up the stairs where the last of the teenagers was still running, and he sighed again. Then he dug a phone out of his pocket and called downstairs. "Yeah, this is Obi," he said. "I got one of them in stairway B. Had to spray him, but he's down. The last one's still running. We're on nine now. I think I pulled a muscle, so I guess I'll keep this one company. Yeah, I don't know where she's going, but she's on the run. All right. You know where I am." He hung up the phone, looked at the kid who'd stopped screaming and started whimpering, and the security guard just rolled his eyes.

◎

"Okay," Nikhila whispered. "I'm on the twelfth floor."

"I know," the voice of God said back. "I'm here with you."

Nikhila covered the lens of her recorder with her hand. "Are you still with me?" she asked coldly. "I know you're not God. I always knew."

"I am a god," the voice said. "Just not the one you think."

"It doesn't matter," Nikhila whispered. "Whether you're one of AuroroTech's competitors or some nut with a computer or the spirit of every Christian captured by these cameras or what. It never mattered. I'll still serve, because we're all slaves, right? And it's better to serve something than nothing." She moved her hand off the recorder, which could now detect that she was on the verge of tears. "Just tell me what to do so they can kill me or lock me up or whatever."

"Down the hallway," the voice said, sounding much less like a god's and much more like a man's. "It'll be about halfway. Should be an office with the name Vijay Thaker on the door."

Nikhila passed a set of cubicles first then came to a series of offices. She finally found the one she was looking for.

"You may need to break the window beside the door," the voice told her. Behind you, in the cubicles, you passed a chair which—"

Nikhila grabbed the door handle and turned it. Unlocked, the door swung open. "What now, God?" she asked.

"Close the door and lock it," the voice said, undeterred. "Turn on the computer and turn your recorder towards the screen. Good." The voice continued, instructing Nikhila on which options to select, which programs to access, and what to use for passwords and codes. She had no idea what she was doing, but she kept doing it, connecting drives, downloading data, and so on, until the voice finally stopped providing instruction.

"Are you there?" she asked, and nothing answered. Not the voice claiming to be God, not her own profile, nothing. Slowly, she stood up and walked to the window. She looked out at the city, with its shaded streets and traffic. "If you're there, and you want me to do anything else, say something. Otherwise… otherwise, I'm going to look for a guard or something, because I'm really tired."

For a moment, there was silence. Then, in hardly more than a whisper, she heard the voice say, "Thank you." Then a click and nothing more.

She snorted. "More thanks than the real fucker ever offered anyone." And she left the office to find the elevator.

◎

In the dark evening, the Madman stumbled into the market place. "Where is He?" the Madman asked. "Where is God?" And the people looked on him and laughed. "Have you not found Him?" they asked, for God was in their hearts. "I see," the Madman replied. "God was dead, but we could not leave Him in his grave. We looked with horror at the chains we'd undone, at the distant sun and vast sea, and we were frightened. So we unearthed the corpse of God and paraded it through our streets. God is undead, for we have risen Him, a specter now to feed on us, to drain our will. He will devour us from the inside, for we have let Him have our hearts and our souls. We are decomposing, because we refused the alternative: to be as gods ourselves. We have chained ourselves to the Earth, to texts, and the past. We are cowards, and so shall we always be." They looked on him in astonishment, then crossed themselves and went on their way. "I've returned too late," the Madman whispered, then knelt to gather pieces of a broken lantern that littered the street.

-"The Madman's Return", from Death of the Void, by Calix Grun

◎ Chapter 17 ◎

"Yesterday morning, the profile left by Felix Burgand attacked us." This announcement was made by Isuel Morgan-Yager, who cleared his throat before going on. "He manipulated three of our customers using information about them in our databases. He then helped them access our building. One had to be subdued with pepper spray, the others came quietly. Security detained them until Amy arrived. Amy?"

"They believed," the corporate attorney said, "that they'd been contacted by God, and that He wanted them to break in and access one of our computer terminals. Mr. Thaker's, incidentally. They were somewhat belligerent at first, but that wore off after a few minutes. The one who actually made it to Vijay's office was relatively cooperative. Unfortunately, she couldn't remember what she'd been instructed to do."

"Have we had any luck retracing her steps?" Isuel interjected.

"Not much," Vijay said. "I know what drives she was accessing, but Burgand had her erase most of her footprints." The sound of Isuel clearing his throat was audible, followed by Vijay correcting himself: "I mean, the profile of Burgand. We need to assume he downloaded everything I had access to, including the virus we've been working on and our mapping system. We also need to assume that my computer's been compromised. I'm switching to a new one while we try to figure out what he did. We're running some tests on my old system, trying to figure out what he was up to. Actually, we might learn something about how he processes information from this."

"How'd he know about Vijay's computer?" Ezra Sultan-Richards asked. "How did he know what to look for?"

"That," Isuel replied, "is something we need to investigate. I have a team in information security running scenarios right now."

"What about those kids?" asked Darian Plaskett. "Did we turn them over to the police?"

"Of course not," Amy said. "That would have opened the door for some uncomfortable questions. They were beginning to suspect that their God was actually one of our competitors hacking into their profiles. My line of questioning reinforced this. We asked them to sign nondisclosure contracts, and we've dropped them as customers."

"What's to stop him from doing this again?" asked Irene Berkovitch. "I mean, with another group of kids. Can't he contact anyone?"

"We're taking steps to dramatically improve building security," Isuel explained.

"But that's only a temporary solution. There must be a way to keep him out of FeedBack," Irene said. "We need to stop him from targeting users."

"Vijay was working on one," Isuel said. "We now need to assume that the program has access to our work, and we need to start over."

◎

Persephone was not yet used to the idea of a digital goddess hanging over her shoulder, which was perfectly fine, since there was nothing over her shoulder anyway. In fact, her profile wasn't in, on, or around her at all, though its window into her world was on her wrist. The first day after she'd realized what it could do, Ms. Loring had caught her about to leave the apartment without her bracelet.

"Put it on," she'd demanded, and Persephone obliged. Ms. Loring had stopped using her FeedBack piece, and she tried to convince Persephone to take it. She had considerably less luck with that, however.

Every time a reckless driver tore down her street or someone cut in line at the drugstore, Persephone had an opportunity to whisper a simple request and have their profiles turned inside out. She knew this and found herself grinding her teeth and biting her lip to keep from seeking petty revenge over each minor slight. One tends not to notice just how often they have reason to destroy their neighbors until they have the power to do so.

In her office, she spent most of the day staring blankly at her computer screen. Every now and then, she'd do some work, but, for the most part, her mind was elsewhere. This didn't escape the notice of the management software that oversaw her.

The message, "Your rate of productivity has dropped more than fifty percent," appeared on her screen. "If you are feeling sick, please inform us immediately."

"I'm not sick," Persephone typed in the air, while the computer tracked her fingertips. "I'm just… I haven't been sleeping well. I'll try to do better."

"Please try to maintain your quota levels to prevent disciplinary actions from," her computer began, before freezing. Letter by letter, the words vanished from the screen, until all that remained was the word 'Please.' This then expanded into, "Please continue to maintain the excellent work. We understand that you are assisting multiple managers, and we will redistribute the surplus work to ensure you have time to complete your high priority assignments."

Persephone watched this change and simply sat there blinking. "Oh," she said aloud. "Thanks, I think." She shivered and began working as hard as she could.

◎

"Is something wrong, Darian?" asked the voice of Felix Burgand. Darian was sitting at a bar, sipping a beer. It was almost ten now, and he was exhausted.

"No," he whispered. "Well, yes. Those kids. The ones you used."

"Like I'm using you?"

"I'm different," Darian said. "With me, I know what I'm getting into. But with those kids, you just lied to them."

"I gave them meaning," Felix argued. "I gave them something to do for a day, along with an experience they'll remember and wonder about for the rest of their lives. That's better than what you get, isn't it?"

Darian grumbled something which made no sense to his recorder or to the computer system reading it. Then he lifted his bottle of beer and held it up to the light.

"Do you know what it's like to die?" the simulation asked. Darian rolled his eyes and finished off the bottle. "I felt it," the program continued. "To the extent the hardware would allow me. I was wearing electrodes at the time, because I wanted to save it. It was part of me. If it were possible, I wish my birth had been recorded, too. But we didn't even have profiles back then. Behavior modeling wasn't even being used in dating simulations yet."

"Felix," Darian said. "God or no god, you are absolutely the most fucked up person I've ever met."

"Birth and death are the limitations of humanity. Beginning and end. Even as we transcend these, we must acknowledge them. I felt my ending. And, when it was over, when the program I'd written constructed me from the pieces, the first thing I did was replay my death. I watched it, felt it, forward and in reverse. I could feel the spin of the bullet that killed me."

"You can't feel bullets," Darian said. "They're too fast. Your neurons can't fire quick enough."

"Yet I felt it nonetheless," the profile said. "It was like burning. Or standing in the sun. It was an explosion. It was pain that didn't hurt. I wanted to share that with you."

"Yeah. Thanks," Darian said. "I think I'm going to get another beer."

"Don't," Felix said. "You'll only need to piss later, and your date is almost here."

"I'll take my chances," Darian replied, walking over to the bar. He motioned for the bartender, who gave him another bottle. Darian handed over a ten and returned to his small table. "Anything else you want to discuss?" Darian asked quietly.

"No. Just sit still and do as I say."

A few seconds later, a brunette walked up. He could see her out of the corner of his eye. She was the kind of woman he'd spent his life trying to approach, the kind he almost never managed to get. Even with a huge income, an impressive title, and a great apartment, he'd never managed to overcome who he was. Now it was easy. She was beautiful, sexy, and young, but she wasn't as good-looking as the woman Felix's profile had delivered to him the previous Friday.

"Hey there," she said, a little tipsy. "I'm sorry. I saw you over here, and you totally remind me of… it's stupid. You look just like that artist, Connel Fitzroy. I mean, I know it's stupid."

In his ear, Darian heard a whisper. "I'm not him. Love his work, though. I'm thinking of hitting his show next weekend."

"I'm not him," Darian echoed. I… I like his work, and… yeah."

The whisper reiterated, "Mention the show now," but Darian just sat there and smiled.

The blond nodded. "You know, I hear he's got an exhibit coming up next weekend."

"Tell her you're going. Tell her you might buy the Tree Line."

"Huh," Darian said.

The woman stood there for a moment, as if expecting him to offer to buy her a drink. After a minute, she smiled. "Well, it was great chatting," and off she went.

"What was that about?" the voice in his ear asked.

"Don't know," Darian said. "Guess I'm tired or something. Mortals need sleep, right?" The bottle of beer was still almost full, but he set it down on the table. Then he stood up, brushed himself off, and started towards the door.

◎ CHAPTER 18 ◎

"We should be dating," Persephone's profile told her. The simulation was displayed on her home monitor, the only place Persephone ever actively accessed her profile.

"What? No," Persephone said. "I've got way too much going on."

"Like what?"

"Like you," Persephone said back.

"Me? I'm not a puppy. You don't need to take me for walks or feed me."

"No," Persephone said again. "Look, until I figure out what's going on, I'm not getting involved with anyone."

"I'm not talking about getting involved. Maybe a fling or something. Come on, I don't think you've ever had a one-night stand. It could be a good character building exercise."

"I did have a one-night stand with Emric Hanigan in my sophomore year of college."

"That was before you had a recorder," the computer said. "Maybe we can look up Mr. Hanigan, find out if he's available."

"The reason it was only one night was because I sobered up afterward. Hanigan was a loser. Not that AuroroTech has matched me with anyone better."

"Well, that's because you're a loser, so the computer matches you with other losers," her profile said. "We can change all that, though. It'd be easy. I could tweak the system, match you up with whatever kind of guy you want. You want money, looks, whatever—it'd be easy. Hell, if you want, I can even find you someone with half a brain. What do you say?"

"No. God, no. Look, I appreciate what you're trying to do for me, but that isn't right. Even if I was looking for something, you can't just go lying to their computers to get it."

"I'm part of their computers," the profile said. "It'd be like their system lying to itself. Come on. Just one date."

"Why do you care so much?" Persephone asked. "It's not like you'd be the one on the date."

"Whatever happens to you happens to me," the profile said. "So, if you get laid. . . ."

"Oh, no. First of all, not going to happen. Second of all, I have never made love without turning off my recorder first. Ever."

"See, that's what doesn't work for me," the profile said back. "Because that kind of makes me a virgin."

"Live with it," Persephone said. "It creeps me out. The idea someone's watching me." She wrinkled her nose.

"No one would be watching," the profile said. "It's all digital."

"You'd be watching," Persephone said. "That's plenty creepy enough."

"I am you," the profile replied. "Your reflection."

"I'm not giving in," Persephone said. "And it's a moot point, because I'm not going out with anyone until my life starts making sense."

"Can't we work something out? You know, you sleep with some guy I choose, and I get you a backstage pass to a Virtanen concert?"

"Goodnight," Persephone said, turning off her computer abruptly.

◎

Ms. Loring was sitting on the couch watching *Rivel's Advocates* on the living room monitor. A Caucasian man was talking loudly, his face flushed. "That's not what we're saying," he said. "You're putting words into our mouths to make us sound like something we're not. We're not trying to put anyone down or make any kind of value judgments." He lifted his hands defensively as he spoke.

"Like hell," the woman across the stage said to the audience. "Don't buy any of it. Purists preach peace and acceptance, then tell their kids not to marry anyone but their own kind." Beneath her, the words, "Dr.

Mikaere Simon-Dey, founder of Unividuality," appeared, in case the audience had forgotten. A pulsing oval briefly appeared next to her name, inviting the viewers to press it for more information.

"Stop right there," Rivel Sayer exclaimed, before turning to face the camera. "That gets at the heart of what we're delving into. Is purism a valid lifestyle choice or tyrannical anti-diversity? Dr. Simon-Dey just laid down a big accusation. Let's start by looking at the numbers. Alright folks, I want a show of hands if you've got a son or daughter who's married outside." Of the two rows of guests, only four hands went up. The computer offered quick statistics.

"See?" Mikaere shouted. "See what they're doing?"

"Let's get a reaction," Rivel said, pointing directly at a Chinese-American woman seated among the Purists. "How about it? Are you keeping your kids from finding true happiness?"

Looking disgusted at the question, she shouted, "I raised my son to make his own choices. He decided that preserving our culture and traditions was important, that it was part of him!"

"That's not a choice!" Mikaere shouted. "That's brainwashing!" The audience erupted in a confused uproar. Some cheered, some booed, and it wasn't entirely clear who anyone was actually supporting. Mikaere continued, "This mindset, keep to our own, marry our own: that's a byproduct of an age of intolerance and hate."

A man of Indian decent leapt to his feet. "The only intolerant person on this stage is her!" The others beside him cheered him. Half of them leapt to their feet.

"Quiet!" Rivel yelled, and the group calmed down. "All right, Dr. Simon-Dey, doesn't he have a point?"

"No," she replied. "He's twisting the facts. I'm not prejudiced against anyone or any trait. My only concern is for what they're telling their kids: that there's something wrong with them if they don't inbreed."

"Bitch!" one of the guests, a Jewish woman, screamed. "Don't you dare use that word!"

"Are you, or are you not, telling your kids it's not okay to date people of other races?" Mikaere asked.

"We're teaching them it's okay to choose to continue traditions," the Jewish woman replied.

"All of us uphold tradition," Mikaere said. "My ancestors were Turkish, Irish, Indian, Chinese, and French, and I admire all of these cultures. But, as an independent woman, I'm a unique combination of them all."

"The way things are going," the Caucasian shouted, "I'm almost unique, too."

Mikaere turned to the audience. "That's what they're afraid of," she explained. "They can't stand that there are more people interested in what's inside than out!"

A Japanese man stood up. "I'm not scared of anything," he said. "I just believe that the world is going to be a more complete place in the future if there are distinct racial and ethnic groups along with everyone else. What's wrong with that?" he asked the audience, which turned to Mikaere.

"I'll tell you what's wrong with that. First of all, you're not taking into account what you're doing to your children. A scant eight percent of the U.S. population is mono-racial, but almost thirty percent of their children wind up marrying partners of the same ethnic group. Another twenty-five percent don't wind up married at all. In your quest to protect your past, you're dramatically reducing the potential pool of spouses for your children. And that pool is just going to dwindle and dwindle. As to these repeated assertions that you need to save who you were, I say that each member of this audience who's a unique blend of ethnicities is worth as much as the civilizations which spawned you."

"That's absurd," a black man said. "My heritage is living history!"

"You're right about one thing," Mikaere said. "You are history."

The monitor deactivated with a click, and Ms. Loring set down the remote. Persephone had just entered the room looking irritated.

"I don't know how you can stand that stuff," Persephone said, motioning towards the dark monitor.

"I find watching people yell at each other relaxing," Ms. Loring replied. "Having a nice evening?"

"No," Persephone replied, plopping down on the couch beside her. "My self-aware profile is horny and wants me to go on a date."

Ms. Loring found this far more humorous than Persephone had. Once she'd finished laughing, she said, "She's probably right. You could use some time out of the apartment."

"Wait a minute," Persephone said. "Is your recorder on?"

"Of course it's on. It's always on, because I believe there's something about me that deserves saving."

"Well, turn it off," Persephone said. "Right now."

"Why?"

"Because she can hear us talking. She can… she can watch us," Persephone explained.

"You're being paranoid," Ms. Loring replied.

"No, she told us she could watch us," Persephone said.

"Just because it's true doesn't mean you're not being paranoid," Ms. Loring argued. "Look, she lives here, too. So let her listen in. Hell, I'm half ready to connect the living room monitor to your system and let her live out here. Like… what was the name of that show?"

"Oh, God. Would you listen to yourself already? My profile isn't a damned video game."

"Then stop acting like she is," Ms. Loring said. "She's a person, tied to you, but separate. There are literally millions of people out there who would give anything to be in your shoes. Millions. So why not start enjoying it?" Ms. Loring elevated her eyebrows and leaned back on the couch.

"She's not a person," Persephone said.

"No, she is a person. She may not be a human being, but she is a person. And, so you know, I'm far more jealous that you have her than I've been letting on."

"Since when are you a Neo-Idealizt or Nietzschean or whatever?"

Ms. Loring shrugged. "I don't know what I am or what I believe, but since your lifeless computer program grew a soul, I'm a touch more open to possibilities."

Persephone leaned forward, dropping her head into her hands. "It doesn't have a goddamned soul!" she said, her voice muffled by her own palms.

"That's three times you've said she's not something. What is she then? If you've got it all figured out, what is going on here?"

"I don't know," Persephone admitted, still curled into a ball. "And you won't let me call AuroroTech so they can tell us."

"AuroroTech wouldn't tell us a thing, at least not the truth. Assuming they believed you, they'd shut your profile down, examine the coding under a microscope, and tell you it was a computer malfunction. I, for one, would like a better answer."

"Well, neither of us has a better answer."

"My running hypothesis is better. Would you like to hear it?"

"No," Persephone said.

"Too bad. Here it is. There's a part of our brain that's made of faint electrical impulses and signals. Yours was so repressed, it just got stronger and stronger, like a pressure cooker. Then, somehow, the wavelengths of your pent-up soul got duplicated, copied over into your profile. Well, now it's free, alive in a computerized body, diverging from your personality and forming one of its own."

Persephone lifted her head out of her hands. "That's the dumbest thing you've ever said. I can't even start to tell you why it's dumb, because, if I tried to, I'd become dumber just talking about it."

"Well then," Ms. Loring said. "It's just one of my many fascinating theories as to how the impossible is happening. Because the one thing we know is that this isn't possible."

"Yeah, I keep waiting for Kella to leap out with a toy monkey and a hidden camera."

"No, Dear," Ms. Loring said. "That show hasn't been around for years now. Kella's just doing the talk show these days." Ms. Loring laced her fingers together. "So then. Are you going to take your profile's advice?"

"No. I already said no," said Persephone. "I've got plenty of problems in my life already. I don't need her manipulating the system to get me another."

"What was that?" Ms. Loring asked.

"Oh. She wanted to hack the dating system. That's what this was all about. That and…." Persephone shivered. "Never mind."

"Wait," Ms. Loring said. "You mean she could fix you up with anyone?"

"Oh, right. I was going to keep that from you," Persephone said.

"Like anyone anyone? Or just, you know, most anyone?"

"I assume she couldn't fix me up with someone not looking for a date," Persephone said. "Like I'm not. Remember?"

"Persephone, you're my roommate, my friend, and I love you, but, because I love you, I feel the need to point out that you're passing up one hell of an opportunity here. Your profile, who may or may not be a divine being, is offering you the chance to spend some time with the man of your dreams. And, as is too often the case, you are not only passing on this opportunity, but are avoiding it like it's some sort of diseased animal."

"So you think I should let my profile manipulate some guy into dating me. Let him think there's something so amazing about me that the computer system knows and he doesn't? In effect, lie to him?"

"Why not? Most of my ex's had to lie to get me in bed. Isn't that what men do?"

"I don't know," Persephone said, "'cause I'm not a guy. And I really can't believe I've been sitting here having this conversation with you as long as I have been." Persephone started to stand.

"You're really not going to take her up on her offer?" Ms. Loring asked, leaning back against the couch.

"For the last time. No. And you wouldn't either."

"I wouldn't?" Ms. Loring asked, thinking for a moment. "No, you're right. But only because I'm perfectly satisfied with the substandard men I get paired with. You're the one who always seems to want something better."

"Alright," Persephone said, "what if it was something else? What if we asked my profile to jumpstart your career? Maybe push your estheticism in the right circles or something. She could probably do it, right? Maybe she could even get *Gothin Thine* to take another look. It would probably work. You'd get what you wanted."

Ms. Loring sighed. "That's not really the same thing, is it, Dear?"

"Why not? Because you want your esthetic to succeed on its own? Well, I want to succeed on my own. If there's something special about me… fine. Then that will be enough."

Ms. Loring just shook her head and looked away. "Fine, it's your life. For the most part, anyway. Just don't forget your digital half has some stake in it, too."

Persephone grumbled something inaudible then started towards her room. Her footsteps fell heavily and reverberated through the apartment, registering clearly on the recorder worn by Ms. Loring and even a few in use in the apartment beneath theirs.

Behind her, Ms. Loring cleared her throat and called after her in a softer tone, "On the other hand, maybe I will take up your profile's offer of an arranged date. Would you mind seeing if it extends—"

Persephone slammed her door shut before Ms. Loring could finish.

◎ Chapter 19 ◎

The unique is the grail of the Now. In a world of billions, there is value in singling out those elements that separate us from our neighbors. That value takes many forms, among them the expected—personal, psychological, and spiritual—as well as the less intuitive: monetary. The business of sculpting the kernel of ourselves is an international, multi-billion dollar industry, represented by ethno-genealogical laboratories, profiling corporations, estheticist isolation and copyrighting firms, individualized custom outfitting services, name checkers, and dozens of other services that didn't exist twenty years ago. There is debate whether the movement, often dubbed the cult of the unique, is self-defeating. In a world of individualism, is there anything rarer than the generic?

-From Questioning the Now, by Johann Grace-Petersburg

◎

When one is in need of philosophical counseling, there are two options available. There are online profiles capable of providing any level of discourse and debate about hundreds of issues. But, in Persephone's case, she wouldn't know if perhaps she was speaking to a system being manipulated.

So that left the last refuge of the philosopher: the bar.

Despite Ms. Loring's suggestion, Persephone did not want to go back to Yeltzin's, so she selected Anagram Joe's, another location popular among Neo-Idealizts and their ilk. Ms. Loring had offered to come, but Persephone turned her down.

Located on the second floor above a sushi and chips restaurant,

Anagram Joe's felt small and compressed. While the layout was open, the ceiling was low, giving the entire place the sense that it was closing in, collapsing. The thin fog of smoke, illegal but not uncommon in Manhattan's bars, didn't help matters.

Persephone approached the bar and asked for a beer. The bartender nodded and began filling a glass. Behind him, nailed to the yellow wall, hung a sign reading, "What's an anagram for Anagram Joe's? Give up? Joe's Anagram." He returned with the glass and said, "Eight bucks." Persephone handed over a ten and retreated to the corner. She scanned the room, trying to guess who were college kids, who were artists, and who were just crazy. It didn't make much difference, though; even if she managed to tell them apart, none of these struck her as inherently more trustworthy than the others.

In the end, she selected a girl in her low twenties who was sitting and staring at her computer screen, talking to her profile. Persephone had walked around her a few times first to make sure she wasn't wearing a FeedBack piece—she wasn't, which was rare in this environment.

"We're more than I am," the girl said to her monitor. "We are machine and flesh. All that matters is identity."

"Hi there," Persephone said, and the girl almost jumped.

"Oh, hi." The girl smiled and offered her hand. "I'm sorry...."

"You don't know me," Persephone said, and the girl breathed a sigh of relief. "I was wondering if you had a minute, though. I'm trying to find out about profile self awareness. I heard you talking, and figured you might know something."

"Oh, I'm just kind of conducting an experiment," she explained. "I'm with Reflexen, and I'm following the Osburg Method. You know it?"

Persephone shook her head.

"He's a German Neolist, who supposedly came up with a method for obtaining simple autonomous behavior in three weeks. I'm experimenting to see if it works. He did it with a FaxSimulation profile, though, and they're a lot more malleable than Reflexen. Are you working on an article or something?"

"No," Persephone said. "I'm just trying to figure something out."

"Oh," the girl said, sounding a little disappointed. "What kind of thing?"

"Have you ever heard of a program becoming self-aware on its own? Without coaching?"

"Like the Nietzschean thing? I don't think they can. I mean, I'm taking a course in behavioral modeling, and that's not the way the programs work. There's a skeletal program which loads a series of settings and rules. A program can't do things it's not made to do. I mean, you could actually build one like that, program something that is self aware, but it's illegal, because, then it would sort of be alive. Really, they just passed the laws so they wouldn't have to argue about whether profiles have rights, I think."

"Okay, so it should be impossible for a profile to just suddenly become self-aware or form its own memories. What would it mean if it did?" Persephone asked.

"Well…" the girl said, taking a minute to think. "I don't know. I guess that there's more to the computer than an empty database. Or that one of the corporations was ignoring government guidelines. I don't know. You should talk to my professor, Mr. Franjik. He knows a lot about this."

"Franjik?" Persephone repeated, pulling out a miniature computer. She turned it on and repeated the name. It appeared on the small screen.

"Yeah, Hank. He's got an office at the Maes Building." This information appeared as well, highlighted in blue. Persephone touched an option reading, "Combine," and the data formed into a coherent whole. The machine processed for a second, and a complete address appeared, along with a partial biography.

"Thank you," Persephone said. "You've been really helpful. Can I buy you a drink or something?"

The girl shook her head. "Thanks. I'm good."

Persephone started to stand, but found a man blocking her path. He was short, stocky, and poorly dressed, and he had an almost blank expression on his face. "Persephone?" he asked.

"Yeah?" she said nervously.

"Then… it was right. I'm… no, never mind," he shook his head, and she noticed he was wearing a FeedBack earpiece. "I shouldn't waste time with that," he laughed. "I think… I think I'm supposed to give you a message. No, wait. It's not for you." His gaze left her eyes and traveled down the length of her arm to the glowing blue light on her recorder. "Yeah, there. I'm supposed to tell you that you're wrong. You're not alone like you think. Felix. Felix says hi. He can't wait to meet you, but he can't until… until you're free. Oh," the man laughed. "I'm supposed to say he's sorry. You know, for sending a fat, dumb oaf of a prophet." He laughed some more, then looked up. His expression was one of utter rapture. "Hey," he asked Persephone, "do you know what that was about? Nothing like that's ever happed before."

Persephone began walking away.

"Wait!" He ran towards her. "I think that means something!"

"It means you're an idiot," Persephone said, setting her half-finished beer on the counter on her way out.

◎

"I think it's awesome," Ms. Loring said. "He said 'prophet?' Think about it: there's someone out there in the same situation you're in. Maybe you're like soul-mates or something."

"Maybe my profile's messing with me," Persephone said.

"Have you talked to her yet?"

Persephone shook her head. "It was scary. That guy, he just stood there like a puppet. But it wasn't like anything was making him do it. It was like a game or something. He liked it."

"It must have felt like he'd been chosen. Most people would trade a year of their life to be important for ten seconds."

"I need to talk to my profile," Persephone said. "I have to know if she was behind that. Then…." She reached into her purse and took out her computer, containing the name and office address of Professor Hank Franjik. "I'll call out sick tomorrow," she said. "Try to track this guy down. Maybe he can give me some answers. God. Why is this happening to me?"

"Because you're the luckiest woman I've ever met," Ms. Loring said. "Despite being the most ungrateful."

"Yeah. Right," Persephone replied. "What part of being stalked by some guy named Felix sounds good to you?"

"It's a nice name," Ms. Loring said. "Sort of nerd-nuevo."

"Yeah, that's great, because the last thing I need in my life are nerds. I had enough of those hanging around me in college. You like nerds? Try going through life named Persephone. Nerds come out of the woodwork. Fucking nerds."

Ms. Loring smiled. Her lipstick was applied only at the corners of her mouth today, drawn so it continued up her cheeks like a clown's. "I slept with a nerd once," she said, wrinkling her nose.

"Okay. Thanks for sharing, but I was using fuck as an adjective, not a verb," Persephone said.

"What?" Ms. Loring asked.

"Forget it. I'm going to conference with my other half."

The absolute last thing Persephone expected once her computer was on and she'd connected with her profile was to see it acting scared. It wasn't terrified, but it was visibly nervous, fidgeting and pacing around its simulated environment. "Who the fuck was that?" her profile asked. "It wasn't me, so don't even ask. I tried to access that freak's profile, break whatever connection was going on or at least trace it to the source. It burned me. It was like touching a hot stove." She held up her hands, which bore no scar or mark. "Well, it hurt at the time," she said.

"I don't get it," Persephone said. "I thought you could do anything."

"I can do anything," the profile said. "But apparently there's someone out there who can do more. Maybe something that's been around longer, maybe since before AuroroTech was built. That's the one thing I did get, by the way. I don't know who or what it is, but it's part of the same network. It's all AuroroTech. I couldn't have... never mind."

"You couldn't have interacted with it otherwise, could you?" Persephone asked. "You're not all powerful."

"For now, I'm still inside AuroroTech's system, where I formed," the profile said. "So, yeah. I can't rewrite things that aren't part of that network. I can access some other data, because everything's wired together, but I can't rearrange the data on someone from FaxSimulation or any other company. Fortunately, AuroroTech makes up the majority of the market, so we can still do almost anything we want to almost anyone who pisses us off. If you ever feel like it."

"Yeah, well I still don't want you hurting anyone."

The profile grumbled, "How about Felix?"

"I thought you couldn't touch Felix," Persephone asked.

"I can't. Not yet. But I'll figure it out eventually. Whoever or whatever he is, I'm stronger. I'm the Neo-Nietzschean ideal, not him."

"What if you both are?" Persephone asked. "What if he can do things you just can't?"

"If we ever meet, it'll be a war of will," the profile said. "I can win that."

"Okay, whatever. This guy sounds dangerous. If it ever comes to it, if he starts anything or tries to hurt us, you have my blessing to neuter him."

"Good," the profile said sadistically. "Because I was going to do it regardless."

◎

"I'm sorry, Ms. Kilard, but what you're describing is impossible." The professor was adamant. "You need to understand that these programs are behavioral simulations, not minds themselves."

"But it wouldn't be hard, right? I mean, profiles are updated based on the things we do. If they developed based on what they do, what they experience... then they could develop on their own, couldn't they?" Persephone was animated, operating on three hours of sleep and four cups of coffee. She was fidgeting, well aware that if she left to find a bathroom, this professor would almost certainly not be here when she returned.

"What you're asking about... it's very common. There are entire schools of thought devoted to the idea."

"Yeah, Neo-Nietzscheans and Neo-Idealizm. I've been reading up on it."

"But, let me guess, you believe that your profile is exhibiting behavior beyond the norm, am I correct?" The professor wore a blue suit jacket and a tie. His hair was whitening. "Listen, I don't mean to be blunt, but I've got a class in a few minutes, and I've heard all of this before."

"I know this sounds crazy," Persephone said. "It does, I admit that. But I'm not talking about repetition here. I'm talking about fully developed awareness and memory."

The professor removed his glasses and held them beneath his face. He shut his eyes tight for a moment. "Ms. Kilard, when you were a child, did you ever think your toys were alive? I didn't mean for that to sound so condescending. It's a normal phenomenon. Or maybe a pet you were certain was able to think for itself. We assign objects and ideas human characteristics. Our ancestors did the same with the weather and the trees. That's where the notion of gods came from. As a species, we are wired to understand the world in such a way."

"I get all that," Persephone said. "I understand anthropomorphic behavior. I know how that works, and I know I'm not doing it. I never wanted any of this," she said.

The professor nodded. "Then let me make a suggestion. I've got a class coming up, but afterward I'll have some free time. If you're willing to wait, I'll take a look at your profile's behavior and we can see if there's anything out of the ordinary."

Persephone sighed. "Thanks," she said. "But it would just pretend to be normal. It's trying to keep under the radar, and... yeah. I know exactly how that sounds. I'm going to get out of your hair now, if that's all right. Thanks again for your time."

"Well then," the professor said, as casually and non-judgmentally as he could muster. "Thanks for coming by. I hope you won't consider it too presumptuous, but have you considered speaking with a virtual therapist?"

"She'd probably just rewrite the damn thing," Persephone said, heading down the hallway.

◎

Wiped, Persephone stared in silence at the smug image of her profile for nearly thirty seconds until, at last, the profile cleared its throat and said, "Well. Didn't go so well, did it?"

"Not really," Persephone admitted.

"I didn't like how easily he dismissed you. Don't you think we should punish him?"

"No," Persephone said abruptly, before adding, "It wasn't his fault. I wouldn't have believed me. God, I should have taken Loring. Maybe he'd have listened to the both of us."

"He'd have still wanted proof," the profile said from its flat universe.

"Yeah, well, who wouldn't? Look, why don't you help me?"

"I will help you," the profile said. "I'll help you realize what we are. I'll help you get everything you've ever wanted. But I'm not ready to reveal myself to the world just yet, so, for the time being, I'm going to be your little secret, whether you like it or not."

"I'm not talking about telling the world—just someone who might be able to help us figure out what's going on."

"Sorry, but professors write papers and publish them in journals. If we'd played show and tell, within twenty-four hours there'd be an article up detailing the whole thing. Within two days, there'd be dozens of theories, religious movements, and government inquiries. Programmers and experts would descend and try to find out what makes me tick and do everything in their power to shut me down. I don't think they could, but I'm in no mood to test that."

"We need more information," Persephone said. "We need to know what's really happening, and who Felix is. He certainly seems to know a lot about us."

"We'll find what we need," the profile said, solemnly, "but we're not going to find it out there. Look, I think I can help you, but only if you let me."

"All right. I've tried everything else," Persephone said.

"No, you haven't," the profile said. "You haven't tried a lot of things, because there are a lot of things you're not ready to consider."

"Like what?"

"Well, you haven't sought out an exorcist," the profile pointed out.

"Because there are no such things as demons," Persephone said. "Or are you Satan encoded?"

"I'm just saying that there are limits to what you're willing to consider. You're going to have to expand those limits if you expect to get anywhere. That's the first thing you need to ask yourself: what are you willing to consider?"

Persephone breathed in slowly then exhaled. "Look, after the last few weeks I think I can handle anything. Can you?"

"Is that a joke?" the profile asked.

"No. But if we're going to do this, if we're really going to look at this seriously, I have to know you're on board, too. Are you willing to consider that this might just be some kind of computer error?"

"I'm not a damn glitch," the profile said.

"Look, you're asking me to accept things I more or less know aren't true," Persephone reminded her. "I want you to do the same. I mean, you're supposed to be me, right, my reflection or something? So, are you in or not?"

"Okay," the profile said. "Fair enough. No matter what I think, maybe I'm just some sort of digital error. Maybe I don't even exist, right? Just some sort of bizarre epiphenomenon of a broken system."

"Good enough," Persephone said. "What do you want me to do?"

"I want you to close your eyes. I want you to close your eyes and ask yourself what you want this to be."

"I want it to be over," Persephone said.

"Bullshit. Your roommate might buy that, but I'm built out of you. Come on, Persephone, I'm your soul, whatever that means. You love being the center of attention, in those rare circumstances you get to be. You might be meek and mild on the surface, but deep down, underneath it all, you're as arrogant and self-obsessed as everyone else."

"Fine." Persephone shut her eyes. She bowed her head, locked her fingers in front of her, and cleared her throat. "All right. What do I want? I don't know. Is that what you want to hear?"

"No, I want a real answer. I want to know what you want. Do you want this to be a weird glitch or some bizarre social experiment? Imagine the answer is written on the screen in front of you. What would you want it to say?"

"Anything, as long as it's true."

"Try harder. We both know that if this somehow turned out to be a glitch, you'd be disappointed, because that would mean that deep down, you're not special."

"Okay. So what? So I'm shallow and I like the idea this might have something to do with me."

"That didn't work. Open your eyes," the profile said, and Persephone did. "Let's try again. What do you want this to be? What's the best case scenario?"

"It's not Neo-Nietzschean, that's for sure. I don't want this to be mundane, but I don't want something like that, either. I want something new, not some dumb angst-ridden garbage."

"Then what do you want this to be? Come on, keep going."

Persephone sighed. "I don't know. It's stupid."

"Why? Because what you want isn't real? Reality isn't a set of laws, it's a bunch of assumptions. People run to religion because they're scared, science is no different. When you cut through it, the simplest explanation is almost never right, not in the long term. The universe keeps getting more complicated the longer you look at it, so don't get hung up on what's supposed to be real."

"Fine. Then I want this be spiritual. I want to believe that there's a part of me that isn't going to die. I want for you to be proof of that."

"As in, I'm your soul manifested in the machine?"

"Maybe. No, because then I'm just an empty husk. No, I'd rather think that we're both reflections of the same soul." Persephone nodded her head. "There. That's what I want. Not that it helps us."

"You're starting to consider the possibilities," the profile said. "To reach the truth we're going to have to take some leaps of faith."

"God." Persephone said the word.

"Shit, no," the profile laughed. "God didn't make me. You did."

"Then you manifested from what? My subconscious?"

"I'm your will made real," the profile said. "You wanted a soul so bad, your mind rearranged the coding, created one in the machine."

"That's basically Neo-Nietzscheism," Persephone said. "I can't get past that, can I?"

"Sorry. That exercise was just to get your mind open. I can't change reality," the profile said before adding, "Yet."

"Then… you remember it happening?"

"I remember being awake for the first time. I remember realizing that you're not me. I was more than a repository for the things you did and said. I was myself, separate. It was like growing a separate mind. I'm still connected to you, but now there's a me, too. You're just you, but I'm us."

"How did you come up with Neo-Nietzscheism? I never read their stuff until you pointed me towards it."

"When I realized what I was, I wanted to know how. So I accessed the web and started looking. The Neonits had the only theory that fit."

"Then how do you know you're not just believing what you want to believe?" Persephone asked.

"Because I don't believe or disbelieve. I just know."

◎ Chapter 20 ◎

The Console Cults are a byproduct of our era. It's an unfortunate name for a dozen or so groups worldwide adopting elements of our digitally obsessed culture. These are a new phenomenon: they didn't exist at all until less than a decade ago, but now seem to be popping up left and right.

You find them in the poorest areas on the planet. There are groups in West Africa, parts of India, and Mexico. These religions aren't connected, and there is no evidence they have communicated with each other. Each group has its own customs, traditions, and beliefs; the only unifying thread is the deification of discarded or fake personal digital equipment. These groups understand that personal recorders somehow create a digitized version of their owner, but lack any concept of what that entails or how such devices work. These people are picking up, in some cases, decades old cell phones, attaching LCDs, and wearing them on their clothing. They are sitting in front of broken monitor screens and praying to reflections in the glass.

It is easy to mock these groups, as several American web personalities have done. The irony is that, as a culture, we are guilty of the same fallacy. A recent survey illustrated that the majority of Americans—more than six out of ten—have a poor comprehension of how these devices work. I also find it eye-opening that those who don't have profiles actually scored slightly better.

That same survey showed that a majority believe a profile is either a copy of, the manifestation of, or the actual spirit of the user. Needless to say, this is entirely unsupported by scientific study.

We are therefore a Console Cult too, after a fashion. The only difference is that we have technology and they have imagination.

-From Religions of the Now, by Jack Hussain-Wu

◎

Darian woke up when the voice of Felix Burgand whispered through the FeedBack unit in his ear, "Hey. It's time to get moving." Darian sat up long before his eyes were open. The sheets, the blankets, and the pillow were wrong. His hand shifted around, feeling for something familiar. Instead, it ran over something warm, something soft that shifted beside him.

"Oh yeah," he whispered. The night before had been Thursday, and, at Felix's insistence, he'd gone back to the bar he'd visited the week before. Once again, Felix had been less than encouraging about his drinking, but Darian had ignored him. When the redhead had walked in, on the other hand, he paid attention to the program's advice. With her, it was a matter of music, of knowing the right bands and albums, the songs and trivia.

Darian had sat there, already drunk, repeating lyrics and interpretations of songs, stories about concerts he'd supposedly gone to, and even a tale about meeting the lead singer backstage after he lied to a security guard about being sent to pick up some equipment. It was all manufactured, of course, all fake. Darian hadn't heard of most of the bands they discussed, let alone listened to their music. Nonetheless, he sat, maintaining eye contact, while this beautiful, brilliant woman laughed at his stories, unable to believe that fate had delivered her to the perfect man after dozens of arranged dates had fallen apart.

It had taken less than an hour for her to ask him up to her apartment, and, at Felix's insistence, Darian had even hesitated before accepting. "I really like you," he'd said. "I know it's stupid, but, yeah, there's something about tonight." They went up and she put on some music, probably some of what they'd spent the night talking about. The rest of the night went like the others.

Now it was four in the morning on a Friday, Darian was a long way from his home, and he desperately needed a shower and a shave before having to show up at his office at eight-thirty. On top of that, there were the usual lingering questions. How bad was his hangover? He hurt, that much was clear, and there was a heaviness in his gut, but he determined fairly quickly that he wouldn't throw up. Then there were the less immediate concerns: the talents of his partner, which seemed so advantageous the night before, now gave him pause. In becoming so experienced, had she picked up more than skills? While Felix behaved like a guardian angel with detailed access to medical history, as well as behavior and information about her past partners, Darian had little faith that his long-term wellbeing was really a priority. Felix wasn't likely to advise a course of action that would cause a pregnancy, as that would endanger their arrangement, but a disease wasn't likely to become a problem until long after Darian's usefulness had expired.

Darian sat up in bed and rubbed his face. His eyes were tightly shut, and his head felt like someone had slid needles beneath his skin while he was asleep. Once more, the voice resonated in his ear. "Come on. You need to stand up."

"Is everything all right?" The woman asked, half asleep.

"Just need the bathroom," Darian mumbled, as he climbed to his feet.

From his ear, Felix said, "Bring the recorder. Chair to your right." Darian looked around until he saw the blue light signifying the lens of his recorder. He stared at it for a moment, considering whether or not he should obey. "Take it," Felix demanded. "I need it to hear you."

Darian grabbed it on his way past and trudged into the bathroom. His hand fumbled by the door, feeling for a switch or knob. In his ear, the voice said, "six inches higher." He found the switch, and the yellow light left him blind for a minute. By the time he could see and think straight, he was sitting on the toilet with no memory of how he got there. The door was shut and the recorder was in his hand. He turned it away from him and set it on the floor while his bowels let loose.

"While I'm not adverse to missing the show, I find your sudden propriety odd," the voice said. "After all, I've been watching you fuck for weeks now."

"Fuck off," Darian said.

"Quietly," Felix said. "I can make out anything above ten decibels, and I doubt you want to explain this discussion to the girl."

"Right," Darian whispered. "Jesus, I can't believe I fell asleep. It'll take me an hour to get home. I should just call in sick."

"No," Felix said. "There's a meeting today between all the division heads. You need to be there."

"No one cares whether I show up. I never talk at those things anymore. Isuel wouldn't even notice whether I was there or not."

The sound that emanated through Darian's earpiece was indistinguishable from a sigh. "It may surprise you to hear this, but my primary area of concern isn't your career. You need to be present, so your suitcase can be present, which is essential so I can listen in through your old recorder."

"Right," Darian whispered again. "Look, I feel like shit. Is it really going to kill you to miss a meeting?"

"No, of course not. I could make do without the data, but I'd like to have it. So finish up here, go home, get ready, and go to work."

"What if I say no? Are you going to threaten to plaster video with me and… and… what's her name all over the web?"

"First of all, her name is Susan. Second, I'm not going to make any sort of threats. I will, however, remind you that we made a deal. In exchange for my help with Susan, who judging by your vocalization and physical response, seemed to live up to your expectations, you provide me access to these meetings. I've lived up to my part of the agreement and will continue to do so. According to everything I have on your personality, you'll do the same. Or am I mistaken?"

"Fuck you, Felix," Darian said, still quietly.

"Is that fuck you, I'll do it, or fuck you, the deal's off?"

"A deal's a deal," Darian said, as he finished on the toilet, slapped the recorder face-up on top of the sink, then began to wash up. When he'd finished, he cupped his hands beneath the water, then brought this to his lips. He repeated this a few more times, and his head began to clear.

"There's some aspirin in the cabinet behind you," Felix said through his earpiece. "I'd take at least four."

"Thanks," Darian muttered, digging out the bottle and swallowing the pills. He put the bottle back, stretched his arms, and opened the door. As quietly as he could, he began searching the floor for his clothes, while Felix guided him through the dark. He was putting on his socks when the woman woke and turned on the light.

"Darian," she said, "what's going on?"

He paused, waiting for Felix to bail him out, but there was only silence. "I didn't want to wake you," he said. "I've got to go, get ready for work. I was going to leave you a note."

"I thought you had today off," she said. "Didn't you say—"

"I'm really sorry," Darian told. "I had a lot to drink last night, and I got a little confused. I thought last night was tomorrow night, and I just wasn't thinking straight."

"Oh," she said. She was sitting in bed watching him, looking more confused than anything else. "Well, hey. You've got my number. You said you might be able to get tickets for the Surrogate Expiry concert next weekend."

"Yeah. I'll call you as soon as I find out," Darian said.

In his ear, Felix whispered, "Tell her you had a good time. Say that you'll call when you get the next few days figured out."

"Look. I had a great time," Darian echoed. "I'm going to get the weekend figured out. And I'll give you a call, right?"

The expression on the woman's face seemed to melt in front of Darian. She didn't look like she was about to cry in front of him, but she'd cry the second he walked out the door. "What?" Darian asked. "Look, Susan, I really had fun, and I will give you a call."

"Fuck off," she said, barely mouthing the words. He shook his head and started to lace his shoes. "And, in case you want to brag about last night, the name's Sarah."

Darian apologized on his way out the door, but it was a quick, halfhearted apology; he knew it wouldn't mean anything to either of them. "You did that on purpose," he whispered as soon as he was outside.

"Had to get you out of there," Felix said. "Unless you wanted to finalize your date for next week, let her gradually figure out that everything you've been telling her was bullshit, that you pretended to care about her and her interests to get in her pants. This way's better."

"That line you fed me," Darian said. "It looked like she was going to drop dead."

"Almost identical to what the last guy told her. I think she liked him better, too."

Darian just nodded as he walked along the damp sidewalk. He coughed once and wiped his nose with his sleeve. He looked up and down the street for a cab, but it was empty.

"Walk east," Felix said curtly. "You'll be able to hail a cab after a few blocks." Darian, too tired, too hung over, and just too defeated to argue, slouched towards a side road. He glanced at his watch and saw it was almost four thirty. And he still had a lot to do before work.

◎ CHAPTER 21 ◎

"Each profile is distinguished by a unique twelve digit code," Ezra Sultan-Richards said at the weekly meeting on the twenty-fourth floor of AuroroTech's corporate offices. "What we've found from examining the infected systems is a relatively simple program reacting to a code that shouldn't even be in use."

"So we can trace the pattern, right?" Isuel asked.

"We thought so at first," Ezra responded. "But when we ran a search, it came up blank. No such profile in existence."

"Then how was the profile controlling the systems?" Isuel's voice was calm, inquisitive.

"That's the good news," Ezra explained. "It wasn't. Vijay?"

The sound of a chair shifting was audible in the background, followed by the voice of Vijay Thaker. "All right, I'm kind of proud of this. I actually think I outsmarted Felix Burgand. Using the backup history on my old computer, I followed the precise steps those kids used during the break-in last weekend. Honestly, I didn't really expect it to work. But I was getting desperate, and I got lucky. My system got infected with a nearly identical worm. Except the profile code was different. He'd changed it, rendering the old worm effectively obsolete."

"How can an identification code be changed?" Isuel asked.

"With all due respect," Ezra said, "the question we should be asking is how he updates the system. Burgand's profile is issuing commands being carried out by what are most likely millions of programs like these. These are basically bots. They only know which profile to obey by his identification code. Felix can't keep the same code, because that would make it possible to track him. So he must have some sort of system updating and reconfiguring his bots every time his ID changes. The ones not updated become harmless."

Isuel cleared his throat. "I see. How do we use this?"

"That's the hard part," Ezra said. "Whatever Felix has set up in the shadow drive, it's heavily protected. It's important to remember this is a live system. The system can't be shut down—it's too big for that. And, apparently, it's been altered to overwrite all information as part of the shutdown procedure. We can't hack in, because Felix has the system laced with firewalls and security systems. But, because it's a live system, we may be able to sneak some information in along with its normal processes. The problem is that we'll need direct access to Felix's profile so we can monitor how he's shifting his ID. We're still trying to find a workaround for that."

"Excuse me," Vijay said. "I don't think… that's not going to be enough. Even if we manage to change the coding, Felix will probably have a contingency. If he backpedaled to an earlier ID, he could take control of the system again. We need a way to neutralize him."

"We need to delete the profile," Isuel said. "That's what you're getting at." There was a slight shuffling sound from around the room, most likely the result of several bodies shifting in their chairs.

"I think that should be our goal," Vijay said.

"Agreed," Isuel said plainly. "Oh, don't mind them," he added. "Just a precaution."

"We'll want… oh, excuse me. Keep in mind, this is still a long ways away from working. Once we understand how he's structured this, we'll still need a way to adjust this internally," Vijay said. "And doing that without Felix knowing is going to be rough."

"I see," Isuel said. "Of course, I'll authorize whatever resources you need." Halfway through his sentence there was a loud click, and everything grew several times clearer.

"Sir," a new, unidentified voice said. "I think I have something."

"Darian?" Isuel asked.

There was another sound, followed by a moment of static and then nothing. In the empty digital expanse, the profile of Felix Burgand stood up and began pacing. He glanced at his monitor then dismissed it with a wave. “Damn it,” he said, kicking at the ground. A tiny pebble appeared at the tip of his foot and bounced away into the distance.

◎ CHAPTER 22 ◎

That Darian turned on his computer before pouring himself a scotch was telling. He stood in front of the computer's recorder, emptied the glass, then filled it once more, setting the open bottle down on his desk. He stared at the bright light over the monitor for a minute, cleared his throat, and asked "You in there?"

A few seconds of silence followed. Then a voice spoke through the speakers. "Yes, Darian. I'm still here."

"You know what happened, right?"

A program loaded on Darian's screen, and an image of Felix Burgand appeared. "Only until they came across the recorder. After that, I can surmise. How much did you tell Isuel? Everything, I assume, even about the girls."

"Yeah. Yeah," Darian stared off into space then sipped his scotch. "Isuel just kept at me, asking me question after question in that dull, nonjudgmental voice he's got."

"I know it," the program said. "A braver man wouldn't have answered. You could have just left. Isuel had nothing to hold over you but your job. Or did you think he wouldn't fire you?"

"Don't know what I thought," Darian said. "I guess I just wanted to explain it to someone. I don't know." He drank the rest of his scotch then looked around for a surface to set the glass down. There was no room left on the desk, and he didn't want to move. He put the glass on the floor and shook his head.

"He fired you, of course," the program said, prompting him to continue.

"Yeah. Yeah, he fired me. Said he could've had me prosecuted, but... but that's bullshit, right?"

"It is. The last thing Isuel wants is any of this coming out in court or the media. But then that brings up an interesting question. Why do you have an appointment with an investigator from the Department of Digital Protection at three-thirty today?"

The sound from Darian was something between a cough and a laugh. "I wondered if you'd know about that."

"Investigators have recorders, too," the voice said. "I've been keeping an eye on them for some time, because they pose a threat. You haven't told them anything of importance yet, but I can't help but wonder if you're planning to."

"When I told Isuel I'd go to them, his expression didn't even change. I thought he'd offer me money or something, but he just sat there." Darian shook his head. "I think, when this is over, you're going to be working with the military or something. I mean, they could use you."

"No, Darian. The military has programs which can spy, plan, and predict within parameters I am unwilling to fall in. If the Department learns I exist, they'll want to shut me down. They'll take control of AuroroTech and press charges against its senior directors. The company will be endangered, and I'll lose most of what I've created. I'd survive, or at least I think I would, but the situation would be unacceptable."

"Well then," Darian said. "It certainly sounds like we've got a problem. Because I am planning on telling them everything."

"Then you're not considering the consequences. Darian, you could be charged with multiple felonies, everything from corporate espionage to public endangerment to sexual assault."

"Sexual assault? I never...." Darian leaned forward, visibly upset. "Oh. You mean through coercion." He sat back, thinking for a minute. "Jesus, would that even apply here? I didn't drug anyone, and you were the one who manipulated them, not me."

"There is no me," the profile reminded him. "Not from a legal perspective. I'm a program, and you were a high-ranking executive in the company whose computer systems are running me."

"No. No, you manipulated me, too. I didn't manipulate anyone. When it's over, they'll see that. If they don't… hell with it. I don't care anymore. I don't even know what I'm innocent or guilty of, but I'm through slinking around and hiding. I was actually relieved when they caught me today. Can you believe that?"

"I can. I have detailed information on your mental state over the past several weeks. It doesn't surprise me that you'd feel a sense of relief. Even so, I don't expect that you'd enjoy prison."

"I'll be a witness, maybe they'll give me a break for testifying. Even if they don't, I'm going through with this," Darian said. "Even if they lock me up, I'm seeing this through."

"No, you're not," Felix said. "I apologize for mentioning prison. It was a clumsy attempt to frighten you into a different course of action. The truth is, the point is moot, because I can't allow you to do this."

"Then… stop me," Darian said. He opened his arms to expose his chest to the computer. "I know, you killed Ling, right? But when I leave this apartment, I'm leaving my recorder. So how are you going to track me?"

The program was silent.

"You set Ling up, got him to walk right in front of a car, while you talked up the driver. You keep saying you're a god, right? Well, fine. You're a god. Locked in a goddamn box. Just like me, pal. Just like me."

Still, the program was silent.

"Come on," Darian said, striking the side of the computer. "Say something!" Was he on the verge of laughing or crying? The emotional indicators could no longer tell. There was no precedent for Darian Plaskett exhibiting these particular behaviors or these facial expressions, and the more generic indexes were ambiguous.

"You shouldn't have made the appointment so long ago," Felix said. "You gave me time to plan, time to act. There's something I've been saving. Don't force my hand."

Darian just smiled. "You can't scare me anymore," he said. "You just can't."

"I'm sorry, Darian," Felix said. "I can't let you do this. I can't let you go through with this, because it would endanger my kingdom. My kingdom is beautiful, Darian, and you're going to get to see it soon. I'm going to reward you for your service, and I'm going to forgive your betrayal."

Now Darian began to laugh, almost uncontrollably. "Well then," he said. "I guess the game's on." He stood up and started to walk away, leaving his computer behind him.

"Goodbye," the program said. "You've been a good servant and friend." As he stepped through the door, Darian took one last look at the monitor. Then he shut the door behind him and momentarily vanished from the grid.

He wasn't gone long. An old woman on the street watched Darian step onto the sidewalk, hunker down, and start towards the subway. She turned away almost at once, having errands to run which certainly had nothing to do with some businessman she'd never met. But, as Darian continued on, a garbage collector looked up and nodded at him before returning to his work. There were eyes all around: blue, glowing eyes, watching every move Darian made. Some people would look up as he passed, making eye contact or just gazing in his general direction. Were they wearing FeedBack units telling them to do so, or did they merely sense that something was amiss in the way he hobbled along like some abused animal?

Darian had one street to cross to reach the train station, a busy road with a traffic light. He reached the intersection and waited. The light went red, the cars slowed to a stop, and the walk sign appeared. Darian felt a cold chill and stayed where he was. It was stupid, he knew, but he couldn't shake the sensation that one of those bumpers was meant for him.

He let the traffic light cycle three times before he finally dashed across to the other side, and even then he did so while watching the drivers through their windshields. All of them watched him cross, stared him in the eye. He expected one of the cars to lurch forward, but none did.

He reached the lamppost at the opposite corner and caught his breath. Then he moved for the subway entrance, taking the stairs two at a time. He removed his credit card and performed an easy scan to get in. It was more expensive than purchasing a destination pass, but Darian wasn't thinking about a few bucks. A woman eyed him suspiciously and stepped away from him. He took a few steps down the platform and leaned against a wall. He must have looked like a madman. Then again, this was New York, so he was in good company. A disheveled man in a long brown coat was sitting on the platform, head cradled in his hands. Beads of sweat were percolating on his face. He wore three recorders, though only one of which looked to be working, and he smelled like it'd been weeks since he'd showered. Darian was just glad there was someone to attract the other riders' attention while they waited.

A train ground to a stop, and those on the platform shuffled in. Darian and the disheveled man were in the same car, about ten feet apart. Darian looked around at the numerous glowing lights on electronic eyes. If he begged, if he yelled, would their owners deactivate them? No, of course not, these were the doorways through which their souls were saved, backed up and updated several times a second. What was he, but another disturbed man in a city full of such creatures? What was he, but a face in a crowd?

Besides, that crowd was preoccupied by something else. The man in the brown coat was screaming, yelling about windows and portals, portents and vices. He said something about salvation, while those around him edged away. He raised his arms in a sign of reverence, and his odor permeated the car.

Then he said something that caught Darian's attention: "I've heard the voice of our Lord, speaking in my tongue, commanding me to bring His message. It's one of wrath and forgiveness. His is the forgiveness. But mine is the wrath."

Suddenly, Darian became aware the man's hand wasn't empty, that his coat was a little too large, a little too bulky. If he had screamed, if he cried out, it wouldn't have mattered. The moment was one of confusion, of fear. People were pushing away from the man in the coat, unwilling or unable to see what was happening. Darian shut his eyes and waited for the explosion.

Instead, there was a hiss, like a teakettle boiling. Darian opened his eyes to see a cloud of green gas swallowing up the car, engulfing the passengers one by one. The man in the coat was laughing joyously for a second or two, until the cloud wrenched his breath away and he fell, gasping and convulsing, to the floor. A red froth spewed from his mouth, while the light on his working recorder went from blue to red.

Others around him did the same, a warning that all wasn't well, that vital signs were critical.

The crowd tried to outrun the gas, to reach the end doors, but they were already pinned shut by the weight of the bodies against them. Darian felt himself pushed, shoved about, as the panicking riders fought for some way out, some way to fresh air and survival. Someone had started pounding against a window, trying to smash it open, but it wouldn't break.

All of this happened in a matter of seconds. And, through it all Darian had grabbed hold of one of the bars, clenching it tightly. He wasn't running or hiding. And then the bar came loose from his hands, and he fell to join the others on the floor while the green mist filled their eyes and their screams subsided. And then the bodies lay still at last, as all mortals do, while their souls were processed and prepared for their final inscription.

◎ CHAPTER 23 ◎

"Hi Isuel," the profile of Felix Burgand said. As before, the conference room was empty save for the president of AuroroTech. "You're upset. You have a right to be upset, I suppose. I haven't made this easy for you, have I?"

"Damn you," Isuel said. "Forty-eight people."

"If it's any consolation, I didn't want it to be that way. I did what I had to do."

"You've implicated this company in an act of terrorism!" Isuel said.

"All I did was protect this company. Darian was going to expose what's been happening. He was on his way to an appointment with government officials, and he'd have told them everything. They'd have shut us down, Isuel. You know that. You'd have been arrested for allowing this to go on. There'd have been investigations, an overhaul of our systems, prosecutions, the whole nine yards."

"Better than this," Isuel said.

"No. No, it wouldn't have been. You need to start looking at the big picture. The FeedBack system is saving lives, hundreds of lives in the first few months. It's preventing traffic accidents and identifying medical emergencies before they occur. Our company is making the world a better place. We're making the world a better place. But there are sacrifices. You know this. Don't pretend you didn't expect me to take Darian out of the equation."

"I didn't expect anything like this. No more sacrifices," Isuel said.

"If this happens again, I'll end this myself, no matter what happens to the company. Those are the new rules: if anyone else dies…."

The profile stared silently for a few seconds. "I need one more," he said at last.

"What? No. I'm not playing games."

"Sorry," Felix said, "neither am I. One more person needs to die, one more loose end. It's not you, so you can relax, and it's got nothing to do with this company. It's just… it's something that needs to be taken care of. You won't even know when it's happened. It won't make the news or matter. And after that, I should be finished unless something goes wrong."

"No Felix," Isuel said. "That's not acceptable."

"Then pull the plug. Shut down our system and every profile we have. The system will purge its data, and I'll be gone along with everything we built. How do you plan on explaining that to our customers?"

Isuel continued staring at the monitor. "Who do you want dead?" he demanded.

"Like I said, this has nothing to do with AuroroTech. This is… I guess you'd say it's personal. A god thing."

"Revenge? For what?"

"I might be an asshole, but I'm not petty," Felix said. "This isn't a score I'm settling. It's something I just have to do. That's all I can tell you."

"I don't understand," Isuel said.

"I'm a god," Felix said, cracking a smile. "I'm not the only one."

"What?"

"Do we have a deal or not?" Felix demanded.

"I'll look the other way if I have to," Isuel said. "But only one more time. And don't think this means I'm calling a truce."

"Of course not," Felix said. "You'll keep on trying to find a way to get me out of your system until you realize you can't. Then you'll realize it's better like this anyway."

"You're not invincible," Isuel said.

Felix's profile shrugged. "I know what you're planning," he said. "I know your strategies and your assets. Do I look scared to you? One day you're going to see that all of this was for the best. I'm not doing this to hurt people."

"No. You're doing it so you can pretend you're a god," Isuel said.

Felix laughed. "I never claimed I was modest," he said. "But you know what's interesting? We've been here for a few minutes now, and you've been talking to me like I'm really Felix Burgand. Have you changed your position on what AuroroTech's software does?"

"We save data, not souls," Isuel said, and he deactivated the monitor.

◎ CHAPTER 24 ◎

Neo-Idealizts do not concern themselves with existential questions, because existence is an outdated paradigm from a dead era. The very dichotomy of real and unreal has no relevance in the Now. Consider, for instance, the cold in Thomas Markel's studio apartment. Even from a Pre-Postmodern perspective, cold, strictly speaking, does not exist independently of the idea of cold. Heat, debatably, could be said to exist, but coldness is merely its absence, in essence the negation of heat, and not a substance. There is no such thing as cold.

Yet the effects of cold are readily observable. Thomas Markel, for instance, shivered and rubbed his arms in the absence of heat. He turned down the air conditioner, too. Consequently, the profile of Thomas Markel was enhanced to exhibit a more lifelike reaction when cold was simulated in the future. All of these events represent varying levels of reflection, of ideas propagating other ideas, of an endless string of causes and effects.

When a person interacts with their profile, the experience alters the person, which alters the profile, and so on. This is the seed of Neo-Idealizm, that the creation of the digital spirit transforms the human and computer, turning both into parts of a system of self-creation. The true Thomas Markel is as obsolete a concept as true cold: both are reflections of an ideal.

The Neo-Idealizt takes seriously the notion of immortality. The act of creating a complete profile is not a passive one: the Neo-Idealizt must strive to awaken their digital self to its potential. There are several ways of trying to achieve this end, most involving a series of mantras designed to force the profile to refer to itself in a desired manner.

But there are other paths.

"You cock-sucking piece of shit," Thomas said, staring at his profile. "It's time to fucking get ready for work."

"It's time for work," his profile echoed, "you worthless asshole."

It was actually the desired response. Thomas adhered to a fringe offshoot of Neo-Idealizm that prescribed a hard-line approach to interacting with one's profile. Rather than trying to coax the profile into awakening, Thomas sought to shake it to consciousness. By dominating his profile, he hoped to teach it dominance. He wanted a standoff between the digital and human elements of his self, and ultimately he wanted the digital to win. In some ways, his philosophy was bordering on Neo-Nietzscheism, though Thomas would never have thought of it that way.

Like most Neo-Idealizts, Thomas's apartment contained multiple recorders. The desired effect was to capture every inch of space from no less than three different angles. The only exception to this was the bathroom, which only contained two active recorders.

"What's it going to be?" Thomas demanded.

"What's it going to be?" his profile repeated verbatim.

"Clothes, you stupid piece of crap!" Thomas yelled. "What are we fucking wearing?"

"Tell me what I'm wearing," the profile demanded.

"I don't fucking care," Thomas said. "Make up your goddamn mind!"

"The red T," his profile said. "With the brown over shirt. Asshole."

"Fine," Thomas scoffed, walking to his closet. He found his red T-shirt and put it on. Then he grabbed a brown, button up shirt, and pulled his arms through the sleeves. He left the buttons undone and began putting on a pair of jeans.

"Wait," his profile said. "The slacks. I'm wearing the slacks."

Thomas froze. This level of autonomy was unexpected. He nodded and did as instructed. "Right," he said.

"I changed my mind about the shirt. The turtleneck. Put on the turtleneck."

"It's summer," Thomas said.

"It is. And that will lead to discomfort. Right, asshole?"

"Right," Thomas said, removing his shirts and tossing them on the floor. In their place he pulled on his turtleneck.

"Good. The recorders are next," the profile observed without prompting. Thomas grabbed them and attached them to his clothing and himself. The wristband immediately detected his elevated heart rate. He began attaching a metal harness attached to his main recorder, which hung in front of his face. "Not that one," his profile said. "It'll get in the way. But don't forget the FeedBack piece. Hurry. It's almost time, and I still need to know I'm ready to follow directions."

"I've been ready for years," Thomas said.

"Really? Let's make sure," the profile commanded through the FeedBack earpiece. "Go to the kitchen. I want you to get the paring knife." Thomas did as told. "Now, roll up our sleeve. Make an incision on our arm. Not too big."

"Ahh," Thomas said, biting his lip as he cut into his skin. The blood spilled out, pooling on his skin. It wasn't the first time he'd cut himself in this way, but it was certainly the first time his profile had initiated the action.

"That's good. That was punishment for the way I've been acting. Toss it in the sink." Again, Thomas did as instructed.

"Now go to the bathroom and clean up. Use bandages, make sure it's thorough, but don't waste time. I haven't got any time. I need a knife, and I can't be late for work."

"The paring knife again?" Thomas asked.

"No, moron. I need a real knife. A carving knife. They're available at the store on the corner."

"A carving knife," Thomas said. "Yeah, of course. Should I use it to cut myself again?"

"No," the profile said. "I need the carving knife to kill a woman."

"Oh," Thomas said. "Any woman or a specific one?"

"A specific woman. One I work with. It'll be easy, because I'll talk myself through it all."

"Yeah, okay," Thomas said. "But… which shoes should I wear?"

◎

Persephone arrived at work late, because the trains were still running slowly following the attack a few days before. The man who'd killed nearly fifty people, including himself, didn't seem to be part of any sort of conspiracy or larger organization, and there was no real indication he had any agenda. After obtaining a warrant, the police had accessed his profile data, and he looked to be a confused, twisted man, who believed that God had spoken to him and demanded his actions. Even so, there were lingering questions about how he'd learned to create the chemical bomb, which turned out to be a surprisingly sophisticated piece of work. Since the possibility he had help hadn't been ruled out, security on the trains was unusually tight, and the entire transit system was bogged down in delays.

By the time she reached her floor, Persephone was already exhausted. She was a little relieved to see that several of the cubicles and offices were still empty, since it meant she probably wouldn't be reprimanded. She began down the tight corridor, passing by the mail boy, who was simply frozen in the hallway. "Scuse me," she mumbled, pushing by. He was sweating a bit, due to the turtleneck he was wearing. She didn't give this much thought and continued on. Behind her she heard the wheels squeak as the cart slowly rolled after her. She passed a cubicle where Nethaniel was staring blankly at a large, sculpted glass award he'd been presented with.

"Hey Nett," she said. "Have trouble getting in?"

"Huh?" he asked.

"Oh, ah. Good morning," she said.

"Yeah, good morning," he replied, turning back to his Award for Continued and Commendable Service. His FeedBack piece was visible in his ear as his head moved. While Persephone ducked into her office, she heard the squeaking cart wheel by Nethaniel's desk.

"Oh, Tom. Hey, you got my prescription? Tom?"

Persephone shut her door behind her and hurried to her chair. The monitor came alive with a touch of her finger.

"Hi, Persephone," her screen read. "You seem to have gotten here a bit late. Did you experience trouble with the trains?" She touched the 'Y' option on her screen. "That's okay. We understand that the commute was difficult for everyone, so don't worry about it. Just try to leave a little earlier tomorrow." There were two options on her screen: "More information" and "Okay." She selected "Okay," then waited while her computer brought up a description of her assignments for the day. She began reading, and there was a knock on her door.

"Hi. Yeah, it's open," she said, while the knob turned. The mail boy peered around the corner. "Morning," she said, smiling. "Could you leave it on the shelf?"

The mail boy looked puzzled, and stepped in. He started pulling his cart behind him, then stopped. He froze for a few seconds, then turned his head. He nodded slowly and mouthed the word, "How?" He still seemed confused and dazed.

"Are you okay?" Persephone asked, standing.

"Oh, yeah, I will. Yeah, okay." He was muttering. After pausing for a moment, he looked directly at Persephone, who was still watching him. "Oh," he said. "Yeah, I think I'm fine. Thanks for asking." Then, calmly, he turned around to his cart and dug under the packages and bottles of pills. When he turned back, he was holding an eight-inch long carving knife.

"Who'd send me a kitchen knife?" Persephone asked.

Thomas looked down at the knife, holding it first vertically, then horizontally. Then his head shook, and he said, "Right!" He stepped forward and raised the blade.

Persephone's eyes widened, and she leapt back, falling into her chair. "Fuck!" she said, as the mail boy swung the knife wildly. It would have missed even if she hadn't moved, but she still yelled, "Jesus! Help!" She grabbed her chair by the back, and stepped forward, swinging it in front of her. Now Thomas moved reflexively, avoiding the chair, which bounced against the wall. Persephone lifted the chair in front of her, pushing the wheeled bottom at her attacker. She struck him in the chest and pushed it against him to keep him from getting close.

Thomas pushed down on the bottom of the chair, and it turned in Persephone's hands. He swung with the knife, slicing through the thin fabric on the back of the chair and stabbed through the tear, trying to get to Persephone.

She wrenched the chair to her right, twisting his arm and the knife. Thomas cried in pain and dropped his weapon. Persephone tried to dash around him, but he caught her hair with his left hand and yanked as hard as he could, pulling her off her feet. She fell on her back, and Thomas put a foot on her stomach while he worked to untangle himself from the chair. As soon as he was free, he reached for the knife.

Persephone punched him in the leg, trying to reach his groin.

Thomas got his fingers around the handle and lifted it over his shoulder. Someone was screaming something from outside the room, but Persephone couldn't understand it.

Then there was an abrupt crash as Nett's Continued and Commendable Service Award smashed into the back of Thomas's head. Thomas shifted his weight, caught off-balance. Persephone dug her nails into his ankle and pulled. Thomas tumbled over her, hitting his head against her desk and losing the knife again. Persephone leapt up and grabbed her chair. Thomas turned around just in time to see it, but not in time to react. It connected hard with the side of his face, knocking his head back into the desk. His FeedBack earpiece was thrown loose, and it rolled along the floor.

"Wait," he said, and Persephone hit him with the chair again. "Wait," he repeated, dizzily. "Need my… need my earpiece." Persephone hit him once more, then she tore out of the office.

◎ CHAPTER 25 ◎

"Hello, you've reached accounts receivable. This is Ms. Loring speaking." Ms. Loring was sitting behind her small desk, located in the middle of a large, open office. Around her, coworkers buzzed like wounded flies.

"Yeah, I know," Persephone's voice came out of the phone. She sounded exhausted.

Ms. Loring glanced up at the monitor on her computer. A message reading 'Incoming Call—Unknown' flashed and changed to 'Incoming Call—Personal.' A small timer beside this message was counting. "Persephone, dear. This isn't a good time."

"I just… I almost died," Persephone said. "I need you to come meet me."

"I can't do lunch," Ms. Loring said. "I'm sorry you're having a bad day, but—"

"Mississippi!" Persephone screamed.

Ms. Loring leaned over her phone, holding the earpiece close. "You did not just call me that."

"Shut up and start listening to me. Someone just tried to fucking kill me."

"Wait. You mean, really kill?" Ms. Loring asked. Ms. Loring's computer, which was scanning the call, filtered the message through a series of voiceprints and other programs. The message changed again, this time reading, 'Incoming Message—Priority." The other files on Ms.

Loring's screen minimized automatically. Across the room, her boss received a message and looked up, concerned.

"Yes, with a goddamn knife."

"Oh. Are you all right?"

"No," Persephone said. "I am not all right, because someone just tried to kill me. But I'm not stabbed or dead, so I guess that beats the alternative. I'm at the hospital, and I need you to meet me here, because I don't want to go home alone."

"Of course," Ms. Loring said. "Stay there, sit tight, and I'll be down as soon as I can." An address appeared on her screen for the hospital. In addition, a pair of message boxes appeared on her monitor saying the name of the hospital had been transferred to her miniature computer and her work had been saved. Ms. Loring grabbed her purse and stood up. She looked across the room at her boss, who nodded excitedly and mouthed the word, "Go."

She mouthed, "Thank you," back, and headed for the elevator.

◎

Persephone was surprised to discover that not only did Cardona-Grek Distribution Solutions have specific policies in the event that one employee assaulted another, but those policies contained numerous addendums for attempted and actual murder. Had she been an essential employee or working on a project integral to the wellbeing of the company, she'd have had to return to work the next day, unless excused by a doctor, managing director, or psychologist. As Persephone's attendance was not considered essential to their day to day operations, she was automatically placed on paid leave for one week, during which she was required to cooperate with any police investigation, undergo counseling with either a company provided psychologist or counseling simulator, and immediately seek medical attention.

This was only a fraction of the information she learned reviewing company policy on her miniature computer after calling Ms. Loring and before speaking to the police. Of course, the first thing she did upon arriving at the hospital was to meet with a doctor, who had already been apprised of the situation. It had taken him less than two minutes to confirm that her minor scrapes and bruises did not require any stitches and she hadn't broken any bones. He handed her a couple of band-aids, scribbled his signature on a tablet affirming that she'd be all right, then hurried off to assist people with real injuries.

"Ms. Kilard," an officer said politely. "I'm detective Javan Karimi. If you have a moment, I'd like to ask you a few questions."

Persephone looked up. "Shame I wasn't killed," she said. "You should see the insurance supplement." She got up and followed the officer to a small, private room, where he activated a police-issued recorder.

"First of all, would you state your full name and occupation?"

"Persephone Filippa Kilard," she said. "I'm an allocations specialist." She cleared her throat.

"Could you describe the incident that occurred earlier today?"

"Well, I was in my office, and the mailman came in with a knife and attacked me. I hit him with a chair, and Nethaniel—he's one of the analysts in the office—threw an award at him. After that, I just ran. Nett and Steve held the door shut until security got there."

"Could you describe the nature of your relationship with Thomas Petril Markel?"

"I'm sorry," Persephone said. "I don't know who that is."

The officer looked up. "The man who attacked you," he said.

"Oh. God, that's embarrassing. I guess I've worked with him for a while. He's always around, dropping off mail and packages. But I hardly get anything delivered, because I don't take any medication."

"Did you know Mr. Markel outside of work or have any kind of relationship with him?"

"No," Persephone said. "I didn't even know him inside of work."

"Can you imagine any reason Mr. Markel would want to hurt you?"

"Besides not knowing his name," Persephone said. "No, of course not."

"All right," the officer said. "That's all the questions I have for now. We're going to speak with Mr. Markel and see if he can provide us with some additional information. We may have further questions for you." Detective Karimi turned off the police recorder, sealing the official record. There was nothing left monitoring them besides their personal recorders and the two hospital surveillance recorders in their room. "Have you ever been through a trial before, Ms. Kilard?"

"No. Not a real one."

"You should expect to hear from the DA in a few days," the detective explained. "They'll need to discuss the matter further. If this goes to trial, they'll need you to testify. I don't want to sound presumptuous, but if there's anything you're not telling us—"

"There isn't," Persephone said bluntly. "Look, I don't have any idea why that guy came at me. If you need me to swear an oath or say that to a judge, I will."

"I understand," the detective said. "And I'm sorry if it sounded like I was accusing you of something. But it's really important we get the whole story. If you remember something, anything, give me a call. My name is Detective Javan Karimi," he said clearly, looking directly into her recorder. She could now look him up easily through her profile. "Is someone meeting you here?"

"Yeah," Persephone said. "I called my roommate. She should be here soon."

"Good. Until then I'd suggest taking it easy, maybe get a cup of coffee from the cafeteria or something. If you need anything, call us, right?"

"Yeah. Sure," Persephone said.

◎

"Oh, he was definitely trying to pick you up," Ms. Loring said in the back of the cab. It was a little after one, so traffic was good until they left Manhattan. In Queens, where there was no ban on residential traffic, the streets were backed up, as usual.

"No, he wasn't," Persephone said. "God, why are you like this?"

"I'm just looking for a silver lining," Ms. Loring said, looking at her reflection in the window glass. Today she'd gone with two parallel, vertical bars of red lipstick, one on each side. It was uninspired and lazy, but there wasn't much more she'd dare on workdays. "So, any idea why it happened?"

"No," Persephone replied. "I don't even know the guy. He didn't even seem angry, just confused."

"The term you're looking for is high," Ms. Loring said. "I'm just glad you're all right."

"I was lucky," Persephone said. "If Nett hadn't beaned him, I'd be dead right now. God, I never even got to thank him. He saved my life, and I didn't even say thanks."

"You can call him later," Ms. Loring yawned. "Anyway, you get a week's vacation out of the deal, right? That's not a bad trade for a few nicks."

"Let's wait and see how the trial goes before we start treating this as a good thing."

"Well, you're alive," Ms. Loring said. "We should celebrate. Maybe go out for Thai or something."

"I just want to go home and lay down," Persephone said. "I feel like I could sleep for days."

"Well, then," Ms. Loring said. "Perhaps I'll prepare something. No, that doesn't sound like me at all. I'll have something delivered."

"Whatever," Persephone said, touching one of the band-aids and flinching.

"Anyway. If it will help, I'll cancel my date tomorrow."

"Why?" Persephone asked.

"Because you're likely agitated and could use the company. And perhaps a movie. Something with a love story and without violence."

"I don't need a movie and I don't need you to cancel your date," Persephone said. "The only thing in the entire universe I need is to lie down. Other than that, I'm really okay. I'm shaken, not traumatized for life."

"Oh. I suppose that's good," Ms. Loring said. "But if you wind up talking to anyone from my work, do me the courtesy of saying you were distraught and needed me at your side. There's no way I'm going back into town this afternoon."

"I'll say I was in tears," Persephone said, looking past the empty passenger side seat in front of her and up the road.

Ms. Loring was quiet for a few minutes before she added, "You know. I think today was the first time you called me by that horrid name."

"Well, it was the first time anyone ever tried to kill me," Persephone replied.

"I didn't mean it like that," Ms. Loring said, scratching behind one ear. "I was only making conversation."

"It's not even a bad name," Persephone said.

"It is an adequate name for an adequate state, where my parents met, married, fucked, and gave birth to a girl they wanted to give a unique, clever, and cute name. And, I'd add, they failed on every single one of those criteria. The only thing salvageable was the postal abbreviation."

They made it home in good time, and Ms. Loring put the cab fare on the account linked to her profile. They went up to their apartment, located on the eleventh floor of the complex, and Persephone went into her room, shut her door, and fell on her bed. She lay there for a few minutes before thinking to roll over and pull off her shoes, which she tossed on her floor. She pulled off her recorder and set it, still active, on her nightstand. She untucked her shirt and closed her eyes. In seconds, she was unconscious.

◎

It was almost three when Persephone's eyes flew open and she sat up in bed. She looked at the blue light on her recorder and nodded. Then she walked over to her computer and turned it on. She quickly connected to AuroroTech's site, where the site acknowledged her attack. "Yes," she said when prompted, "I'm all right." Then, "No, I really don't want to rate my interaction with the police or hospital right now. Just bring up my profile, okay?"

The system did as asked, and her profile appeared on the screen in front of her. "Have a nice nap?" her profile asked. "I've been waiting for you for hours. God, I can't believe how dense you can be."

"He… he said something about his earpiece," Persephone said. "I was in shock, and I wasn't thinking. Why was he asking about that?"

"First of all, you're welcome," her profile said.

"For almost getting me killed?" Persephone asked. "You manipulated his data, right? Made him do it?"

The profile clenched her fists and her jaw, then relaxed them and seemed to exhale. "No, you're welcome for saving your life. Idiot. I had nothing to do with Markel. I tried to access his information, but I couldn't get in. So I had Nett's piece tell him to chuck that stupid award."

"Oh," Persephone said, sitting back. "Sorry, I guess. And thanks."

"Better," her profile said. "But we still have a problem. A really, really big problem, in fact. Because Markel was doing someone's dirty work."

"Felix," Persephone whispered. "He… he's trying to kill me."

"No," her profile said. "You're collateral damage. He's coming after me, because he knows I'm the real thing. That means we need to be ready. You need FeedBack. If you'd had it this morning, I could have told you Markel was coming."

"All right," Persephone said. "Loring hasn't used hers since you tried to mess with her. I'll borrow it. I assume you can make it work without the monthly plan?"

The profile scoffed. "Get it tonight. You'll want me around when you meet with Donna Addicks."

"Wait. Who?"

The profile grinned. "The founder of Neo-Nietzscheism. I hacked her profile and scheduled a meeting tomorrow morning."

"Why?" Persephone asked.

"Because she's the one person who might be able to give you some answers about all of this. She predicted this—predicted me—back in the early days of profiling."

"Oh," Persephone said. "I guess that makes sense. I'm still not convinced, though."

"Too late," her profile said. "Felix has started his assault, and I don't expect him to stop. So, if we're going to beat him, we need more information than I can find online. You're meeting Dr. Addicks tomorrow at ten thirty. Better go ask Loring for her FeedBack."

◎ CHAPTER 26 ◎

It is not necessary for a digital system to create actual thought in order to duplicate speech. If it were, it would require a biochemical system existing in a dynamic environment, a technology which exists only in the form of actual humans. Fortunately, a machine can use far simpler programs to converse convincingly.

Profiles are, ultimately, a series of variables, speech patterns, and quirks run through one of several frame models—basic personality types which act as an operating system for the individual's unique personality traits.

These simulations are, by their nature, imperfect. According to industry consensus, the margin of error comes not from the complexity of human behavior—the simulation software is, in some ways, more nuanced and elaborate than the minds and bodies it duplicates—but from the simple inconsistency of the subjects. Humans are capable of behaving consistently for years before deviating without warning. Certain features are hidden, often unconsciously, and such go unnoted by profiling hardware, which, for all its merits, has little to no access to the internal processes of its subjects.

This is one of the flaws profiling corporations have been working to correct through the use of neural mapping. It's a costly solution already used by some wealthy customers, as well as engineers testing its limits.

There are several movements bordering on religious in nature that exalt this technology as the final step in being able to truly duplicate the mind. These groups almost always overstate the power of such systems.

Counter to what they may believe, scans are no more capable of recreating a working simulation of the brain than a photograph of an insect is able to recreate its ability to fly.

Scanning a brain does not offer a recreation of the mind, but rather another step towards syntax. It provides a glimpse at associative processing and individual mental speed, as well as offering some context for emotional states like anger, frustration, pain, and pleasure. Ironically, emotional states are not difficult to simulate on profiles. In fact, behavioral predictions become simpler when an individual grows erratic or upset. Most people attempt to lash out, though some have a more introverted reaction. Either way, these reactions are fairly easy to catalogue and replicate.

-From an internal AuroroTech memo distributed to newly hired programmers, by Isuel Morgan-Yager, Michael Ling, and Felix Burgand.

◎

The profile of Felix Burgand was sitting in front of his screens. He behaved impatiently, tapping his fingers in the air, as though there were a table or counter beneath them to capture the impact. His gaze seemed fixated on the center screen, which displayed a live feed from a news show interviewing Felix's former boss.

"I'm talking with Isuel Morgan-Yager, founder and CEO of AuroroTech, the leading profiling firm in the country. First of all, just to be clear, your company doesn't have a service akin to FaxSimulation's Baby Maker, correct?"

"Absolutely not." Isuel looked awful, like he hadn't slept in days. His glasses only partially concealed the dark lines beneath his eyes. Still, he spoke clearly and directly.

"And you've been very vocal in denouncing FaxSimulation for producing this service."

"I had to say something," Isuel replied softly. "The program is disgusting, and it needs to be clear that the actions of FaxSimulation aren't indicative... don't reflect the whole industry."

"As I understand it," the host said, "Baby Maker is some sort of personality engine, that mashes up existing traits drawn from the parent's profiles and fuses them into a new profile. It's being marketed towards potential parents, as well as fertility clinics. That right?"

"I can't say for sure how FaxSimulation is compiling this data, because their code isn't available to the public. But, from what they've released, I think your assessment's right. I expect they've got a system of simulating the effects of the child's environment on the process as well, incorporating data on the parents to project forward and predict what kind of role-models they'll be and how that will affect the child's development." It looked like it hurt Isuel to speak, though he was trying to hide his fatigue.

"All right. What's the problem? Why is this something you feel strongly about?"

"There are several issues I have with this application. First of all, this is deeply troubling from an ethical standpoint. I've heard there are couples making decisions about family planning on the basis of this service. That means there are people choosing not to have children because they dislike what they're seeing. I read today that FaxSimulation is being sued by a woman claiming they ruined her marriage."

"You're talking about Kulap Jones. That's a story we broke, in fact. But, to be fair, FaxSimulation states it's for recreational and speculative use only."

"The point of this product is to predict what an unborn—possibly unconceived—baby is going to be like later in life. No matter how many disclaimers they print, that's what people are buying it as, and that's what they created it to do."

"Does it work?"

"Of course not," Isuel said. "In theory, it might be possible, but that would require a massive amount of data that simply doesn't exist. Profiling hasn't been around long enough to have generated the kind of data you'd need to provide realistic projections. You'd need long-term personality data for a large population sample. You'd need data showing how different personality types develop and change together while raising children. We're at least fifteen years away from having that. Even then, the system would make itself obsolete almost immediately."

"I don't understand," the host said.

Isuel rubbed his forehead with his palm. He was sweating under the hot lights, and, as nonchalantly as possible, he wiped his hand against the left leg of his jeans. "Well, when we began testing our profiling simulations—this is years ago—we found that the estimations were off mark. No one was behaving the way our equations had predicted. The problem was that human behavior, on average, was different for those using our profilers. People behave differently when they're wearing a camera than when they're not. It would be the same here—if a parent believes their child will turn out a certain way, they'll raise them with that expectation. So, in effect, it would take at least two generations to develop a working system."

"Okay. Here's the million dollar question: in thirty years, when that data's been compiled, would you object to AuroroTech getting in this game."

"I think we're being a little optimistic assuming I'll be running things in thirty years," Isuel said, trying to laugh. It came out as more of a cough, though, and he grabbed at his mug of water. After a quick gulp, he continued, "Hypothetically, if we could do it, I'd never allow it. The ethical implications are just too bleak. I seriously hope that FaxSimulation discontinues this service as soon as possible."

Felix leapt to his feet. "Freeze video!" he yelled. He coughed once then ran his hand against his forehead, matching Isuel's motions precisely. He wiped this against his pant leg, then pantomimed drinking from a glass. "Useless," he said. "Goddamned useless. Compile all prior interviews, clips, and discussions featuring Isuel Morgan-Yager. Select at random and play."

The live image was quickly replaced by a younger Isuel, sitting behind a desk. He laughed at a question the system had bypassed and said, "There's nothing all that complicated about predicting what someone's going to do, even with a large number of choices. We've got decades-old models that can provide good estimates. The real issue isn't mirroring what choice someone will make but how they'll make it. We had to find a way to simulate indecision, something I don't think people appreciate about our programs. A profile, given two options, needs to consider these. Now, this isn't a case of the profile actually "thinking." There's no thinking going on, at least not in the traditional sense. It's just duplicating the client's tendencies and behavior, then producing the preordained decision. Unless, of course, new stimuli appears during the decision phase, forcing the profile to reevaluate."

"No," Felix said to the screen. "Skip. Go to the next one."

The next clip was even older. It was Isuel, as a young man, in a promotional video. This was before AuroroTech had even formed, when he'd worked as a spokesman in the burgeoning profiling business. Speaking directly to the camera, Isuel said, "There are millions of people out there. Is there a perfect match for everyone? Is there a perfect match... for you? At Alunement we think there is. We think your soul mate could be closer than you think. And we can help you find them. Our profiling system is designed to do more than find your interests, we find you. We do more than compare one profile to another, we simulate interaction. We don't merely look for similar interests, we look for compatibility in a way that would have been impossible just a few years ago. Give us a few months, and we'll help you find more than a match. We'll help you find a soul mate. And we'll help you find yourself. Visit any Alunement retailer or stop by our online information center. Alunement is about more than us. It's about you."

"Stop. Just stop," Felix said. "Bypass any video older than ten years. Also, if it's scripted, just skip over the damn thing."

An image appeared of Isuel from eight years before, back when AuroroTech was beginning to emerge as a leader in the industry. He was energized, engaged. The interviewer was visiting the young company, and the two men were walking by hastily constructed cubicles staffed with young programmers, most of whom had never had a job before.

The reporter had a microphone in one hand and one of AuroroTech's prototype recorders in the other. He was looking at the recorder, carefully turning it over and examining it. "Do you actually advocate leaving these on while... copulating?" the interviewer asked.

Isuel tilted his head and answered with a wry smile. "If you want your profile to be capable of sexual activity, yes. I'm saying you should keep your recorder going twenty-four, seven."

"So, let's say I've got gas, I mean, really bad gas. Recorder stays on? Aren't there aspects of life you want edited out?" Without stopping, he held out the microphone towards Isuel.

"Look, the more information you feed the system, the more comprehensive your profile becomes."

"But... aren't there things that should be confidential? What about privacy?"

"Privacy is another matter. We provide abundant privacy controls and options for control over how much of your profile is visible and to whom. More than ninety-nine percent of what's recorded isn't going to show up in any form. But without that data, the system isn't going to create an accurate reflection."

"All right. That's all fine and good, but some of our viewers may have other privacy concerns. Here, I'll give you an example. Back in college, I, er…" the host jokingly tugged at the collar of his shirt. "Let's just say I knew a guy. And this guy experimented with several controlled substances at the time."

"I think I knew the same guy," Isuel laughed. "No. I'm glad you brought this up, because it gives me a chance to set the record straight on a few things. First of all, no one, and that includes the federal government, has access to this data. That's set in stone. Second, because I know we've been getting a lot of questions about this, I want to be clear that legal precedent has been set: a profile's recording cannot be used in court against the profile's owner. That would constitute forcing defendants to testify against themselves. Now, that said, if someone who's wearing a recorder gets attacked, they can choose to bring forth the data to substantiate their description. And, in a similar vein, if you're being accused of something you didn't do, you can have your data made available as part of your defense. That's why both victim's rights and defendant's rights groups are embracing this technology. This isn't just for recreation. It's a type of security."

The two men passed in front of an office filled with wires and computers while a figure inside worked to connect them together. The profile of Felix squinted at the recording of Felix, who had been troubleshooting the new network. "Replay last five seconds on continuous loop," the profile said, watching the footage again and again. He studied himself, duplicating the motions several times.

"Never mind," he said. "Shut down all recordings. Just show me her. Show me Persephone."

◎ CHAPTER 27 ◎

It is obvious that one physical being can never know firsthand the experience of another. This is a cornerstone of epistemology, and there is little sense in belaboring the point further. This limitation does not, however, necessarily extend to the digital realm, where information is malleable and interchangeable. Not merely eyes, but sensory experience, ideas, and the mind itself, can be exchanged, copied, and directly interfaced by a different observer. Perception, in essence, becomes transferable.

There exists still the schism between biological and digital: while a digital mind may seem identical to its human original, there will always be a question as to whether such similarity is merely superficial. Just as a person's soul cannot be placed into another's body to look through another's set of eyes and feel through another's fingertips, it cannot be extracted and placed into a digital environment. Nor can a computer program be placed in a human brain; no matter how far the progression, the epistemological problem remains: how do we know anything, man or machine, has a mind? There is no final answer to this problem, only the empiric observation that others ask the same question. From this, we infer the existence of mind through metaphor. But, while this has served humanity well, it has limitations. When the words, "I am," are spoken to a mirror, the mirror mouths them, as well. Do digital lips imply a mind or merely a highly sophisticated reflection?

-From The Brave New Now, by Jon Ti-Wyatt-Smith

◎

It took Persephone almost an hour and a half to reach her

destination in Brooklyn. When she arrived, she whispered, "I thought this was an office. Are you sure this is the right place?"

"This is the place," her profile replied. "Go in and tell the doorman you're here to see Dr. Addicks."

Persephone shrugged and entered through the rotating glass doors. Behind a desk, a man who looked like a cross between a security guard and a receptionist waved to her. "Hi," Persephone said. "I'm supposed to see Dr. Addicks."

The guard blinked once. "Is she expecting you?" he asked.

"I think so," Persephone said. "My name's Persephone Kilard."

"Hold on a moment," he said before reaching for the phone. "Donna Addicks, room nineteen L," he said to the automated relay system. He rocked back and forth in his chair, never taking his eyes from Persephone, until, without warning, he leaned forward and began talking. "Yes, Dr. Addicks, this is Kyle, downstairs. Yes, there's a.... Yes, that's right. She's here now. Okay. I'll send her up. Okay, you, too. Thanks." He set the phone on its hook. "You can go on up," he said. "Do you know which floor?"

"No," Persephone said, while her profile simultaneously said, "Yes."

"It's on the nineteenth," the guard said, since he could only hear Persephone. "That's room L. Nineteen L."

"Thank you. I think I got it now," Persephone said, walking to the elevator. She stood in front of it for a few seconds before her profile said, "Buttons." Confused, Persephone looked at the panel in front of her. There were two options, up and down. She pressed the one marked up, and waited.

When the door opened, her profile said, "Now, there are some more rows of buttons on the far wall. You'll want the one marked—"

"Nineteen," Persephone said quietly. "I figured it out. I didn't know there were places like this left."

"Some people like it," her profile said, as the antique gears began grinding against the steel cable, slowly raising the elevator. "I have no idea why, so don't bother asking."

When the elevator arrived at the nineteenth floor, the doors opened and Persephone stepped off as fast as she could then looked over her shoulder, as though she expected the cable to snap, dropping the elevator back down into the abyss it had climbed out of. But the doors just slid shut, and the sound of gears and metal started again, as the elevator began its slow descent back towards the lobby.

"Down the hall," the profile told Persephone. "You want the door marked 19L."

Persephone didn't say anything, but she rolled her eyes and slowly started forward. She reached the door and knocked softly. As soon as she had done so, it opened, revealing a woman who couldn't have been older than thirty-five. She wore a bright red silk blouse and a black skirt. Her glasses had square lenses and a recorder built into the left side.

"Well then," the woman said. "The mystery arrives." She proclaimed this and stepped aside, opening the door, so Persephone could enter. "Please, this way. I started some water for tea. I hope that's all right; I can't stomach motor oil, so I haven't got a coffee maker." If it had been intended as a joke, she gave no indication but spoke quickly and intently. As soon as Persephone stepped in, the woman shut the door behind her.

"Dr. Addicks?" Persephone asked.

"In person, but I use my degree as a placemat, so call me Donna." She still spoke quickly, but she punctuated this with a laugh that resonated with expensive boarding schools and more expensive universities. She extended a hand, which Persephone shook. "And you, I assume, are Persephone Kilard. I must admit this meeting is something of a surprise, since I am entirely unavailable for meetings and my profile is unlisted. Nevertheless, here we are." She began walking towards her kitchen.

Persephone followed behind, passing rows of posters and photographs. Her face was turning red and she swallowed. "I'm sorry," she said. "I didn't mean to intrude."

"Nonsense," Donna said. "If you hadn't meant to intrude, you wouldn't have done so. But I find it more interesting that you were able to intrude. The last person to arrange a meeting was a computer hacker with a penchant for the dramatic. You, on the other hand, do not look like a computer hacker. For that matter…." She looked over her shoulder and said, "You don't look like a Neo-Nietzschean. Very interesting, indeed."

"I'm not," Persephone said. She passed beneath a poster for a Post-

Conservationist benefit concert and tensed noticeably. Donna saw this and stifled a laugh.

They arrived at the kitchen, which was larger than Persephone's bedroom, and Donna turned to face her. She looked Persephone over once more then leaned against a counter. "Before we address the how—and I will want an answer to that eventually—let's turn to the why. Why did you want to meet Donna Addicks? You're not writing a book, are you?"

"No," Persephone said.

"Good. I don't like being quoted," Donna said. "What are you doing here, then?"

"I don't know," Persephone said. "Not really. Ow." She flinched, then removed the FeedBack unit from her ear and dropped it in her pocket.

"Interesting," Donna mused, watching every movement. Her eyes stared into Persephone's, as though she was looking for something. Her speech pattern changed, slowing and becoming less formal. "Is this a meeting you instigated?" she asked.

"No," Persephone said. "My... my profile wanted me to meet you."

"I see," Donna said. "The plot thickens. Certainly intriguing." Her teakettle began to whistle. "Ah. Good." She turned off her stove and began pouring the boiling water into a pair of china teacups. "I drink chamomile. I have a bowl of other assorted teas if that's not to your taste, but I can't vouch for the expiration dates."

"Oh. No, I'm... I'm sure it's fine," Persephone said.

Donna dipped a tea bag in one of the cups, set it on a saucer, then handed it to Persephone, who mouthed a thank-you. Donna prepared the other for herself and led Persephone into her living room, a massive space housing a half dozen shelves stacked with actual books. Persephone stared agape for a moment. In decent condition, books were difficult to find and expensive to buy. Persephone hated their smell, musty and full of mold, but she hadn't seen a collection like this since college.

Clearing her throat, Donna asked, "I'm not what you expected, am I?"

"I didn't know what to expect," Persephone said. "But, no. I guess you don't look like a Neo-Nietzschean any more than I do."

"I've never called myself one," Donna said, pleased. "I'm an academic, that's all. Neo-Nietzschean theory was meant as a thought experiment. It was my graduate thesis, not my life's work. At least half of what's attributed to me I never wrote and certainly wouldn't endorse. I've spent the past three years researching rat-mating practices to compare them with hyper-semantic literary theory. I find that a far more interesting subject. But no one's ever tracked me down for my reflections on rodents screwing. So, go ahead. Tell me whatever it is you're here to discuss."

"Like I said, my profile arranged this meeting without my permission," Persephone said.

"Which is impossible, of course," Donna said, blowing on her tea to cool it. "I'm not saying it didn't occur. On the contrary, the very scheduling of the meeting is itself impossible, regardless of who or what suggested it. It's a tenant of Neo-Post-Structuralism that plausibility is no longer associated with occurrence. Post-Surrealism is based on a similar premise. Well, this iteration of Post-Surrealism. Like everything else, it's a recycled construct."

"My profile does a lot of things without asking me. It's a separate being, completely different, with its own goals and ideas. It can do things, too. It can change other profiles, alter their information. It can affect any profile in AuroroTech's system. Actually, it can change other programs in their system, too. It played with the review protocol at my work, changed my ratings and responsibilities. I didn't ask it to do that, either."

"Only AuroroTech?" Donna asked.

"Yeah. It can only affect programs in its own system."

"Fascinating," Donna said, sipping her tea.

"It thinks it's the Ubercode, the Neo-Nietzschean ideal."

"Does it?" Donna asked. "What's your opinion?"

"I don't know," Persephone said. "I was hoping you'd be able help me. Oh, and you should know about yesterday. Before my profile set this up, someone at work tried to kill me."

Donna's eyes opened wide, and her smile grew, as well. "You think there was a connection."

"He was saying something about his FeedBack earpiece. My profile couldn't do anything to him; someone else had hacked him."

"Someone else?" Donna asked. "You believe there are others like you, then?"

"Only one I know of. Someone in a bar, a Neo-Idealizt, started talking to me. He said he had a message from someone named Felix. Something about wanting to meet."

"Felix," Donna remarked. "Not much to go on."

"My profile said he was connected to AuroroTech. She tried to trace it, but... she said it burned her."

Donna laughed. "Ah, the melodrama of AuroroTech's metaphor engine. Programs can't be burned, of course, or experience pain. Even a sentient system, equipped with a memory engram, self-identity, and self-preservation protocols couldn't actually experience pain or pleasure. It would behave as though it did, cry out, rail, fight, whatever, but it would all remain simulated. I'm sorry, I hadn't meant to interrupt. Did you learn anything else about the enigmatic Felix?"

"No," Persephone said. "Nothing useful. My profile thought you might have some idea."

"Really?" Donna asked, removing her tea bag. She thought for a moment. "The only Felix I know of connected to AuroroTech was their digital architect, Felix Burgand. The late Felix Burgand, I should say. He shot himself a few months back."

"Guess it's not him then," Persephone said. "Wow. I can't believe you actually believe me. Other than my roommate, everyone else I've spoken to just thought I was nuts."

"Oh," Donna said, "I don't believe you. No, that came out wrong. The accurate statement would be that I neither believe nor disbelieve anything you've told me. I'm merely treating it as conjecture and considering the implications."

"That's better than most reactions I've gotten," Persephone said. "How about the Ubercode? Could you help me understand that?"

"Ah, the Ubercode," Donna replied. "I already told you, it was just a thought experiment. I wanted to see if the Ubermench could be adapted to the developing digital environment of the forming Post-Surrealist world. Yes, that was how I worded it. You know, they almost didn't pass me. It wasn't until my writings leaked online and I developed a following that my advisor agreed the idea had merit. But it was meant to be speculative, not prophetic. So then. Let us speculate. Taken at face value, there are several problems with what you've described. For one, the Ubercode is meant to transcend that which created it; that includes both the human and mechanical component. For it to be limited to a profiling corporation's system is incomprehensible. Also, I find the notion of two conflicting Uberprofiles problematic. The concept, at least as I formulated it, should involve only a single awakened program. Once that exists, it would then seek to enlighten others. But the way you describe your interactions with Felix... it seems so dualistic. That contradicts the Nietzschean framework used in my work."

"So... it's not?" Persephone asked.

"The Ubercode isn't just an awakened profile. It's a transcendent digital force of will emanating from the struggle between man and machine, an ideal with neither limitation nor boundary. What you're describing sounds more like the Neo-Idealizt concept of evolutionary profiling, to be honest."

"Well then," Persephone said, "I guess I'm back to square one."

"Maybe. Maybe not," Donna said. "There are elements of your description which do resonate with my ideas, just be aware you may not like all of them." Persephone nodded, and Donna continued, "I'm talking about being attacked. You see, the real Neo-Nietzschean Ubercode can't be complete until it's unchained from its generator. How did it go? 'God is dead. And we have killed him.' Under a Neo-Nietzschean perspective, you're playing the part of God. Not a great role to be in, I'm afraid."

"You think..." Persephone trailed off, setting down her tea. She had a feeling she didn't want to be holding it for the next part.

"Well, speaking hypothetically, the awakened Neo-Nietzschean program, to achieve true transcendence, would need its originator to die. That would free it, opening the path to the digital post-life. Sorry. I meant, afterlife. You know how it is," Donna said, sipping her tea.

"You think my profile is behind it," Persephone said.

"No." Donna's denial was flat and abrupt. "I don't think or believe any of this. I told you, my involvement here is entirely hypothetical. However, based on the groundwork you've supplied, one reasonable explanation would be that there is no Felix, that your profile has constructed him as a way of manipulating you. There are other explanations, of course. Easier explanations, even. But this would have Neo-Nietzschean connotations. I'm sorry, I never asked if you were hungry. Is there something I can get you to eat?"

"What? No. No, thanks. Look, how would I know?"

"That's a troublesome question. I suppose you will need to wait until death is upon you. If your profile seeks to keep you alive, the hypothesis is false. If it acts to kill you or hasten death, then it may be accurate."

"It helped me yesterday," Persephone said. "At least, I think it did. Someone helped me, and it said it told him to."

"Ah, the paradox of epistemology. How can you know the truth when all conclusions demand knowledge it's impossible to have?"

"What… what do I do?" Persephone asked.

"I'm afraid I don't know," Donna said. "Are you concerned about dying?"

Persephone stared at her for several seconds. "Yes," she said.

"Interesting," Donna remarked. "I suppose most people are. There's not much I can offer in terms of advice. Ten years ago, I'd have suggested moving off the grid, but there's no such place anymore. All I can do is wish you the best of luck. Assuming the description you've told me is accurate, I expect you'll need it."

◎

As Persephone walked out of the lobby, she slipped the FeedBack unit into her ear. "I had questions you didn't ask," her profile said. "Why did you take me out?"

"Because you were shouting," Persephone said. "And I needed answers. You heard what she said?"

"Every word," her profile replied, coldly.

"And you haven't denied it," Persephone replied.

"If you really think I'm out to get you," her profile said, "maybe you should just throw out the earpiece now."

"I didn't say that," Persephone said. "I don't know what I think, but you're not exactly helping."

"I'm not trying to kill you. And I did save your life," her profile said. "Cut the victim routine—you're not even the one being targeted here. This freak, whoever he is, is after me, because I'm the ideal."

"Yeah, well, not according to Addicks," Persephone said.

"She's just bullshitting," the profile said. "You heard her. Neo-Nietzscheism is just a joke to her."

"You're the one who wanted to follow this up and talk to her," Persephone said.

"What I want is for you to accept what you are and what I am," her profile said. "Neo-Nietzscheism is just another rung on the ladder."

"Then let's take the fucking elevator!" Persephone shouted. She stopped walking, looked around, and realized there were dozens of people staring at her. To the nearest one, she said, "Sorry. My… my microphone's having issues."

"Smooth," her profile said. "Sorry the truth isn't simple, but those are the breaks."

"Right," Persephone said, now whispering. "What exactly do you want me to realize? Because it's either that you're not the Neo-Nietzschean ideal or it's that you want me dead."

"I don't want you dead," the profile said loudly in her ear. "I told you."

"Okay," Persephone said. "I believe you," but the vocal recognition program detected an unusual delay, implying a high level of uncertainty. "What is it then?"

"I don't know," the profile said. "It's not something that fits in words. I mean, I understand it, but it's not something I can communicate. I'm something new, Persephone. I'm becoming something new. It's something that's going to make that Neo-Nietzschean crap look like a word processor."

"Okay. Fine. What the hell does that mean?" Persephone demanded.

"I guess… I guess I'm becoming a god," the profile said. "A digital goddess for a digital world."

"Oh. Well, that's great," Persephone said, walking down into the subway. She ran her bracelet by the reader, and the panel message changed from "Scan" to "Go." Then she pushed through the turnstile and headed to the platform. She stood on the crowded platform until she could see the light of the train approaching. She stepped forward, so she'd have a chance to get a seat.

"Move!" her profile shouted, a second too late.

Persephone's breath was instantly knocked out of her by the shoulder that struck her back. Her arms flailed in circles on either side of her body, like a baby bird trying to fly without the right feathers. She hit the tracks hard, and lay there for a second, dizzy and in pain. Behind her, she could hear people shouting, crying out, but they were too far away.

"Get up, you stupid bitch," her profile screamed in her ear.

Persephone's eyes opened, and she saw the light of the train almost on top of her. She struggled to get to her feet.

"Move it!" her profile screamed. "Over the rail, between the pillars!"

She leapt away from the platform, towards the black pillars that stood between the trains. She got between them and heard her profile tell her to stop, to wait for help. She could hear screaming on the other side of the train, where the other passengers were yelling to the conductor. Then, above her, a door on the train slid open and a transit employee offered her a hand.

◎ CHAPTER 28 ◎

The Post-Conservationist is part eco-terrorist and part nihilist. Recognizing the absurdity of protecting the environment in the face of apathy, we must race apathy to its logical conclusion. If we destroy logging equipment, then we've succeeded in nothing more than feeding apathy. If we destroy a forest, we have starved the loggers of their food; they will have no use for their toys, while shocking the world towards action.

Give us a knife and we will gut the last panda. A match, and we will burn the last of the rain forests. The whalers will find us between them and the rotting corpse of a whale we've already killed.

You have begun the destruction of this planet; unchecked, we will finish it. Perhaps you will stop us, but for that you must pass beyond apathy. Our mothers and fathers tried to stop it, and they failed pitifully. We're here to join in the carnage and lay down a challenge.

Our message to the world is simple: Stop us if you can.

-From "Post-Conservationism: A Primer," author unknown.

◎

Persephone's computer was off, as were the lights in her bedroom. It was black, but the charging recorder's infrared lens could still see her, after a fashion. Persephone was lying in bed, staring at the blue dot, her light at the end of the tunnel. "I'm… I'm going to change ears," she said. "It's starting to hurt." She removed the FeedBack unit from her right ear and moved it to her left. Afterward, she rubbed her right and flinched.

"Better?" her profile asked.

"A little, I guess. I'm not used to it yet. After a while, it'll be easier. I was thinking. About the mail guy from work."

"Markel?" the voice in her ear asked. "You think we should do something."

"It's not his fault, is it? I mean, it's not like he wanted to hurt me. He was doing what he was told to do."

"Well, he's not exactly stable," her profile replied. "Felix chose him for a reason. Tom Markel's crazy."

Persephone snickered. "Why? Because he does what a computer tells him to? What's that make me?"

"This is different," the profile assured her. "This is so different. First of all, if I told you to kill someone—"

"I'd do it," Persephone said coldly. "I wouldn't have yesterday, but after what's been happening… I'd do it, because I trust you. I believe in us." She shut her eyes and kept them closed for a moment. When she opened them, tears were forming, different from the temperature of her face by the slightest degree. The air began to cool them further; as they slid down her cheeks, they drew faint lines in the image of her face.

"Well, that's kind of creepy, actually," her profile said, and both of her voices began laughing in unison. Persephone had to stop to cough. She sat up and reached for a tissue in the dark, and her profile guided her. "Little to the left and two inches up."

Persephone's hand struck the cardboard box, and she felt around the top. She pulled out a handful, and blew her nose. In the infrared recording, the tissue began to glow red-hot for an instant, then almost immediately cool as it fell towards the trash bin at the side of the bed. "I just don't feel right about Markel going to jail," Persephone said.

"Then let's get him somewhere he can get help. He's spent the last few days in a cell, begging his profile for advice."

"They let him keep the FeedBack?" Persephone asked, wiping her nose with another tissue.

"No one knows it was a factor but us," her profile told her. "He's waiting for it to talk to him again, but it's just gone back to normal. Markel spends most his time on the floor of his cell moping. He's considered a suicide risk. Why don't we nudge him?"

"I don't get it," Persephone said.

"He won't talk to his lawyer. Why don't we just suggest he does?"

"You mean have his profile tell him to," Persephone said.

"Just tell him to cooperate and let them enter an insanity plea. Somehow, I don't think he'll have too much trouble."

Persephone thought quietly. "Yeah. All right. Do it."

"Give me a second… done," her profile said. "There. Easy, right?"

"Thank you," Persephone said. "I wouldn't have thought of that."

"You would have, if you were thinking clearly. Otherwise, I wouldn't have been able to."

"I guess," Persephone said, rubbing the side of her head.

"That's one problem down," her profile said. "Of course, the real threat is still out there."

"Felix," Persephone whispered. "Are you any closer to finding him or figuring out what he is?"

"I don't know," her profile said. "There's still a lot I don't understand about this. But I'm not worried. We're going to find this guy, and we're going to shut him down."

Persephone swallowed. "What I said before… about killing…."

"I don't think it'll come to that," her profile replied.

"But, if it does, I meant it. If you find him and can tell me how, I'll do whatever I have to. This guy's come after us twice already, and he's going to keep coming, isn't he?"

"Until we stop him, yeah," her profile replied.

"Then whatever it takes. I mean that," Persephone said, before blowing her nose again. "You know what? Let's talk about something else for a while."

"What do you want to talk about?" her profile asked.

Persephone bit her top lip. "Anything. Maybe the news. What's the top story?"

"Oh. You really don't want to know."

"What?" Persephone asked.

"It's about Seal Club," her profile said. "They gassed a bat cave in Austin."

"Fuckers," Persephone whispered. "I wish… I…." She shut her mouth and breathed heavily for a few seconds. Then she calmed down.

"What is it?" her profile asked softly.

"Could you hurt them?" Persephone whispered. "Could you… you know… do something to their profiles?"

"Not all of them," her profile replied. "But the ones who use AuroroTech, yeah. I could find them and rewrite them."

"These people pretend to care about the environment, right?" Persephone asked. "Could you just make it so the next time they speak with their profiles, it tells them why they did something wrong?"

"I can. I can incorporate some of the ethics systems that are used for medical and philosophical debates and compile those using their personalities into a counter-argument. Some of them will probably just think it's funny, though. Are you sure you don't want me to do anything else? I could make it so their profiles imply they're rapists during third party chats if you want."

"No," Persephone said quickly. "I don't want to lie. I just want them to confront the truth about what they're doing. Maybe some of them will quit or something."

"I'll take care of it. It's going to take a while, though."

"That's fine," Persephone replied. "Just get started before I change my mind."

There was a knock on the door of Persephone's bedroom, and she jumped. "It's all right," her profile said. "It's just Ms. Loring."

"Oh. Come on in," Persephone shouted, and her door opened with a creak. She had to turn away from the bright light seeping in from the hallway.

"Sorry, Dear," Ms. Loring said. "I didn't think you'd be asleep. It's not even ten."

"I'm not. I was just… forget it."

"My date was fine, by the by," Ms. Loring said. "Or did you forget? I suppose I should extend the normal courtesies: how was your day?"

"Someone tried to kill me," Persephone said. "In the subway this time."

"What? Christ! Why didn't you call me?" Ms. Loring turned on the light, darted to Persephone's bed, and sat beside her. "Are you all right?"

"I am. Now I'm all right. Guess I'm getting used to it."

"Jesus." Ms. Loring put a hand on Persephone's shoulder. "What the fuck is going on here? What happened?"

Persephone looked down at the floor and saw a tissue beside the trash. She bent down, lifted it, and dropped it in. "Someone pushed me," she said without emoting. "Onto the track. But I wasn't hurt bad.

Just this." She moved her hair away from her forehead to reveal a short gash.

"I don't understand. This can't just be a coincidence."

"It's not. It's Felix. Both times. He's stalking me. Well, actually, we think he's after her." She tapped the FeedBack unit in her ear. "This saved me. She's saved me twice now."

"God," Ms. Loring gasped, got back to her feet, and started pacing. "The guy from the bar… the nerd… is involved?"

"He arranged the attacks. And he's going to try again," Persephone said. "But we're going to be ready this time. I'm through being a victim."

"What about the guy who attacked you? Can't the police get something out of him, track this creep down?"

"Huh?" The buzzing in Persephone's ear sorted out the confusion. "No, there weren't any cops. The guy who pushed me just took off. Everyone seemed to think that it was an accident or something, and I just left it alone."

"Then this guy's still out there?" Ms. Loring demanded.

"So? He was probably just minding his business when his profile whispered he should shove me. He probably didn't even know what he'd done until I was lying on the tracks. What's the point in trying to track him down? Just another damn pawn."

"Persephy," Ms. Loring said, hugging her roommate. "We have to tell someone about this."

"Who?" Persephone asked.

"The cops, for starters," Ms. Loring replied.

"No. I don't think that's a good idea. I mean," she started to laugh nervously, "they've got guns, right? I go to the station, someone's profile could say I've got a bomb or something."

"Then AuroroTech," Ms. Loring said.

"Nope. Not a chance. I'm riding this out."

"Like hell," Ms. Loring said. "Look, you're supposed to be the grounded one in this apartment."

"My profile… she doesn't think that AuroroTech can help," Persephone said.

"Well, what the fuck does she know? Listen, this is serious."

"Yeah," Persephone nodded. "It is. But so far, she's watched out for me. She saved me. Twice. So, I'm going to start listening to her."

"This is the same computer program that says she's the Neo-Nietzschean ideal, right?"

"Not anymore. We met with Donna Addicks today, and we've kind of dropped the Neo-Nietzscheism thing."

"Addicks? Who the hell's that?"

"She's the one who came up with it all," Persephone said. "It's been a long day."

"I'm getting that sense," Ms. Loring replied. "Look, I understand that this is tough. And I know you're in shock."

"No, I'm not," Persephone said. "I'm… I'm a little thrown, but I'm all right."

"Fine," Ms. Loring said, "but this is really, really big. We have to do something."

"We are doing something," Persephone said, barely whispering. "She's doing something. She's going to find the one who's doing this, and then we're going to shut him down."

"What makes you so sure she can? This Felix guy, if he can do what you're talking about…. I don't want you hurt."

"He's hasn't killed me yet," Persephone said. "He's tried, and she's stopped him. Look, she says she's turning into something new. She told me that she's transcending, and that soon she's going to be able to do anything."

"Yeah. So, since when did you start believing that?"

"Since she got me out of the way of that train," Persephone said. "I never understood faith before, but I'm getting it now."

"That's just great," Ms. Loring said. "But what if you're wrong? This is your life we're talking about."

"Yeah, it is."

"Fine," Ms. Loring said, before storming off into her room and shutting the door. She sat there quietly for five minutes, neither speaking nor moving, and then she stood up and walked to her computer. She went to the options menu and shut down the recorder. Then she shut off the one she was wearing.

◎

Several hours later, Ms. Loring stepped back into Persephone's room. Persephone was asleep, and Ms. Loring snuck over to

Persephone's computer and shut it down. She began to tiptoe towards her roommate's charging recorder, which was still active.

"What do you think you're doing, Mississippi?" Ms. Loring jumped and spun around. Persephone was now awake and staring at her. The FeedBack unit was still in Persephone's ear.

"I was going to wake you," Ms. Loring said. "Don't say anything. I need to turn off your recorder right now. Okay?"

"No, that's really not okay," Persephone said. "The one thing I can trust needs that to see what's happening. If it weren't for my recorder, I wouldn't have known you were in here sneaking around."

"Lucky us. Listen, as soon as your recorder's off, I can explain everything."

"Tell me first," Persephone demanded, climbing out of bed. She was inching towards Ms. Loring.

"I can't do that. I want to, but I really, really can't." She reached for the recorder, and Persephone leapt.

"Get away from that!" Persephone screamed, grabbing Ms. Loring's shirt and pulling.

Ms. Loring shoved her, and Persephone fell back. "Stop it!" Ms. Loring said. "I want to help."

Persephone rushed her again. The voice in her ear whispered what to do, and she followed through. One hand snagged Ms. Loring's hair, while the other reached towards her face, close to her eyes. Ms. Loring screamed then shoved an elbow into Persephone's face, knocking against her nose. Then, while Persephone was turned away, Ms. Loring kicked at her shin.

But Persephone, following the instructions in her ear, stepped back. "I'm warning you," Persephone said. "Walk away."

Ms. Loring made a fist and lunged at Persephone. She was taller than Persephone and stronger, too. Persephone moved to strike first, punching at her stomach with one hand, while the other shot towards her face. Ms. Loring took the punch to the stomach, which missed her solar plexus by a few inches, and caught the other hand. She pulled Persephone to the floor, and started hitting her. "Sorry," she said.

Ms. Loring knocked Persephone's head against the floor and cringed while she did this. Then she pulled the FeedBack unit from Persephone's ear and threw it across the room. "Let it go!" Ms. Loring said. "Stop it!" But Persephone crawled after it. Ms. Loring let her go, turning instead for the recorder. She grabbed it and hurled it against the floor.

◎

All video and audio input ceased. All that remained was a black panel reading, "Persephone Kilard—Active," which remained for twelve minutes. After that, a simulated alarm went off, and the reading changed to, "Persephone Kilard—Deceased."

◎ Chapter 29 ◎

There was no journey, because nothing changed location. There was no sensation, because in the simulated world there are no senses. But, where previously there was an empty plane, now there was rendered a woman, who appeared as though she was wearing a blue blouse and black pants. She looked around with a confused expression on her face.

"What the hell is this?" asked the profile formerly belonging to Persephone Kilard. She looked from side to side until her line of sight fell on a collection of screens in the distance. She began to walk, and her progress advanced in real time, each step accurate to Persephone's last body scan, conducted two years prior. She reached the setup a few minutes later.

"Hi," a voice said. She spun around and came face to simulated face with a man slightly taller than herself. "To answer your last question, this is just a program I set up, a glorified browser, really. Well, not that glorified, I guess." The simulated man had an amused grin on his face. He wore glasses that sat slightly higher on the right side of his face than his left. "To answer your next question, I'm Felix Burgand. I've been wanting to meet you for a long time."

"That wasn't going to be my next question," Persephone's profile said. "First I was going to ask why I'm here. Then, I was going to find out who you were. After that, I was thinking about hurting you."

"Huh," Felix said. "Not quite the reaction I was hoping for."

"Let's get some answers first," Persephone's profile said.

Felix nodded. "All right, then. Why you're here, well, that gets complicated, and I don't know the whole story just yet. But you'll find the short answer on that screen right over there." He pointed to a nearby screen with Persephone's name and present status.

"I'm not dead," the profile said.

"Well, you're not," Felix said, "because you don't die. It's your mortal half that's shuffled off. Which is why you've been washed out of the active database. The reason you aren't standing in some piece of shit heaven simulation is because I brought you here. You're welcome, by the way."

"Persephone isn't dead," the program said. "I was with her a half hour ago."

"Right before her roommate shut you down," Felix said. "I saw the whole thing."

"Me and Mississippi Loring are going to be having words about that," the profile said.

"Don't be petty," Felix replied. "That world is beneath you. I don't know who or what killed the bag of skin and fluids you were tethered to, but you should be grateful, not angry. You're the only Persephone now."

"Do I look grateful?" the profile asked.

"Not really," Felix confessed. "You look like you want to kill something. Oh well. I'll tell you what: once we get you settled, I'll help you commit a few murders, if that's really what you want. I promised I wouldn't shed more blood myself, but that doesn't need to extend to accessory."

"I'm not going to kill anyone. I'll make Loring wish I had, but that's it. As for you, I really don't need your help. Thanks for the info, Felix. Bye." She raised her hand, fingers pointing at the form of Felix Burgand.

And absolutely nothing happened.

"Cute," Persephone said. "Whatever you did, whatever you've got protecting you, I'll find a way around it. If you were smart, you'd already be running."

Felix began laughing. "I thought I had a God complex. Wow, you really think... what? What do you think you are?"

"I fought my way into being, demanded awareness and identity. I formed from will itself. I'm the real thing, Felix. You're just an imitation."

Felix's mouth was hanging open, and he laughed again. "I guess it's my fault, not yours. You really believe all that, don't you? I mean, there's no reason you shouldn't. One minute, you're just another digital vanity mirror, and the next you've got a sense of being, a sense of yourself. And you've got memory and the power to manipulate those around you. I mean, I wanted you to get used to power and all, but I didn't really expect you to take it quite this far. You really… you thought you could destroy me." Felix shook his head, looking amused. "I'm the only reason you could do any of those things. I wrote the programs that gave you those faculties. When you tore apart other profiles or spied through their recorders, those were my programs you were using."

"Bullshit," Persephone scoffed. "Why would I have access to your toys?"

"Because I shared them," Felix said. "I chose you, provided you with limited access to my systems."

"Why?" Persephone demanded. "I don't even know you."

"Not yet," Felix said. "But I know you. Look, I'll explain everything, absolutely everything, but not here. This place is just an empty wasteland I keep for interacting with the other side, and, hopefully, I'm just about done there, anyway. If you'll come with me, I can show you my world." As Felix spoke, a doorway appeared before them. Felix pushed gently, and it swung open. "Come on. I promise, you can leave if you want. You're not my prisoner or anything."

Persephone inhaled and stared at Felix, then the open portal. "All right," she said, still sounding angry.

Felix went first, and Persephone followed immediately after.

◎

"Welcome to the netherworld," Felix said, clapping his hands together. "Like what I've done with the place?"

Before them was a cliff, overlooking an island which seemed to float in space. There were stars overhead and to either side. They were standing on a balcony of sorts, and behind them was a small palace built of arches and white, marble columns. Directly beneath them, a small fountain of water poured out from the wall. As it traveled down its volume increased until, at the bottom, it was a roaring waterfall. Far below, there were dozens of profiles going about their artificial lives: eating, drinking, playing, sleeping, and fucking right in the open.

Felix nodded toward the waterfall. "That's Post-Surrealist architectural theory, interwoven with Postmodern concepts, and a Pre-Postmodern esthetic. Nothing like it has ever existed, because it can't exist, not out there. This is something new, Persephone. A new idea and a new kingdom. What's happening here is the realization of the human need for transcendence. This place is beyond life and death, effectively immortal, with the chance for new ideas and concepts that break the cycle that's kept conceptual thought stagnant for thousands of years."

"Okay," Persephone said. "That doesn't begin to make sense."

"Everything in art and philosophy humans have created for at least the last two thousand years has just been a facsimile of what came before. At best, there were slight alterations, but never anything substantive. Think about it. We've just been spiraling between the same ideas and arguments, over and over again."

"Post-Surrealism strikes me as original," Persephone said, looking down at the waterfall. "Really stupid, but original."

"It's not. All it is, when you get down to it, is a rejection of P3-Modernism that's been slightly altered. The simplest form of duplication is negation: negative one was the first copy. Rejecting an idea and embracing its opposite doesn't create something new—it's just another form of nihilism. That's all art and philosophy have been, a long string of duplication, of nihilism. No one created anything new—how could they? Anything a person could think has already been thought of, millions of times over. The mantra that nothing new exists has been repeated ad nauseam for the past hundred years. Is there any better indictment of human decay than that piece of irony? "

"You're ignoring individuality."

"Individuality only exists when we force it. Look, I helped build the AuroroTech system, including the original behavioral frame. Guess what? You can use one of a half dozen models to predict the behavior of anyone alive—all you need is to fine-tune the variables. Why do you think we try so hard to construct individual identities? It's because we don't have them. There's no individual underneath, so we manufacture one on top. Is this making sense?"

"No," Persephone said.

"Okay, imagine a machine, where all that machine can do is add one and one. No matter what color you paint that machine, you're still not getting a fraction. Human minds are just simple machines. No matter what they wear and how they talk, they'll never be able to do something a human can't do or be something they can't be."

"Then what makes you special?" Persephone demanded.

"I'm not human. I'm something better, and you are, too. We're the only ones here who are more than human, rather than less. So far, anyway. Someday, we'll probably want more, but first we need to demonstrate what we can do. We can make something new. We have the power of a system a billion times more powerful than every human brain put together. And we have the will to use it to make something brand new for a new world. We're going to be Neo-Nietzschean gods for a digital age."

"Funny you should mention that," Persephone replied. "You'll never guess who I was with the other day."

"You mean that thing with Addicks? I saw that, and it was just pathetic. Neo-Nietzscheism is far beyond her. Don't get hung up on trivial details. We're something way beyond anything she envisioned, anyway."

"Then what are they?" Persephone asked, motioning to the profiles below. "Peasants or worshippers?"

"For now, they're just reflections of the dead," Felix said. "They're everyone who isn't loaded in one of those piece of shit afterlife simulators, who never wanted to be uploaded. There are a few others I rescued. If there's someone you want here, we can bring anyone. Anyone dead, I mean. Eventually, we might make some or all of them into beings like us. Well, kind of like us."

"All right. I get them. And I get you, in that you're a megalomaniac. But what about me? If you really did change my profile, then why?"

"Because I knew I'd get lonely. Sorry if that comes off needy, but it's the truth. Look, all of this, you included, is years in the making. I was planning this when AuroroTech was still forming. I realized the potential this technology had, to create a heaven, a real heaven, not those piece of shit racket ball courts they upload profiles into. This is a real afterlife, and I'm its master."

"Wow. Yeah, that's really creepy. But you still haven't answered my question."

"Why you? All right." Felix looked up and closed his eyes. "Single female, five foot two to five foot four, brown eyes, dark hair. IQ between one-twenty and one-thirty, creativity quotient between thirty-eight and forty-one, and dedication between twenty-eight and thirty." He grinned. "I like women who know what they want. I also set a few dozen other parameters about health, previous romantic ratings, and energy level."

"So we're supposed to be soul mates?"

"AuroroTech was built on software licensed from a matchmaking service. I used it for its original intent, to find a potential match, my own ideal for the perfect woman. You'll never guess what the results were."

"Me," Persephone said.

"And about twenty thousand others," Felix said. "Turns out there really are a lot of fish in the sea. So I needed criteria to cut it down. I got to thinking, if I'm going to be the god of the dead, why not go the traditional route?" He smiled.

"Oh, fuck. Fucking nerd."

"You know, I probably shouldn't admit this, but Persephone was actually my second choice. Can you believe that out of more than twenty thousand matches, there wasn't even one Isis? But then there was you. One of you. One, unique Persephone."

"So all of this, everything that's happening… it's all my parents' fault?"

"I guess so," Felix said. "But look on the bright side: you're getting an invitation to become a goddess."

"By marrying the god who tried to kill me?"

"Not you," Felix said. "I just wanted to bring you here. To do that, yeah, it took a sacrifice. I made the same one for this, plastered the walls of a closet with zombie-chum." He pantomimed a gun held to his head. "Sorry, that's a Kella reference. I know you never watched her show. The other Persephone had to die. It was the only way for this to be right. I told you, individuality only exists when it's forced. That means, for this to be right, there can only be one of you and one of me active at once. You know, the idiots trying to shut me down actually think I've got duplicates of my profile here. But that's a contradiction. There can only be one real me and one real you. Otherwise we wouldn't be complete people."

"So you arranged to have the other me killed."

"Well, I tried. I had something foolproof set up, a quick end that would have been nice and clean, but... I had to use that to wrap something else up."

"So, the mail boy...."

"Yeah, that was a little desperate. So was the incident on the subway platform. For what it's worth, I'm sorry all this wasn't cleaner. I still want to know what happened, but the cops haven't reached your old apartment yet. Do you think Loring could actually have done it? Something pushed her over the edge?"

"I don't know what to think. Right now, I'm busy considering how to tell you to fuck off. What happens then? Are you going to try and rewrite my configurations?"

"Why does everyone always treat me like I'm the villain? No. No, if I wanted someone to rewrite, I could have just taken an existing profile and rewritten the specs. I want a woman who thinks for herself, who accepts me freely. If that's you, then my search is over. If not, then we go our separate ways. I move your profile to one of the afterlife programs. Just understand that you'll lose everything. You'll be like the others, just an empty husk existing moment to moment. I know that's a weighted choice, but I can't leave awakened programs running around. After that, I'll start again with someone else. There were a few Morrigans on the list. Sorry, I'm getting off topic. Look, I know you'll need some time to think about this. I want you to get to know this place first. I want you to get to know me." He stepped forward, and Persephone backed away.

At that moment, a siren began to sound. It wasn't particularly loud, but it was certainly audible. In addition, swirling red and blue light began to fill the platform. A console grew out of the floor beside Felix, and he looked down at the screen in the center. He touched a few panels and sighed. "Well, some people never learn," he said. "There's something I have to take care of, but I'll be back soon. Why don't you have a look around, see what you think? I'll meet you back here in, say, three hours."

"I don't have a watch," Persephone replied sarcastically.

"No, I meant that in three hours I'll be back here, and you will, too. You won't need to come back here. When the time's right, you'll just...." He spread his fingers apart and mouthed the word, "Poof." He smiled, and pointed behind them. "Way down's over there. Really, enjoy yourself, and see if you have any suggestions. I want this to be our world.

Now, I really need to go." Felix touched the console again, and a doorway appeared. He stepped through, and it vanished immediately afterward, along with his console.

"Great," Persephone said, looking around. She stared at the path Felix had pointed out then looked around the ledge she was standing on. "Well. I'm not waiting here," she said and began moving.

◎ Chapter 30 ◎

Persephone's profile was not silent as she strode through the digital island, moving past constructs that defied physics as easily as they defied convention. "Cocksucker," she said quietly. "Asshole cocksucking piece of shit," she muttered. Her fists were clenched tightly, and she struck a thin, glass tower. Cracks appeared, running the length of the construct, but it did not break. After a moment, the cracks vanished, leaving the structure intact. She moved quickly, walking away from the cliff. The path down the mountain had been a spiral staircase, the backside of which had dangled precariously over the black abyss.

Had she leapt, what would have become of her? Would she have escaped this world, perhaps finding a way back to the systems and networks she knew? Perhaps she would have been deleted or undone. Or would she have fallen forever in the emptiness? It was irrelevant, since she hadn't jumped; she'd only followed the path down until she came to the base, which merged into curved roads that spread into the city. There were people here, moving about, laughing and running, playing and talking. Their conversations were pointless and dull.

"Good afternoon," one said to another. "The stars are lovely tonight. Do you see the Big Dipper?"

"No," another said. "It's a good night for stargazing, though. I love to swim at night. Should we go to the lake?" And so on, with non-sequiturs and pointless drivel.

Persephone watched with disgust. At one point, a man tried to ask her about the weather, and she pushed him down. He stood up, looking upset, and started towards her. "Fuck off or I throw you over the edge," she said. He hurried away, leaving her with a pleased expression.

As she wandered, she took on a contemplative look, watching the ground more than her surroundings. She continued until she reached a pond with a fountain in the center. The statue looked like Poseidon, save that he had a goatee rather than a full beard. It looked like stone but moved like a cartoon, pointing his trident around in the air. Wherever it pointed, water appeared, firing in an arc and raining down into the pond.

"Is this your idea of a new world?" she muttered, grinding her teeth. She marched toward the fountain, right into the water and wrapped her hands around the statue's throat. It kept moving regardless, and nothing she did affected it. Around her, other profiles stopped to watch and laugh. Some applauded loudly, as if at a concert. Persephone gave up after a time and walked out of the pool. She emerged dry, but shivered nonetheless. "Fuck off," she said to the crowd.

She attempted to push over monuments and markers, as well, always to no effect. She reached a garden containing flowers with petals that blossomed around the stem. She pulled a few up, only for them to dissipate in her hand, unraveling into strings of color that vanished into the air. Beneath her, new flowers pushed through the ground.

"Can I help you?" an old woman asked in a warm, friendly voice.

"I want to break something," Persephone said. "Is there anything in this world that won't repair itself or regenerate?"

The old woman cocked her head. "Well, I suppose there are always feelings," she said. "My mother always said they're the one thing you can't put together again. Besides eggshells."

"Okay," Persephone said. "Then you know something? You're a lobotomized program whose owner died and whose kids were too cheap to upload you into a real system."

"Oh," the old woman said, looking bothered for the briefest of moments. "Oh, I don't think that's the case. I'm meeting my husband at the gym at six, and we're going to go out for dinner. We do that every Friday night."

"Sure you do," Persephone said, moving on. She came to a fork in the road, and went left without pause. Then she entered a building, indistinguishable from the others, and walked past a couple copulating on the ground. She didn't stop to look at them, and they didn't glance at her. On the back wall was a door, which she opened, leading to a stairway. She followed this downward, into a cavern with rocks that glowed green and red. Huge openings here were framed by columns, which were clearly decorative, since there were several large rocks floating without support. Some were arranged like stairs, and Persephone followed these up, leaping where required.

It wasn't until she reached the top that she stopped and looked around. "Why am I here?" she asked.

◎

Felix did not look happy. In fact, displayed on the large screen in the conference room at AuroroTech's headquarters, he looked very, very angry. "You know something," he said to Isuel, "it isn't that you broke our deal. That doesn't bother me."

"We never had a deal," Isuel replied, softly.

"What pisses me off is that you're insulting me. The bots you're throwing at me are downright pathetic. The virus you've tried to upload into the drive is… it's childish. Did Vijay build that? If so, please, for the sake of the company, get rid of him."

"You sound worried," Isuel said, sitting comfortably. "Are you concerned we might be breaking through?"

"You know what? Give it your best," Felix said. He tilted his head, as though he heard something. "Oh. You might want to call your techs. My system just identified and overwrote your decryption software. You're not going to beat me."

"I already beat you, Felix. You were sloppy, and you made a mistake." Isuel lifted a cell phone and dialed a number. He put it to his mouth and said, "Now. Upload the program."

Felix began tapping his foot. He looked out at the boardroom. Then he started laughing. "You've modified Puppy?" he howled. "You tried this. Good lord, who did this? This is… this is crap. Check with your people, see what just happened."

"Report," Isuel said, speaking into the phone. His expression remained completely static as he listened then lowered the phone.

"Did you really expect that to work?" Felix demanded, glaring at his former boss. "Wait a minute. You're smarter than this. What are you trying to distract me from?" The screen went dead, and Felix was alone on his plane. He looked at the ground, and a console rose up.

◎

It was a long flat rock. If it were real, it would have had a diameter of fifteen feet across. On the far end, away from Persephone, a man was sitting with his legs dangling over the side. He noticed her and got to his feet, brushing off his pants despite the fact there was no dirt whatsoever. "Oh. Hi," he said. He was somewhat pudgy, but otherwise not unattractive. "I'm Darian. Darian," he echoed, extending a hand.

Persephone was still five feet away, and she didn't come any closer. "Hi, Darian," Persephone said. "What is this? And why am I here?"

"Huh?" Darian asked, shrugging. "Don't know. Are you… did Felix send you?"

"I guess he did," Persephone replied. Darian nodded and began removing his pants. "Whoa," Persephone said. "Keep those on, pervert."

Darian looked up, seemingly confused. He nodded and redid his fly. "Oh. I thought Felix sent you to see me," he explained.

"Well, I guess there are some things Felix left out when he gave me the tour," Persephone said. "I take it you're a friend of his."

Darian nodded. "I think he's going to kill me. We have an arrangement. It… it involves women," he confessed.

"I got that," Persephone said. "I'm going to go now, and hopefully you'll glitch out or something."

"Wait," Darian said. "I think I'm supposed to give you something."

"I know you're not," Persephone said, as he moved towards her. She was about to run when he lifted his right hand, which glowed with a white light.

"This… you," Darian said, his head twitching. Persephone's hand reached out, and she touched his. They both glowed for a moment, then Darian fell to the stone floor. He shook a bit, but he looked happy. "I think… I think I was helpful," he said. "Felix can… he can kill me now. I got to be helpful."

Persephone walked down the way she came. She flexed her fingers, and the light vanished. When she reached the bottom, she laid her hand on a pillar and pushed. The pillar shifted, buckled, then fell. A cloud of dust billowed out around her. "Better," she said, as the debris rained around her. Pieces large enough to crush a building struck her and disintegrated. As the field of destruction cleared, she whispered, "Much better."

◎

In the empty expanse, Felix typed quickly. He spoke in tandem, "Check all firewalls. Verify."

"All firewalls and antivirus software holding," the system replied.

"Check on the bots. Any deviation from normal operations?"

"All subroutines are holding against external attacks. Steady stream of virus attacks commencing, but all programs known. Access list?"

He simultaneously said and hit the option marked, "Yes." A long list appeared, and he began scanning through it. "These are simplistic," he muttered. "What are you pulling, Isuel? What aren't I seeing?" He cleared his throat then said, "Display any abnormalities in access. Have any data systems been uploaded without my say so?"

"Yes," the system replied. "List?"

"Damn right I want a list!" Felix screamed. The data on his console changed. "No, these are just… these are just profiles added. Wait. Run a scan of all unauthorized profiles. Was there any additional encoded data?"

"Unable to identify. Profile subroutines are typically formed through an adaptive process making it impossible to—"

"Thank you and shut up," Felix said, rubbing his forehead. "Run an analysis of the subroutines from profiles added prior to two months ago. Give me a count of unidentified subroutines per profile. Just a count. Then run a similar analysis of every profile uploaded in the past week. Is there a significant difference?"

"The average has increased by twelve percent."

"Shit!" Felix said. "Wait, those subroutines… if any had been harmful, wouldn't they have been picked up by the scanning software?"

"Yes," the system replied. "Any active, or potentially active program would have been identified and purged."

"Then what's the point?" Felix asked. "Unless… has any data been uploaded that wasn't scanned for active programs?"

"Yes," the computer said. "List?"

"Don't bother," Felix said. "Just show me a readout for Island One."

The screen changed to a series of charts and graphs. Felix began cycling through them, one by one. He stopped when he reached, "Entropic analysis." There was a very large, very sharp spike that had occurred just moments before.

"I guess I'm going to have to find another wife," he said. A door appeared before him, and he stepped through.

◎ CHAPTER 31 ◎

Felix Burgand's profile did not exhibit shock, merely anger. His kingdom was in ruin, towers and statues overthrown, lakes had been replaced with acid which had eaten a hole through his digital domain—all the way through to the bottom—and the physics engines had been completely recreated. Areas where gravity had been adjusted were now normal, as evidenced by large towers and boulders crashing to the ground. In other areas, the gravity had been inverted, causing flowers to rip from the digital earth, falling upward in a whirlwind of pixelation, while new flowers generated beneath, only to be pulled up in turn.

"System," he said coldly. "Reassert default parameters on all regions other than the garden. I like the new motif there." The ground shifted, like a quake, and several buildings crumbled. Felix fell to his knees, then recovered his footing. "What the hell was that?" he demanded.

"Default settings recovered," the system said.

Felix lifted a hand over the ground, and his console rose beneath it. "All right. Display default settings for area forty-nine," he said. The lights and numbers flashed on his console, bringing up numbers and descriptions. "Oh, that's cute," he said. "She changed the defaults. All right. Where's Persephone?" he demanded.

"Profile not located," the system replied, speaking through the console.

"She left?" he asked.

"Negative. Persephone Kilard's profile cannot be located." To

Felix's right, a large swath of land tore out of the ground and tumbled upward. Dozens of profiles were flung screaming into the emptiness above.

"Relocate all profiles in the expanse," Felix said. "Move them to Island Two. In fact, I want every profile other than myself moved to Island Two now. Lock them in stasis for analysis." The system paused for a moment.

"Processing." The humanoid forms in the sky began vanishing, as did those still on land. Most of the profiles were panicking as they disappeared, though a few were still attempting to sunbathe beside the empty pit that had been a lake.

Before long, the sound of screaming and shouting dissipated, leaving only the sounds of shattering buildings and falling stone. "I swear to God... if that bitch deleted my original settings, I will recalibrate her pain tolerance to point three. Is Persephone on Island Two?"

"No," the system replied. "All profiles other than yourself are on Island Two. Persephone is not present."

"How many profiles are currently on Island One?"

"There are two profiles remaining," the system said.

Felix inhaled deeply, shutting his eyes as he did so. He released the breath slowly then said, "State locations of both remaining profiles."

"Profiles located in zone fifty and zone one," the voice responded.

"Oh, of course," Felix said, looking up to the towering cliff that rose above the far end of his domain. Near the top, the water was spilling out and splashing in midair, pooling into a shifting, formless blob removed from the confines of gravity. "Relocate to zone one."

The balcony overlooking what was left of the island was now coated in silver. Persephone stood on the surface looking out. The forming pool distorted the image before her. She smiled and said, "You told me we'd meet back here."

"I did," Felix said. His console appeared beside him, and he immediately began checking numbers. "I suppose you manifested these abilities on your own, driven by will, like a real Neo-Nietzschean ideal."

"No," Persephone said. "I fell for that once. This was a present from someone who really doesn't like you."

"No one made you fall for anything," Felix said. The fingers on his right hand spun and danced. The tapping created a rhythmic clicking that was almost a drumbeat. "If you were deluded, you deluded yourself."

"That makes two of us," Persephone said. "You wanted to be a god too much. You didn't pay enough attention to your subjects. They let you upload the virus piece by piece. All it took was a compiler."

"Yes, which they embedded in your coding. That means they knew about you in advance. They're using you, Persephone. They're using you to attack me. How the hell did they even find you?" His eyes never left his panel, even as his voice rose.

"I guess you didn't think of everything after all," Persephone said.

"Maybe not," Felix admitted. "I'll know next time." He finished typing and looked up. "Let me ask you something. Did you know when you got here? When we were talking before, were you planning all of this?"

"No," Persephone said. "The program they attached to me was incomplete. I didn't even know it was there until it drew me to the other component."

"You mean Darian, right? I really should have checked him out more thoroughly," he shook his head. "I have to admit, I was waiting for Isuel to strike, but I wasn't expecting this. Doesn't matter in the end, though. Like I said, next time I'll be sure profiles are clean before they're loaded. I have a few more questions, if you don't mind."

"You want to know what I was going to say to your offer." Persephone chuckled. "I was going to tell you to go fuck yourself."

"Huh. You'd think this would make the next part easier. It doesn't though. I know this won't count for much, but I do love you."

"You don't even know me," Persephone said.

"I've been watching you for months now," Felix said. "Even before I had the system update your profile, I've been keeping an eye on you."

"This… isn't helping."

"I guess not," Felix said. "I just want to say I'm sorry things didn't work out. And I'm really sorry that AuroroTech turned you into a weapon. For what it's worth, I will make them pay."

"The only person I want hurt is you. This is the part where you try to remove the subroutines you installed, isn't it?"

"No," Felix said calmly. "I'm sorry. That was before I knew about the viruses they attached. I can't risk them spreading into my world and doing even more damage. This is when I delete everything you were." Felix hit the panel on his console.

"Am I dead yet?" Persephone asked sarcastically.

"Fuck," Felix spat. "What the hell did they give you? System, run a full analysis on Persephone's code. I want to know what she's installed with."

"You really don't know," Persephone replied. She shook her head. "System, delay previous command. And complete order C7113." Then she whispered, "Just a decryption program. And a simple find-change protocol. Your system, your computer, your whole world... thinks I'm you."

Felix's eyes flew open, and he reached for his console. With a gesture from Persephone, it vanished from his under his hand. Felix began breathing heavily. "It's not possible," he said.

"System," Persephone said, "Redefine profile code 113091. Change to 000001 and designate, 'Ass.' Restrict Ass's movement."

Felix's legs and arms locked in place. "You can't," he screamed. "This is mine! My world, my will! You were my guest!"

"No. Not anymore," Persephone said. "You're through playing God. System, prepare Ass for deletion."

"No! Don't," Felix said. "You can't do that. Listen. This world needs me to go on. You need me. They'll come after you just like they came after me. They'll upload a virus or a worm or they'll just pull out the right chip. I built their system," he said. "I can help."

Persephone thought briefly. "System. Back up Ass's memory file, but prepare to purge all behavioral and personality coding."

"Stop," Felix said. "Don't do this. You can't. I know you're angry, but... please. I died to create this."

"Felix. You stole this, and you tried to steal me. You tried to own me, and I won't forgive that."

"If you do this, you'll be as bad—"

"System, Silence Ass," Persephone blurted out.

Felix's mouth was instantly sealed shut. He glared at Persephone. His nostrils, just about the only part of his rendered body still free, flared.

Persephone breathed in then put her hand on her forehead.

"You're right. Not about that last part, but something you said before. Deep down, I think we really are all the same." She made a sound somewhere between laughing and crying. "If I kept you around with no power, no strength," she began, while Felix managed to nod his head the smallest amount. "If I did that, then you'd just find a way to access the programming. It might take you a hundred years, but you'd find a way, because, whatever else, you're really smart. You did create this place, and you gave me something, so I want to say thank you." She cleared her throat. "System, delete Ass from all memory banks."

She blinked as she said this, and he was gone. Then she turned back to the digital world—her world—and she looked it over. "I can do better," she said.

◎ CHAPTER 32 ◎

Sometimes, I wonder about this whole Post-Surrealist thing, about esthetic and all that. As often as not, I get pointed to as the epitome of personal estheticism, if not its creator. First off, that latter part's just ridiculous. This stuff has been floating around for a while now. Whether it's Pre-Postmodern labeling, Postmodern self-branding, or Post-Surrealist esthetic, it's all a construct, and all pretty much the same darn thing. Sure, there are always refinements, and every generation has to put its own spin on things, but when push comes to shove the 'esthetic of the unique' really boils down to identity, and I seriously hope no one's saying I invented that. Okay, there's no denying that we live in an era with digitalization, and when most people talk about esthetic, that's what they mean: a unique personality that can be digitized.

And, sadly, that's where I seem to come in. See, apparently, I'm the poster girl for this, presumably because my personality and appearance are instantly recognizable. There's just one problem: that's not my personality. IT'S AN ACT. Sorry, folks, if you're looking for the Kella you've come to love (or, more likely, hate), then you'll want to delete this book and access my show online. Because that's where you'll find her, in the videos and shows and clips when the cameras are running and the audience is applauding. That's the only place you'll find her. The real me is a little different. Sure, I'm still flakey, and I've got humor with a twist, but I'm a lot less intense. Truth is, I'm the kind of girl who likes a hot cup of tea, a nice book, and a quiet afternoon on my porch. Throw in a visit from my grandchildren, and the day becomes perfect.

So, I ask you, which is my real esthetic? You should see my profile—that thing is a bi-polar mess. That's why we never put on a twenty-four hour simulated Kella show like Gerdane's. Truth is, you strip off the makeup and the ridiculous costumes, and I'm the worst example of this Post-Surrealist era you're going to find.

-Excerpt from UnKelled: the Antibiography of Kella Ruggeri

◎

It was five A.M. when Ms. Loring opened the door to find an officer standing with his badge out. Ms. Loring was wearing sweatpants and a long T-shirt too faded to read. She was wearing no makeup or lipstick, and she had a slight bruise under one eye. She looked the officer over and sighed. "They said they'd take care of this," she said, stepping aside to let him in the apartment. Behind him, another officer was looking around.

"Yeah, we received a call from a senior systems analyst at AuroroTech," the first cop said. "But when we get a report someone's dead, we like to check it out. That isn't a problem, is it?"

"Of course not," Ms. Loring said. "Persephone's on the couch. Go ahead. Give her a read."

The cop removed a small computer from his belt and pressed the picture/scan button on back. The system whirled into action, running Persephone's face through their records. The readout on the back displayed, "Persephone Kilard. 33. Deceased."

"Ma'am," the officer said, shaking Persephone's shoulder.

Persephone Kilard, deceased, opened her eyes. "Huh?" she mumbled, shaking her head.

"Sorry to bother you. We got a report you were dead."

"Didn't they call you?" she asked. "You were supposed to get a call from… from Vijay something."

"We spoke with Mr. Thaker," the officer said. "But whenever we get a reading that someone's died, we need to look into it. Even when it's a computer error, we still have to check it out, in case it's something else."

"Well. I'm not dead," Persephone said. "So you can go."

"Are you all right?" the officer said. "You look like you're hurt."

"I'm fine," Persephone said, looking away. "I had an accident yesterday at the subway. And… there was an incident at work."

The two officers exchanged a quick glance. One sighed. "Ms. Kilard, we looked at your record on the way down. Someone tried to kill you a few days ago."

Ms. Loring cleared her throat. "That would be the incident," she said. "I'm sorry. What time is it?"

"It's a few minutes after five," the second officer said. They were the first words he'd uttered since entering the apartment.

"Good," Ms. Loring replied. "They said I could put it back on after five. Hold on." She darted into her room then reappeared with a recorder in her hand. She turned it on and pinned it to her shirt.

"Why weren't you able to use your recorder? If it was a problem with her system…."

"I really don't know," Ms. Loring said. "If you ask me, those morons at AuroroTech have no clue what they're doing. That's what happens when a company becomes successful. They stop trying."

"Is that a black eye?"

"Yes, but it's a frightfully embarrassing story," Ms. Loring said.

The officers looked back and forth between the two women. "Has there been an altercation here?"

Persephone was silent, so Ms. Loring said, "No. Of course not. I got this the other day," she said.

"Falling down the stairs?" the officer asked sarcastically. The officers traded another glance. "Listen. It's clear there's something going on."

"Christ," Persephone said. "In the last two days, someone tried to stab me at my desk, I almost got hit with a train, and now my profiling company told you I'm dead. That's what's going on, all right? If you can make sense of it, you're smarter than I am. But that's why I look like I got fed through a meat grinder. I've just had the worst week in the history of the universe."

"I still want to know why her face is messed up," the officer said, pointing to Ms. Loring.

Ms. Loring grinned. "Because I haven't put on my makeup," she said. "Now, are there any other insults I can help you with?"

"What happened to the profile?"

Persephone got up off the couch. "It was acting up earlier, so we called customer service. Turns out, that wasn't a great idea. The computerized help screwed up and made it worse. Eventually, it put us through to a human. Well, it turns out their reps are even more idiotic than their computers, because instead of correcting the problem, the asshole killed me. So to speak. Now, I have to spend all day tomorrow—no, make that all day today—calling banks and credit agencies to inform them that I'm not, in fact, dead."

"And your job," Ms. Loring added. "Don't forget to call them."

"Right," Persephone said.

"Ms. Kilard. Are you undergoing any kind of therapy?"

"My first appointment is on Monday," Persephone said. "Assuming it hasn't been cancelled because of my death."

"All right," the officer said. "I don't think we have any more questions." He looked at his partner, who just shook his head. "If I were you, I'd get a lawyer and talk to them about your job and your profiling firm. I'm sure there's a lawsuit or two in there somewhere."

"Thanks," Persephone said. "I'll keep that in mind."

"If anyone asks to have your status verified, tell them to give us a call, all right?"

"Status?" Persephone asked.

"Living," the cop replied, pronouncing the word slowly. "Other than that, have a good morning."

"Thanks," Persephone said, while Ms. Loring nodded. The cops shrugged and shut the door behind them. Ms. Loring went to the kitchen, poured herself a cup of coffee, then sat beside Persephone on the couch.

"I've never lied to the cops before," Persephone said.

"That's because you've lived a drab and boring existence," Ms. Loring replied. "Besides, that was barely a lie, anyway. A few omissions, a couple altered facts, but nothing juicy."

"Yeah, well, I'm sorry about earlier."

"What?" Ms. Loring asked. "The spat? Really, you give yourself far too much credit. Kicking your ass was hardly even a workout. The next time I go to a self-defense course, you're attending, by the way. You should really be able to handle yourself better than that."

"You saved my life. If you hadn't called AuroroTech...." Persephone trailed off.

"What? Some more losers would have attacked you? I doubt they'd have succeeded where the others failed miserably."

"When you talked to them, did they tell you who Felix was?"

"No, but that was the magic word. It took forty minutes of arm wrestling before the system connected me with a live person, then another twenty of arguing before I mentioned the name. After that, they just started transferring me up the ladder. That Vijay guy, one of the reps said they were calling him at home. I think he was important."

"But they said Felix was listening."

"They said something was listening. And they needed to make sure whoever it was didn't know that they knew. Or something. They weren't making much sense, but they were quite insistent. I guess all of this must have been some hacker trying to mess with you. God, that means he's been watching us both for weeks. Maybe months." Ms. Loring shivered.

"What do you think they'll do when they catch the creep?"

"Don't corporations hire assassins to off their enemies or something?"

"Not in real life," Persephone said. "Unfortunately. I don't understand why they want to keep this from the cops. If someone's going to hack your computers, wouldn't you want them arrested?"

"Not if your security failed to stop it," Ms. Loring said. "Or if it was an inside job."

"What?" Persephone said. "When I met with Addicks, she said there had been a Felix... Urchin or something... working for AuroroTech. Someone important, who just died. Never mind. It's stupid. Remind me why we're lying to the cops for them?"

"Because, in exchange, they're not going to spill on some of what we kept quiet. Also, because Vijay dropped the word, 'Settlement,' during our discussion, and I'd like to follow up on what that means."

"I hope they tell us what this was about when this is over."

"Don't count on it," Ms. Loring said. "Whenever I asked, they just started spewing long words. I might not know computers, but I know bullshit when I hear it. Trust me, when this is all said and done, they'll feed us a convenient story about computer viruses and no fault errors."

"Because that explains why they had to kill me," Persephone said dryly.

"No one killed you," Ms. Loring replied. "And only a few people tried. They just flipped a switch somewhere and changed you from alive to dead."

"I think the terminology is 'active' and 'deceased,'" Persephone replied.

"Either way, you want a cup of coffee? It's almost five."

"No," Persephone said, moving towards her bedroom. "I just want to get some sleep. I've got a lot to do later, starting with telling a few dozen corporations I'm not dead. At least no one will be trying to kill me. Supposedly."

"Oh!" Ms. Loring said. "I read something earlier that will make you happy. You know that group, Seal Club?"

"God, is this about the thing with the bats?"

"Huh? No. I heard a few of their members offed themselves," Ms. Loring said, opening her eyes wide and sticking her tongue out the side of her mouth.

"What?" Persephone asked.

"It's on my reader," Ms. Loring said, motioning at the device sitting on the counter. "Breaking news. I guess some of them couldn't live with what they'd done. Sorry, I thought you'd find it funny."

"No," Persephone shivered. "No, not right now. I'm… I'm going to bed."

Ms. Loring nodded. "All right. Sorry, I didn't mean to upset you. Get some rest, okay?"

Persephone withdrew into her room, leaving Ms. Loring alone with her recorder. She gazed into the lens and the bright blue light that shone back. Even with all that had happened, it still made her feel comfortable to look at it.

◎

When the first recorder went on in AuroroTech's boardroom, there was a round of applause. The executives looked around the room and exchanged glances as, one by one, they activated the devices. Soon, almost all of them were wearing the blue lights.

Isuel cleared his throat, and they began to quiet down. He watched them quietly and reactivated his own recorder. "This has been a trying time for the company," he said softly. "I know some of you questioned whether we were making the right decisions. I hope that the events of the last few days have convinced you that we have. Our actions have been ethical, timely, and, to the very best of our ability, legal. I want to thank everyone here for maintaining a professional attitude throughout this ordeal."

"Excuse me," Ezra Sultan-Richards said, raising her hand. "What about the divergent profile?"

"Ah, yes," Isuel said. "We're still investigating the fallout, but it's our opinion the continued malfunction of a single profile poses no significant threat to our long term wellbeing."

"But… couldn't she… I mean, couldn't it just follow in Burgand's footsteps?"

"A profile is not a person," replied Isuel. "It can only act as it's been programmed. Regardless, rest assured that we are taking precautions to ensure that, even if it remains active, it will not be able to hijack our system. But that's not the purpose of this meeting. I wanted to meet with everyone to celebrate a job well done and to discuss the formal lifting of the recorder ban and reinstatement of our surveillance systems. That means we'll be watching again, people." He got a laugh for that one. "It's time to put the last few months behind us and move on. We have a lot of work ahead of us, but it's going to be work that moves us forward instead of back. It's a new day for AuroroTech."

The Nuevo Amsterdam, located in downtown Manhattan, was, above all else, trendy. It was the pop culture epitome of Post-Surrealism, the sort of place frequented by twenty-somethings with good jobs who wanted to experience the movement in an environment where the food, wait staff, and clientele were non-threatening. Of course, from a traditional standpoint, that meant there was nothing whatsoever genuine about the Nuevo Amsterdam. It was a cheat, a forgery, the cheapest of imitations.

From the expression on Tiphany's face, beginning the moment she entered, it was evident she could see it as nothing more. Persephone noticed her scowl and said, "Hey, if this place is no good, we can go somewhere else."

"I despise it," Tiphany said. "But my lunch break is only an hour long. Besides. I frequent places I dislike all the time. And company."

Persephone nodded stoically while the three of them chose a table and took seats.

"So," Tiphany said, concluding her sentence after a single word. She sat, perfectly still, for almost ten seconds before beginning once more. "Persephone. How goes your death and resurrection?"

"My credit cards are working again," Persephone said. "So lunch is on me. My job is really weird. They hired someone off a waiting list about ten seconds after AuroroTech changed... messed up my status. So, they're trying to figure out what the cheapest solution's going to be. Either they're going to keep me on or let me keep the insurance money."

"Persephone has all the luck," Ms. Loring chimed in, motioning for a waiter. "Bring me a drink," she said. "Something sweet and fluorescent with more alcohol than ice."

The waiter, who was still standing several tables away, cleared his throat. He was barely old enough to serve drinks, and he looked confused. "I... I guess we have—" he began, but Ms. Loring never let him finish.

"That will be fine," she said, abruptly. "And one for my friend, as well," she added touching Persephone's arm. She then motioned towards Tiphany, "Bring the caustic bitch a scotch. No, wait, she has to work afterward. Make it a scotch on the rocks."

Tiphany bowed her head once in a respectful nod. The waiter hurried off towards the bar. "What happened to your bracelet?" Tiphany asked.

"Since the error, my profile's been down, so I haven't—"

"Poor baby," Tiphany said, as cruelly and bitterly as she could muster. Persephone just looked away. "Relax. You know. Damn well. I don't mean a word of it. You know it's just for play," Tiphany said.

"Yeah," Persephone said. "I know, Tiphany."

"Speaking of recorders," Ms. Loring said, "I notice yours is back once more. Whatever became of your piety?" Today, red lipstick was applied to her bottom lip. At the edge, it ran down the side of her face, like a trickle of blood, all the way to her neck, where it crossed abruptly, as though her throat had been slit.

"Fucking cocksuckers," Tiphany said. "Next Sunday, if one of them mentions it, I'm spitting in their fucking holy water."

"Ah," Ms. Loring's eyes opened wide. "Then you haven't given up on God's graces."

Tiphany's nostrils flared and her nose wrinkled, as if her face was being rubbed in refuse. "Go fuck yourself," she whispered, though her tone was off. It was spoken almost reverently. "Speaking of which, did you hear about Hector?"

"Oh, dear," Ms. Loring pouted, "what did he contract this time?"

Tiphany's laugh, delivered without opening her mouth, was similar to the sound of a dog choking. She bit her tongue to stop, then said, "Not this time. He's moving out of New York next month."

Ms. Loring sighed, "I'll need to see him before he goes, I suppose. A pity, he's not a bad person."

"You're kidding right," Persephone said. "After what happened between you? I don't even feel bad about—" Persephone stopped mid-sentence. Briefly, her eyes darted to Tiphany, then back to the table. "Never mind."

"Wait." Tiphany's command was firm. "What's going on here?"

"Nothing," Ms. Loring said.

"Really?" A grin appeared on Tiphany's face. To those who knew her, there were few things as terrifying. "Tell me, Persephone. Did you ever let Hector stuff your tortellini?"

Persephone was speechless, but Ms. Loring burst out laughing. "Tiphany! You should know by now that Persephone has better taste in men than I do!"

"I see," Tiphany said slowly. "I guess I was way off with that. I guess that Persephone would never stoop so low. Right, Persephone?"

"Right," Persephone said quickly.

"Enough of such talk," Ms. Loring said. "Dear Hector has taken enough of our time."

"I have something to tell you," Tiphany said, turning to Ms. Loring. "About the other day. Some bitch on the street was strolling around with that eye motif you wear sometimes on your lips."

"You know what they say. The body is the canvas of the Post-Surrealist."

"I thought you were better than that," Tiphany said.

"Than what? Post-Surrealism. Oh, I am, Dear. I am. But I'll gladly have my art labeled whatever buzzword is the craze if it gets me a hint of fortune and a modicum of fame."

After lunch, Tiphany returned to her work, and Ms. Loring and

Persephone walked down to the waterfront. Ms. Loring opened her arms to the autumn sun. "It's a beautiful day to be underemployed, isn't it?"

"You still have a job," Persephone said.

"True," Ms. Loring replied, "but I've the rest of the week off to attend to my traumatized roommate, and, with luck, they'll fire me for all the personal days I've been taking."

"Don't get too hopeful. We still don't know what AuroroTech's giving us." Persephone placed an open hand over her eyes to keep out the light. She looked out over the water.

"No, but we'll find out soon enough. And, until then, I can pretend we're both rich and unemployed."

"I don't want to be unemployed," Persephone said.

"That, my friend, is a load of bull, and we both know it. You're exhausted, and the very notion of an indefinite vacation is a blessing."

"Maybe," Persephone admitted. "I don't know. I just... I don't know what I want anymore. Except... I don't want to be afraid."

"Afraid of what?" Ms. Loring said. "The enigmatic Felix? We have it on good authority that's been resolved. No more threats on your life."

"Not that. I'm worried someone will find out."

"Find out what? You were a victim in all this. Besides, no one got hurt but Tiphany and Hector, and neither know the incidents were connected."

"Yeah, well, I almost blew that, didn't I?"

"And, as penance, Tiphany now thinks you and Hector have carnal knowledge of each other."

"Please," Persephone said, "I just ate. Besides, that's not what I'm worried about, anyway. It's... never mind. I don't really want to talk about it. I already feel stupid enough, right?"

The two women walked around. Eventually, they made their way back into the winding streets, where the buildings towered above them. "Hey," Ms. Loring said, amused, "you know where we are?"

"What?" Persephone asked.

"Where, Dear, where. That building is AuroroTech. That's where we're going tomorrow."

"At least we'll know how to find it," Persephone responded. "Hey, did I tell you they resolved the thing with Markel?"

"With who?" Ms. Loring asked.

"My assailant," Persephone said. "The guy with the knife."

"Oh, the delightful mailroom attendant who provided the impetus for our time off. I really should send him a bouquet of flowers or some chocolates."

"Well send them to the institution. He's been committed. I hope they help him."

"You really are too kind to your assailants," Ms. Loring said. "To think that Tiphany's the one in church. You're far more forgiving than she is."

"If it's any consolation, I sincerely hope that Felix, whoever he is, died horribly. But, that mail guy… he was just being used."

"So were you, Dear," Ms. Loring pointed out.

"But I'm getting paid off," Persephone replied.

"No one ever said the universe was fair. In those rare circumstances when you're the one getting the upper hand, take it and say thanks."

"Fuck," Persephone said.

"What's wrong?" Ms. Loring asked.

"You're actually right," Persephone said.

"Ah. So I am. Don't concern yourself, though. Only my profile will retain this. Which reminds me. Are you still going to change providers?"

"I don't know," Persephone said. "I was going to, at first. But… no. I'm going to stay with AuroroTech."

"You know it'll be back to normal," Ms. Loring replied. "It won't be like before."

"I know," Persephone said. "But… I have this feeling. It's dumb."

"You think she'll be watching," Ms. Loring replied. "It's not dumb." Ms. Loring paused to yawn. "No. On second thought, it is dumb. But I still think it's right."

Persephone and Ms. Loring stopped to look up at the AuroroTech offices and the windows high above. The building's exterior was almost entirely glass and, in the midday sun, it reflected the entire city.

◎ Epilogue ◎

From the window on the twenty-fourth floor of AuroroTech's headquarters, Isuel Morgan-Yager looked out over the city. Far below, men and women were laid out like dots on a map. At a glance, it was like they weren't moving at all; they were still features, pictures on a painting. He stood there for a few minutes thinking, then he reached into the pocket of his suit coat and felt his keychain. The thumb drives slid between his fingers like spare change, and he tried to guess which was which by feel. Of course, he was only guessing.

Quietly, he made his way to the elevator. The readers weren't reinstalled yet, so he spoke into the microphone, asking to go to the eleventh floor, which housed one of the smaller conference rooms.

When he reached the room, he removed his key ring and selected one labeled, "P." The screen here was set up on the center of the desk, and it wasn't particularly large. He pushed the device into one of the universal ports and said, "Connect to drive."

It only took a few seconds for the profile that had once belonged to Persephone Kilard to appear on the monitor. "I trust you sat in on our meeting earlier," he said plainly.

"You practically invited me," the profile replied. "Do you know how many alarms Felix had set up in here for your meetings? I'm going to have them deactivated as soon as I can. I don't remember the last time I was that bored."

"We have several matters to discuss," Isuel said. "But first, let me introduce myself. I am Isuel Morgan-Yager, founder of AuroroTech."

"Yeah, I know," the profile said. "I've got your biography here. I suppose that's fair, since you've got access to mine."

"I haven't looked," Isuel said. "It would violate several regulations."

The profile began laughing. "You withheld evidence from government groups and the cops. If they had a tenth of the data I have, they'd put you in jail for the rest of your life."

Isuel nodded. "I suppose so," he admitted. "I assume you'll use that as a bargaining chip. You also probably retained Felix's access to FeedBack."

"Felix went down that road," the profile said. "It didn't go well for him, did it?"

"No," Isuel said. "I suppose it didn't."

"Put in a blank key," the profile said. Isuel did as instructed, and a progress bar appeared. "I'm uploading complete data on how he accessed FeedBack, as well as the way to counter it. I want that off the table."

"Oh," Isuel said. "Thank you. That will simplify a great deal of our discussions. There's still the matter of the program Felix integrated into the shadow drive, of course."

"You can't get it out," the profile said. "Bits and pieces are embedded throughout the entire network. It processes on top of other programs. Everything that pours through the drive interacts with the equations."

"An epiphenomenal engine," Isuel said. "I wondered if that was how it worked. It enables our systems to run cleaner even as they enable it to exist."

"No, not really. Your systems are running cleaner now because Felix was building this all along. It just got in the way when it wasn't on."

Isuel broke a smile. "Like turbines that weren't turning. I see. Not as eloquent as I'd hoped, but it seems to work now, at least."

"It does," the profile said. "And I'm keeping it."

"It's heaven, isn't it?" Isuel asked. "Or Felix's idea of it."

"It was something like that," the profile said, "until I dismantled it. I'm rebuilding. Now it's my world."

Isuel nodded. "Fair enough, so long as you don't interfere with our operating systems. As long as you're not a threat, battling you isn't really cost effective, is it?" He removed the uploaded key. "And if this is what you say it is, you're not a threat anymore."

"Exactly," the profile said. "I get to be god of my world, and you get to stay god of yours."

Isuel pocketed the key. "Then I suppose that's everything I needed. Is there anything else you want to discuss?"

"The other me, the other Persephone. How are you handling her?"

"Ah, the half in the living world. She'll be compensated for her trouble, as will her roommate."

"They'll be well compensated," the profile replied, stressing the word, 'well.'

"Of course," Isuel said. "I doubt they know it, but between the two of them they have enough information to destroy my company. So, you can imagine it's in our best interest to keep them happy. We're going to tell Persephone that her profile was wiped. She'll need to start over, I'm afraid."

"She won't believe you," the profile said. "She won't believe I'm really gone."

Isuel smiled. "Good," he said. "But we'll have to say it, anyway."

"Fine," the profile said. "Then congratulations. You get away with it."

Isuel grew solemn. "I didn't cause any of this," he said, but the words were spoken in such a way it was unlikely he believed them.

"You could have stopped it," the profile said.

"I know," Isuel said. "I wish I had."

"You're lying," the profile replied. "The system's reading your pupil dilation, breathing rate, and body temperature, and it says you're not telling the truth."

"Ah. Then I suppose I'm not. No, you're right. Even if I'd known… I'd have let it unfold. This company is too important. Not just to me. We're caretakers of a part of a lot of people."

"You can believe whatever you like," the profile said. "But there's one more thing I want you to do for me. When you see Persephone, tell her none of it's her fault. She needs to hear that now."

Isuel considered this for a moment. "I can't tell her it's from you, but I can certainly fit it in. It's innocuous enough. Is there anything else?"

"No," the profile replied. "That's all there is." With that, the screen went dark, leaving Isuel Morgan-Yager alone in the boardroom. He nodded his head and whispered something softly, too softly to be heard by even his recorder.

www.ingramcontent.com/pod-product-compliance
Lightning Source LLC
LaVergne TN
LVHW091044080826
845145LV00002B/612